Cheryl Holt

Wonderful

Copyright © 2014 Cheryl Holt
All rights reserved under International and Pan-American Copyright Conventions

By payment of required fees, you have been granted the *non*-exclusive, *non*-transferable right to access and read the text of this book. No part of this text may be reproduced, transmitted, downloaded, decompiled, reverse engineered, or stored in or introduced into any information storage and retrieval system, in any form or by any means, whether electronic or mechanical, now known or hereinafter invented without the express written permission of copyright owner.

Please Note

The reverse engineering, uploading, and/or distributing of this book via the internet or via any other means without the permission of the copyright owner is illegal and punishable by law. Please purchase only authorized electronic editions, and do not participate in or encourage electronic piracy of copyrighted materials. Your support of the author's rights is appreciated

No part of this book may be reproduced or transmitted in any form or by any electronic or mechanical means, including photocopying, recording or by any information storage and retrieval system, without the written permission of the publisher, except where permitted by law.

Thank you.
Cover Design Angela Waters
Interior format by The Killion Group
http://thekilliongroupinc.com

PRAISE FOR *NEW YORK TIMES* BESTSELLING AUTHOR CHERYL HOLT

"Best storyteller of the year..."
Romantic Times Magazine

"A master writer..."
Fallen Angel Reviews

"The Queen of Erotic Romance..."
Book Cover Reviews

"Cheryl Holt is magnificent..."
Reader to Reader Reviews

"From cover to cover, I was spellbound. Truly outstanding..."
Romance Junkies

"A classic love story with hot, fiery passion dripping from every page. There's nothing better than curling up with a great book and this one totally qualifies."
Fresh Fiction

"This is a masterpiece of storytelling. A sensual delight scattered with rose petals that are divinely arousing. Oh my, yes indeed!"
Reader to Reader Reviews

Praise for Cheryl Holt's "Lord Trent" trilogy

"A true guilty pleasure!"
Novels Alive TV

"LOVE'S PROMISE can't take the number one spot as my favorite by Ms. Holt—that belongs to her book NICHOLAS—but it's currently running a close second."
Manic Readers

"The book was brilliant...can't wait for Book #2."
Harlie's Book Reviews

"I guarantee you won't want to put this one down. Holt's fast-paced dialogue, paired with the emotional turmoil, will keep you turning the pages all the way to the end."
Susana's Parlour

"...A great love story populated with many flawed characters. Highly recommend it."
Bookworm 2 Bookworm Reviews

BOOKS BY CHERYL HOLT

WONDERFUL
WANTON
WICKED
LOVE'S PERIL
LOVE'S PRICE
LOVE'S PROMISE
SWEET SURRENDER
MUD CREEK
MARRY ME
LOVE ME
KISS ME
SEDUCE ME
KNIGHT OF SEDUCTION
NICHOLAS
DREAMS OF DESIRE
TASTE OF TEMPTATION
PROMISE OF PLEASURE
SLEEPING WITH THE DEVIL
DOUBLE FANTASY
FORBIDDEN FANTASY
SECRET FANTASY
TOO WICKED TO WED
TOO TEMPTING TO TOUCH
TOO HOT TO HANDLE
THE WEDDING NIGHT
FURTHER THAN PASSION
DEEPER THAN DESIRE
MORE THAN SEDUCTION
COMPLETE ABANDON
ABSOLUTE PLEASURE
TOTAL SURRENDER
LOVE LESSONS
MOUNTAIN DREAMS
MY TRUE LOVE
MY ONLY LOVE
MEG'S SECRET ADMIRER
WAY OF THE HEART

WONDERFUL

10 February, 1814

Evangeline,

You are reading this letter, which means I have passed on. I don't know if you will grieve for me, but should you be so inclined, please don't. I lived a long and full life, and I am content with my choices—as you must learn to be with yours.

I've watched over you since you were a girl, and I often found it to be a burdensome trial. At this late date, I don't say this to upset you. You're aware of my opinion.

You have a flamboyant character that does not suit the world in which you must live. I understand it is more natural for you to flaunt yourself, to sing and perform and have others watching and applauding. But these traits will not take you any place you would wish to be. You must seek gratification in other ways. You must learn to be happy with smaller, more pleasing pursuits.

By now, you will have learned that I betrothed you. Your dowry has been paid and the contracts signed. I'm not sure you are suited to being a wife, but life spent as a spinster would be even worse for you.

Your fiancé is a vicar, and a vicar's wife is constantly busy with important tasks. In this role, there will be many chores to calm your hectic mind, and you will spend your days helping others. It will be a rewarding path for you. I am convinced of it.

We have quarreled frequently over the years, but I will not apologize for my attempts to guide you and mold your character. Please accept the vicar and the life I selected for you. While at first, you will be vexed by my choice, I know you will ultimately find peace and contentment.

Your mentor
Miss Peabody

CHAPTER ONE

"Will there be anything else, Miss?"

"No, no, I'm fine."

Evangeline Etherton stood still as a statue, observing as the housemaid walked to the door, about to leave Evangeline to her own devices. A smile of joy was bubbling up, and Evangeline could barely hide it.

At the last second, the girl said, "Oh, I forgot. Cook wanted to know if it would be all right to serve your supper in the small dining room."

"Where is it usually served?" Evangeline asked.

"Well, if Lord Run is here, he uses the larger dining room, but it's quite big and grand. Cook felt you might rather use the smaller one."

"The smaller one will be perfect," Evangeline insisted, "and please tell everyone there's no need to make a fuss. Just feed me once in a while, and I'm happy."

The housemaid dipped a curtsy, which was very polite but completely unnecessary. "I'll spread the word to the other servants."

"Thank you."

She left, and Evangeline was finally alone.

She listened as the maid's footsteps faded down the hall, then she lifted her arms and twirled in merry circles.

The suite she'd been given was too beautiful to be believed. With sitting room, bedroom, and dressing room, it was fit for a princess. The furniture was expensive and tasteful, the wallpaper a warm shade of yellow that seemed to glow.

She might have been dropped into a fairytale.

The dressing room had a silver bathing tub, the cupboards full of plush towels and scented soaps. The entire place was so much more than she'd expected, and she'd get to stay for a whole month, but she deemed the sojourn a fair reward for what was coming after that month ended.

There was a door that led out onto a balcony, and she slipped outside to gaze at the manicured garden and rolling hills beyond. The manor was called Fox Run, and she wondered what it would be like to own such a property. She couldn't imagine.

At age twenty-five, she had no prior opportunity to experience opulence. She'd been orphaned as a toddler and sent to Miss Peabody's School for Girls. Supposedly, a kindly benefactor had paid her tuition, though Miss Peabody had refused to say who it was or why charity had been extended.

Evangeline had been reared under Miss Peabody's watchful eye, had received a brilliant education and, after graduation, had been invited to remain as a teacher. Her skills at singing, theatricals, and playing musical instruments had guaranteed her a spot on the faculty that had included her two best friends, Rose Ralston and Amelia Hubbard.

They'd both been orphaned girls too, and had grown up with Evangeline and been hired as teachers by Miss Peabody.

But Miss Peabody had passed away, the school was closed, and their days as spinster schoolteachers were over. The next phase of their lives was just beginning.

Through the trees, she could see the steeple of the church in the village, and it was a reminder that *her* future was about to arrive, and very quickly too. She tamped down a shudder and went back inside, not eager to stare at the church and be unnerved by the sight.

She'd promised to come. She'd promised to proceed. It was too late to worry or second guess.

She was to wed Vicar Ignatius Bosworth. Miss Peabody had contracted the betrothal shortly before her death. Evangeline had never planned to marry, and didn't actually wish to marry now, but she'd had no alternative.

She hadn't met the vicar yet and had been provided with only a few facts about him, those contained in a one-page letter of introduction he'd personally penned.

He was forty and had two hobbies—he liked to read in front of the fire at night, and he liked to study Scripture. He'd never been wed, but was at a spot financially where he could support a wife.

In the miniature portrait he'd furnished, there'd been no attempt to enhance his features. He was balding, severe in appearance, clean shaven, and a tad gaunt.

Homely as mud. The spiteful thought was awful, and she shoved it away.

If she'd previously fantasized about someday having a handsome, dashing husband, those were juvenile dreams and not worthy of the woman she'd become. She wasn't fickle or immature, and she wouldn't judge the man by his looks. She had *no* option but to marry, and she was in no position to be picky.

They'd get on fine. They would! She was fun loving and cheerful, and she made people happy with her singing and other musical talent. She'd make him happy too.

Suddenly, her pulse was racing. She tried to picture herself sitting by the fire, listening to her husband expound on obscure Bible passages, but the vision left her so anxious that she felt nauseous.

She swallowed down her burgeoning panic and hurried to the bedchamber to unpack her portmanteau. From her years under Miss Peabody's tutelage, she knew that useful activity was the best medicine for stress and unease.

Miss Peabody had been a stickler for proper behavior, and Evangeline—with her singing and flamboyant character—had been a constant trial to the older woman. Evangeline had been scolded and punished so frequently that she'd never understood why Miss Peabody had kept her on as a teacher.

Evangeline had learned to tamp down her outbursts of gaiety, to ignore her true inclinations. She'd learned to never reflect on how ill-suited she was to the only choices available.

In a world where she was required to exhibit a modest, humble demeanor, she loved to show off and perform, and if she could have arranged the perfect future for herself, she might have been an actress on the stage in London. But of course, such a sensational path would be insane, and she could never figure out why she was overcome by such wild ideas.

She had to find a way to take her mind off her troubles, so she decided to go exploring. The manor belonged to Aaron Drake, Lord Run, a viscount who was son and heir to George Drake, Earl of Sidwell, but also a distant cousin to Vicar Bosworth.

Lord Run was rarely in the country, the house standing empty most of the time. The vicar's mother had contacted him, and he'd agreed that Evangeline could stay at Fox Run during the month leading up to her wedding.

She was certain her duties as a country vicar's wife would be very dreary, so during her visit, she intended to revel. She would secretly pretend the property was *hers*, would act as if she'd been born to luxury and extravagance, and she often wondered if she hadn't been.

Occasionally, she dreamed of mansions and fancy carriages and elegant attire. Her dreams were so disturbingly real that she suspected they must have some basis in her past, which she didn't remember.

Evangeline had had no choice but to accept her engagement,

and she'd sworn to herself that she'd work hard, that she would be the best vicar's wife who had ever lived, but she couldn't quite believe she fit the role Miss Peabody had selected for her.

She went to the wardrobe, but she owned only a handful of clothes, so there was little to put away. Three dresses—all gray with white collars and cuffs. A nightgown. Underclothes. A wool cloak for winter. Winter boots too.

And one very pretty day dress that she'd saved for years to buy. It was a fetching violet shade that highlighted the blond of her hair and the deep sapphire of her eyes. When she wore it, she felt she was someone other than a boring spinster and schoolteacher.

She took a last look at the meager pile, having to admit that—with her marrying a vicar—it was probably all she'd ever possess. Somehow, she didn't imagine there would be money in the household budget for frivolities such as stylish gowns.

Finished with her chore, she marched out, ready for an adventure. Such an ornate residence would have a music room filled with instruments, and she was eager to locate it.

She roamed about, poking her nose into deserted galleries and salons. It was late afternoon, and the house was very quiet, the servants likely in the kitchen and having tea. So it came as a huge surprise when a woman's sultry laughter drifted by, when the low rumble of a man's voice answered the woman.

Evangeline slowed and began to tiptoe, worried over who it might be. Was it Lord Run? What would it mean if he was suddenly on the premises? Could she remain a guest at Fox Run until her wedding?

Oh, she hoped so! She'd only just arrived. She would hate to have to depart so soon.

She found the pair at the end of the hall in what had to be the house's most ostentatious suite. It was decorated with mahogany furniture, maroon drapes and rugs. Every item bespoke comfort, wealth, and pleasure. Evangeline neared and peeked through the crack in the door.

They were in the sitting room, the man lounged in a chair, the woman—very beautiful, very exotic—prancing about in front of him. With fiery auburn hair and big green eyes, she was tugging the combs from her hair, letting it fall down her back in a curly wave.

She was about Evangeline's same height of five feet five inches and probably Evangeline's same age of twenty-five, but the similarities stopped there.

Wearing a lush emerald gown that hugged her voluptuous figure, she was glamorous and confident in a manner Evangeline had always struggled *not* to be.

As to the man, he was incredibly handsome. Broad shoulders, flat belly, dark hair, blue, blue eyes. He had a face like an angel. Or maybe a devil. He hadn't shaved, so his cheeks were stubbled, making him appear dashing and reckless and dangerous.

His skin was bronzed from the sun, and he was robust and vigorous. Since he was seated, it was hard to guess his height, but Evangeline suspected he'd be very tall, six feet at least. He was dressed in expensive clothes, black riding boots, tan trousers, a flowing white shirt that was open part way, providing a glimpse of his chest, and Evangeline's innards tickled at the sight.

It was horrid to spy, but she'd never seen such a delicious male specimen and couldn't look away.

"You want me," the woman was saying. "You know you do. Admit it."

"If I do or if I don't, Florella, how can it matter?"

"Not matter!" the woman, Florella, huffed. "This has been brewing between us for an entire year. Why not get on with it? We'll both be happier once it's over."

"Doesn't Bryce have an exclusive arrangement with you? What's he paying you *for* if not for your exclusivity?"

"He might be paying me to be his mistress," she saucily retorted, "but he doesn't own me, and he doesn't pick my friends. When he's not around, he can't dictate who I can entertain and who I can't."

Evangeline was so shocked to hear the word *mistress* that she could barely bite down a gasp of astonishment. Living as she had at a girl's boarding school, she'd never associated with loose or disreputable people. If Florella was truly a mistress, then she qualified as being the most scandalous person Evangeline had ever encountered.

Florella was unbuttoning her dress, the fabric falling away to reveal a very shapely bosom. The man watched, seeming bored, as if he regularly viewed naked flesh and was too jaded to be moved by it.

Florella's sleeves were next, as she exposed a very frilly, very elaborate corset.

The man arched an arrogant brow. "Bryce spends enough to keep you in very fine undergarments."

"Yes, he does. Lucky me." Florella grabbed her breasts, as if offering them to the man, and she grinned. "Are you hungry? Would you like a little nibble?"

"If I said yes"—the man shrugged—"how would I explain it to Bryce? I'm too honest for my own good, and I'd feel compelled to tell him."

"I'll tell him myself. You won't have to."

"He's my friend," the man insisted.

"So he won't mind sharing."

Florella hiked up skirt and petticoat and climbed onto his lap, straddling him so her bosom was directly in his face. She was riffling her fingers through his hair, fussing with his shirt. She leaned down and touched her lips to his in a brief kiss that thrilled Evangeline, riveting her with a peculiar sort of excitement she didn't understand.

She'd had very limited experiences with men in her life, had never had a beau, or even a close male acquaintance. She'd been kissed several times, but it had been when she was an adolescent and allowed to attend the harvest fair. She'd sneaked off with a few boys and had found the groping and pawing to be particularly stimulating, but much of the exhilaration was due to the danger involved.

If Miss Peabody had ever learned of the indiscretions, there was no predicting what might have happened. Evangeline would likely have been expelled, and as she'd gotten older, she'd had the sense not to flirt. So it had been years since she'd participated in a romantic interlude, and she'd never seen two adults kissing.

She'd always heard risqué stories about how adults behaved when they were alone, but she'd never expected to witness such antics. Her rampant curiosity was one of her worst traits, and she wasn't about to creep away before she saw quite a bit more.

"Bryce won't care," Florella persisted, her lips brushing the man's again. "He's very generous, and he likes me to be happy."

"And you'd be happy if we were lovers?"

"Yes, absolutely."

The man scoffed. "If you think Bryce would be nonchalant about it, you're mad."

"If he's upset by it, we can switch. I'll leave him, and *you* can have me instead."

"Me! I have no desire to support you. I'd have to take out a loan merely to keep you in undergarments."

"I have very expensive tastes."

"Poor Bryce. How does he afford you?"

"I'm worth it," Florella claimed.

The entire moment was so erotically charged that Evangeline could scarcely breathe. She felt as if she'd stumbled on an alien world she hadn't known to exist. She wanted to burst into the room, to question them about their relationship, their opinions on sin and morality.

How could they so flagrantly eschew decency and decorum? How did they rationalize it? How would they carry on later, when they were seated across from each other at the supper table?

Florella appeared frozen, as if waiting for something special to transpire, but the man wasn't inclined to oblige her. Ultimately, he said, "I'll ask Bryce. If he gives me permission, I'll consider it."

"Oh, you beast. Didn't you travel to the country to enjoy yourself? If you're going to be a stick in the mud, what's the point?"

"The point is I won't deceive a friend."

"You men!" Florella snorted. "As if you have any loyalty."

"I have *some,* not a lot, but some. I wouldn't waste it on you."

Florella began massaging her breasts, her crafty fingers circling round and round as if trying to mesmerize him. The movement had Evangeline eager to touch her own breasts. Her nipples were throbbing with an ache she'd never noted before.

Her skin was tingling, her ears ringing, and she was so fixated on the pair that a wild bull could have raced up and she wouldn't have noticed.

"Boo!" a man whispered from directly behind her.

"Ah!"

Evangeline yelped with fright and lurched away from him, and it pitched her into the room where the lovers were still together in their chair.

At her sudden arrival, they both stiffened with surprise, then Florella leapt to her feet, shoving her skirt down her legs. She whipped away, showing Evangeline her back, yanking at her sleeves and bodice.

The man who'd snuck up on Evangeline was probably thirty, and he looked enough like her, with the same blond hair and blue eyes, to be a relative. He snapped, "For God's sake, Florella, cover yourself."

"Sorry, sorry," Florella said.

"You're such a whore," the blond man declared, but without any rancor. "I don't know why I put up with you."

As with the prior word *mistress,* Evangeline had never previously heard a person utter the word *whore,* and she was stunned to the core of her being. What type of asylum had she entered, and what was she to do now?

"She wanted a tumble," the dark-haired man explained, "but I thought I should check with you first to see if you'd mind."

"Honestly, Florella," the blond man scolded, "we're all aware that he's richer than me, but stop being a mercenary for two seconds, would you?"

"Sorry," Florella said again. She turned toward Evangeline, which meant they all three turned.

"What have we here?" the dark-haired man asked, still

lounged in his chair as if nothing odd had occurred.

"The door was ajar. She was peeking through the crack."

"Well, she certainly got an eyeful."

"I scared the devil out of her." The blond man approached and made a slight bow to Evangeline. "I'm Bryce Blair." He waved dismissively at Florella. "This is my good—and very disreputable—friend, Miss Florella Bernard. And this"—he gestured to the man in the chair—"is Aaron Drake, Viscount Run."

Evangeline's heart sank.

Lord Run was the owner of the estate, her host, and cousin to Evangeline's betrothed, Vicar Bosworth. What was she supposed to say? How could she justify her conduct? What if he tattled to Vicar Bosworth? Evangeline's engagement would likely be over before it had begun.

"Hello," she glumly mumbled.

"And you are...?" Lord Run inquired.

"Miss Evangeline Etherton." He gaped at her, clearly not recognizing her name, so she added, "I'm your houseguest."

"*My* houseguest?" Lord Run said. "I don't have a houseguest."

"Yes...ah...the vicar's mother, Widow Bosworth, arranged it with you."

"That's very curious. I don't remember her contacting me."

The three of them were staring as if Evangeline had grown a second head, but Lord Run's assessment was the most intense of all, his shrewd gaze probing for information and details that Evangeline had no idea how to supply. She flashed a tepid smile, hoping to generate a hint of a smile in return, but he simply glared and pointed to her gray dress.

"Are you a nanny? A governess? What?"

There was no way to hide her identity. She had to reveal herself. He'd learn who she was soon enough.

"I'm the vicar's fiancée."

There was a shocked silence, then Mr. Blair asked, "Vicar Bosworth—as in Ignatius Bosworth?"

"Yes," Evangeline said.

"He's marrying? Truly?" Mr. Blair persisted.

Miss Bernard chimed in with, "He's marrying *you?*"

"Yes."

Lord Run seemed the most bewildered by the news. He studied her even more intensely. Finally, he said, "*You* are engaged to Cousin Iggy? Seriously?"

"Yes." It might have been the sole word Evangeline could speak.

There was another fraught silence, then the trio burst out

laughing in loud, rude guffaws.

Evangeline had never been more mortified and didn't know why they were so amused. Was she an inappropriate bride for the vicar? Was she too far beneath him? Or was the vicar inspiring their hilarity? Were they surprised by his betrothal? Were they humored that he'd settled on Evangeline? Why would they be?

Was Vicar Bosworth horrid? Was Evangeline the only one who hadn't been apprised? What sort of mess had Miss Peabody orchestrated?

What's so funny? she yearned to demand.

But instead, she spun and ran, their chortles following her down the hall.

CHAPTER TWO

"Hello, Miss Etherton."

Aaron smirked as she jumped a mile high.

It wasn't that late, but he'd had too much to drink, and with Bryce and Florella having traipsed off to bed, he'd been brooding and moping. He'd traveled to the country specifically to improve his mood, and his pouting seemed to defeat the entire purpose of the journey.

"Lord Run!" she snapped. "You can't be in here! What are you thinking?"

"I have no idea," he admitted, which was the truth.

He was in her sitting room, and he'd been there for quite awhile, lounged in a chair and listening to her stomp about in the dressing room. It had sounded as if she was pacing and venting.

She hadn't come down to supper, and the notion had vexed him enormously. He'd questioned the staff and had been advised that she'd had a tray delivered. Most likely, she'd been too humiliated to join them.

Ultimately—after several stout whiskeys—he'd decided he should find out for himself. By blustering in as he had, he'd already made a dozen bad choices, but he couldn't help it.

After she'd stumbled into the middle of Florella's failed seduction attempt, he'd felt awful. His queries to the housekeeper had confirmed that yes, she was his cousin's betrothed, and Iggy's mother, Gertrude, had arranged for her to stay in the manor as the wedding approached. Gertrude had claimed she'd written to Aaron about it, so the housekeeper hadn't given it a second thought.

Of course no such correspondence had occurred. Aaron would certainly have granted his permission, but Gertrude wouldn't have dared to ask Aaron for such a favor. She liked people to assume they were close, but they really weren't.

No doubt she was simply hoping to impress Miss Etherton with the Bosworth's connection to the Drake family. Gertrude was overly concerned with status and lineage, and usually Aaron was too, but Gertrude exhausted him with her fussy ways and stuffy manner. She reminded him too much of his father, Lord Sidwell, and if Aaron had wanted ridiculous posturing, he'd have remained in London.

"Go away." Miss Etherton tried to shoo him out as if he were a strange dog that had wandered in.

"No."

"Go!" she said more sternly.

"No."

"I'm in enough trouble because of you. Don't make it worse."

"Because of me? What did I do?"

"I met your dissolute friends! I saw Miss Bernard bare her...her..."

Her cheeks turned such a bright shade of scarlet that he was surprised she didn't ignite, and he laughed uproariously. He couldn't remember when he'd last laughed about anything, and it made him feel better than he had in a long, long time.

"What's so amusing?" she fumed.

"You are. You're absolutely hilarious."

"*I* am hilarious? I'm so glad I could be of service!"

She gave a theatrical bow, her nose nearly touching the floor, which humored him even more.

"Why were you skulking about and snooping in my bedchamber?" he asked.

"I wasn't skulking. I'd just arrived, and I was exploring the house. The housekeeper told me I could. You were the one carrying on in full view of anyone who chose to look. If you don't want innocent parties to witness your salacious conduct, you should shut your blasted door."

"I should, should I?"

"Yes. And speaking of doors"—she pointed to hers—"mine is open. You may walk through it whenever you're ready."

He studied her, fixated on her slightest move and gesture. That was the real reason he'd come.

When she'd been in his bedroom, he'd only had a minute to take stock of her, but he recalled her as being stunning. He'd been anxious to evaluate her again, to see if she was actually as exquisite as his memory had painted her.

She was.

Her glorious blond hair was piled on her head in haphazard disarray. Her striking blue eyes were flashing daggers. She was amazingly pretty. Shockingly pretty.

Her features were perfectly sculpted, her body curvaceous and alluring. There was a fascinating air about her that was so riveting it was almost carnal in effect. A potent, joyful vigor rolled off her in waves. Was she aware of it?

She was standing across the room, and he could practically feel her beckoning him closer. He wanted to stroll over and rub himself against her. Would sparks flare? In his entire thirty years of living, he'd never encountered such an intoxicating force.

"You claimed I'd gotten you into trouble," he said. "What kind of trouble?"

"With Vicar Bosworth. I haven't even met him yet, and you caught me spying on your naked acquaintance."

At her voicing the word *naked*, her cheeks grew even redder—if that was possible. He probably should have had mercy on her, should have told her not to worry, but he was from London where people deliberately tried to be boring and dull and never exhibit an ounce of emotion.

Her energetic personality was greatly enlivening.

"Is that why you had supper up here?" he asked.

"I've never seen such outrageous behavior in my life. I couldn't have sat at the dining table with Miss Bernard. I'd have died of embarrassment."

He laughed again, finding her silly and fetching and interesting in a dozen ways he hadn't expected.

"You won't tell him, will you?" she pleaded.

"Who?"

"Vicar Bosworth." She swept over and fell to her knees in front of him. She clasped his hand and gazed up at him, her blue eyes beseeching and miserable. "Swear you won't tell him about it."

"I won't," he murmured.

"If I lost his good opinion—"

"You won't lose it because of me."

"Swear that you mean it."

"Yes, I swear."

"Oh, thank you, thank you."

"You're welcome."

She pressed her forehead to his hand, almost as if she was whispering a prayer of relief. Had she been up here fretting? Had she been terrified Aaron would rush over and tattle to Iggy?

Aaron never talked to his cousin if he could avoid it, but she didn't know that.

"Get up, Miss Etherton," he quietly urged. "Get up, would you? There's no reason for all this upset."

"Easy for you to say," she grumbled. "Should I leave Fox Run? I've packed my bag. I can go at once."

"Leave? Why would I want you to leave?"

"Well, you can't want me to stay. Not after how I acted."

"It was nothing," he scoffed, although he was quite ashamed of himself.

Typically, he was a model of decorum, and Florella was a horrid doxy who had no scruples or sense. Why Bryce continued on with her was a mystery, but Aaron was mortified that Miss Etherton had observed him with Florella.

Though it was disgusting to admit, if Bryce hadn't barged in when he had, there was no predicting what Aaron might have done. He'd always been attracted to Florella, but so was every man in London.

She was a renowned actress who loved to have rich oafs panting after her. Bryce was the latest fool—in a long line of fools—to be snared in her web. She'd be more than happy to substitute Aaron for Bryce, but Aaron didn't keep mistresses, and he was greatly irked that Miss Etherton had seen him at such a weak moment.

Not that he'd confess as much to her. He deemed women to be frivolous and exhausting—and indiscreet.

She staggered to her feet, those luscious blue eyes still focused on him, and he couldn't believe how she held him rapt. She recognized the odd swirl of emotion flitting between them, for she frowned and whipped away. She went over by the door and leaned her back against the wall.

"I'm not usually so rude or uncouth as I was this afternoon," she said.

"I'm sure you're not."

"I was walking down the hall, and I peeked in your room. Miss Bernard is so beautiful, and I paused to look at her—only for a second—then suddenly she started removing her clothing."

"She has a habit of that."

"I was so shocked I didn't know what to do."

"Neither did I. I was minding my own business when she slinked in. I can't imagine why she assumed I was interested in a dalliance. I've never given her cause to suppose I would be."

Miss Etherton studied him, then she smiled, and it was such an arresting smile that it illuminated the space around her as if someone had lit a very bright lamp. He was glad he was sitting down. If he'd been standing, the force of it might have knocked him over.

"Mr. Blair is your friend?" she asked.

"Since we were boys."

"And Miss Bernard?"

"She's *his* friend."

"You're too polite. I heard her true role."

"She has a low side to her character, but mostly, she's an

actress, which I guess isn't much better."

The word *actress* caught her attention. "She's an actress? In London?"

"Yes."

"She appears on the stage?"

"Yes. She's very famous."

"You're joking."

"No. Bryce and I came to the country for a few days of rest and relaxation, and she begged to tag along. Bryce thought she would enliven our party."

"Has she?"

"Not yet."

He assessed Evangeline, trying to picture her as his cousin Iggy's wife. She was so fresh and vivacious. Iggy was pretentious and curt and set in his ways. How could anyone have imagined them a suitable pair? Weren't they marching toward decades of misery? But what did he know about marriage or romance?

His own wedding was in six short weeks. His fiancée, Priscilla Cummings, was a fussy, spoiled shrew who was twelve years younger than Aaron and totally wrong for him, so he was hiding in the country, eager to forget the entire mess for a bit.

His father, Lord Sidwell, had arranged the match, but Aaron couldn't bear to proceed. He had to come to terms with the situation, had to muster the temerity to return to London with a smile on his face and peace in his heart. As his father kept pointing out, the union would bring an enormous amount of money and property into the family, and a man didn't wed for love. He wed for wealth and personal gain, and Priscilla delivered them in spades.

"How did you end up engaged to my cousin?" he asked.

"I received an inheritance as a dowry, and a friend of mine contracted it."

"But you haven't met him?"

"No."

He could practically see her mind whirring. She was dying to inquire about his cousin, but it would be completely inappropriate for them to discuss Iggy. Aaron hadn't a kind word to say, and she needed to form her own opinion.

Still, he hated to have her fretting. What were her circumstances? Iggy was marrying for the same reason Aaron was marrying: for his bride's dowry. Why was Miss Etherton marrying? It had to be for stability and security. Who could fault her for that?

"My cousin is all right," he said, anxious to reassure her.

"Is he?"

"He can be a tad stuffy, but then he's a vicar. I think it's in their blood. They have to be stuffy."

She seemed relieved by his comment, and she smiled again, the beauty of it washing over him like a cool rain, and it occurred to him that he'd like to linger in her company all evening. She attracted him as no other female ever had. The sensation was peculiar and novel, and it made him nervous, made him wary.

He was in an awful condition himself, and he had no business flirting with her, no business gaping at her as if he'd like to gobble her up. But she was just so damned pretty. How could he mind his manners?

He had to force himself out of the room before he thought up a hundred excuses as to why he should remain. He unfolded from the chair and walked toward her. At six feet, he was much taller than she was, and he towered over her.

She watched him come, her gaze guarded and tense, as if she was afraid of what he might do, and he had to admit, he was curious himself.

He approached until he was close enough that the toes of his boots slipped under the hem of her dress. Sparks ignited, the air charged with an electric energy.

"You'll stay at Fox Run—as my guest—until your wedding."

"Thank you."

"And don't be embarrassed by Miss Bernard or what you saw. I'll send her away tomorrow."

"No! I don't mean to impose. It's a huge house. I'll keep to myself. You won't even know I'm here."

He doubted that. Where she was concerned, he could detect her scent—as if he were a hound chasing a fox.

"I insist you join us for supper every night, as well as for any of the amusements we plan."

"I shouldn't, Lord Run."

"I insist! Florella will be on her best behavior, and I'll try to be on mine."

She considered his request, and he held his gaze firm, pressuring her with his male presence, with his greater size and position.

Her shoulders slumped. "All right, and I'll be on *my* best behavior too. No more peeking in bedchambers for me. I learned my lesson the first time."

"Good."

They stood, grinning. He felt as if there was something else he should say, something he should tell her, but he couldn't figure out what it might be.

It was the moment for him to depart, but he couldn't move.

Eventually, he reached out and touched the tip of his finger to the tip of her nose. She appeared surprised, but didn't back away.

He traced it down across her lips, her chin, her neck, to the bodice of her dress. Sparks were exploding, the air hissing with the excitement generated by their proximity.

"Have you a dress that's not gray?" he asked.

"Just one."

"Is it blue? Is it the color of your eyes?"

"It's violet."

"Wear it for me tomorrow."

"I will, Lord Run."

He pulled his finger away and hurried out, wondering what on earth was wrong with him. Was she a sorceress? Had she cast a spell on him? If so, what insanities might he perpetrate?

The notion didn't bear contemplating.

He shook off his eerie sense of bewitchment and continued on. Behind him, she shut her door and spun the key in the lock.

"Play it again! Play it again!"

"Yes, yes, please do!"

Aaron halted in his tracks.

Down the hall, a group of people were laughing and clapping as if a party was in progress. It was nearly midnight, so who was up and raising a ruckus?

After leaving Miss Etherton, he'd gone to his own bedchamber, had written some letters and drunk more liquor, but he hadn't been able to relax. He'd given up and had come downstairs again, thinking he'd head to the estate office and review the ledgers. Nothing would put him to sleep faster than adding up long columns of numbers.

But to his surprise, he'd encountered the merry gathering. It could only be the servants, but why weren't they in bed? They all had chores early in the morning, with many of them having to rise before dawn.

The noise was emanating from the music room, and he tiptoed toward it.

He wasn't a musician himself, but he kept the room for entertaining and also for the unlikely chance that his brother, Lucas, might visit someday. Lucas was a renowned rake and scapegrace, but also an accomplished keyboardist who would enjoy the spot should he ever have occasion to use it.

Aaron stopped outside the door and peeked in.

To his astonishment, Miss Etherton was seated at the pianoforte and belting out a bawdy song. Eight footmen and housemaids were scattered around the box of the instrument.

Even the housekeeper was present, and as Aaron listened to Miss Etherton sing, he swiftly understood why they were so enamored.

He was a regular theater goer in London, had attended many musicales that boasted recitals by the most famous voices in Europe. But he'd never heard anyone sing as she could sing. She had a throaty, sexy alto, and her love of performing was blatantly apparent. Her eyes sparkled with mischief, her cheeks were rosy from her efforts, and she reveled in the acclaim of her small audience.

In that, she was very much like Lucas, who relished the opportunity to have a crowd applauding and telling him he was marvelous.

The local parishioners were very fortunate to have her coming into their midst, but how would she fare as Iggy's wife? It was the strangest mismatch in history. Who would have arranged such an odd pairing? Obviously, it had been carried out by an idiot who didn't recognize Miss Etherton's flamboyant nature.

She arrived at the chorus of her song, and the servants heartily joined in. He supposed he should have been incensed by their raucous exhibition, but he'd never seen them in such a state of gaiety, and Miss Etherton was simply too mesmerizing to ignore. When she sang like that, how could a person *not* join in?

She finished off with a whisk of her fingers up the keyboard. She was laughing, the servants clapping, and Aaron was grinning like a fool.

What a breath of fresh air she was! What a fantastic addition to his dreary abode! How lucky that he'd traveled to Fox Run during the brief period she would be in residence.

"Now then," Miss Etherton was saying, "I must head for my bed."

"No, no," they all protested, and there were pleas of, "Just one more!" and "Don't quit yet!"

"I'm sure Lord Run would be upset if he learned we were cavorting in here," she told them.

There were comments of, "Lord Run won't find out," and "We won't tell him."

Aaron thought it was a moment fraught with danger. At any second, they might utter derogatory remarks about him that he shouldn't hear.

He'd moved to sneak away, when a housemaid glanced over and saw him. She gasped and nudged the footman next to her, and very quickly, they all straightened, their jollity vanishing. They looked like guilty children bracing for punishment.

He hated that he'd wrecked their merriment, and he blustered in. "There's no reason to stop, Miss Etherton. Don't mind me."

She leapt to her feet. "It was all my doing, Lord Run. I was wandering the halls, and I stumbled on the pianoforte. I was being much too loud, and they came in to discover what was happening. I apologize."

"No apology is necessary."

"Please don't be angry."

"I'm not." He smiled and, hoping he appeared cordial, he let his gaze drift across the assembled group. "Miss Etherton is quite amazing. You have my permission to listen to her sing whenever she decides to grace us with her talent."

Miss Etherton's cheeks flushed in that delightful way he was coming to enjoy.

"You're too kind, Lord Run," she murmured.

"I'm absolutely stunned by you. Thank you for your performance."

The servants were completely intimidated by him. They were elbowing each other, nodding to the door, slipping out one by one.

"Good night," Aaron said to each of them as they passed by.

They dipped curtsies and hurried off, clearly terrified that there would be consequences, and he felt awful that they viewed him as being so imposing. His father was the sort to terrorize people. Not Aaron.

Very rapidly, he and Miss Etherton were alone.

"You certainly know how to empty a room," she saucily said.

"It's my best trait," he replied, and he wasn't joking. He was a renowned boor, a notorious fusspot and stickler for the proprieties.

Lucas was the easy-going member of the family. He had the knack to fit in to any situation, to make any person comfortable, but then he took after their long-deceased mother. Aaron, to his chagrin, mostly took after their father who was famous for his conceit and snobbish ways.

"How did you learn to sing like that?" he asked as he walked over to her.

"I've always been able to. It comes naturally."

He pointed to the keyboard. "And the playing?"

"I had teachers at school. I caught on right away."

"Were your parents musically inclined?"

"I have no idea. I'm an orphan and was a charity case at school. I have no information about them, but I suppose I must have inherited my talents from them."

Aaron wondered which was worse, to never have known one's parents? Or to know them and realize you possessed all their same foibles and flaws?

He leaned his elbows on the box of the instrument, and it

placed him very close to her.

"Play something just for me," he insisted.

"I couldn't. I'd be too embarrassed."

"Why is that? Can you only perform for the servants? Is that the audience you prefer?"

"No. I just...just..." She halted, shrugged, then said, "You make me too nervous."

"*I* make you nervous? Why would I?"

"I want you to think I'm good."

"Trust me, I think you're very, *very* good."

"Do you mean it?"

She inquired tentatively, as if she wasn't sure of her ability, as if maybe she'd been denigrated for it in the past.

"Yes, Miss Etherton, I'm bowled over by you."

"You're being serious? You're not jesting?"

"I'm not jesting."

She graced him with her beautiful smile. On seeing it, his heart actually lurched in his chest.

"And you're not angry?"

"No."

"I'd hate to have you be cross with the servants because of me."

"While you are my guest, you may perform in any fashion and at any volume you like."

"What if I keep luring the servants from their duties, and they don't serve you a brandy fast enough? Won't you be irked?"

"With you and that voice in my home? You must be joking. I haven't heard a singer as grand as you in any of the theaters in London."

"That's the sweetest thing you could have told me."

"Have you ever considered singing on the stage?"

"I dreamed about it when I was younger, but of course, I eventually grew up and had to accept that it's not a suitable path for a woman."

"It's the very dickens, isn't it, being an adult?"

"Yes, the very dickens," she agreed.

She leaned her elbows on the box too, so there was hardly an inch of space between them. She scrutinized him, as if she didn't know what to make of him. Was he an enigma? He'd like to imagine he was, although the truth was that—for all his pomp and circumstance—he was very dull and ordinary.

Very quietly, very surprisingly, she said, "I like you. I probably shouldn't, but I do."

"I like you too, Miss Etherton. Very much."

They stared and stared, a thousand comments swirling that couldn't be spoken aloud. A strange wave of destiny swept over him, as if it was his fate to have met her, as if they were supposed to find themselves alone in this very spot.

Before he realized his intent, he closed the gap separating them and kissed her. In the entire history of kisses, it was very brief, very chaste. And very, very *wrong*.

She was his houseguest—his *engaged* houseguest—who was betrothed to his cousin. So what was Aaron thinking? He wasn't thinking; that was the problem.

For the fleetest moment, she allowed the contact, then she jumped back. If she'd slapped him, he'd have deserved it, but he was relieved to see that she was smiling.

She wagged a scolding finger at him. "You shouldn't have done that."

"No, I shouldn't have."

She paused, apparently waiting for him to apologize, but he didn't because he wasn't sorry. He wanted to kiss her again. He wanted to drag her over to the sofa, lie down with her, and kiss her until dawn.

He was being pummeled by a confused sort of yearning he didn't understand. Once again, there were a thousand comments swirling, and he clamped his teeth together, terrified he might open his mouth and blurt out any wild, inappropriate remark.

"Say good night, Lord Run," she said.

"Good night, Lord Run."

She laughed, the sound sultry and alluring and extremely dangerous to his equilibrium.

"Go." She pointed to the door.

"You first."

She studied him for an eternity, then nodded. "Yes, me first. I definitely think I'd better."

She scooted around him and left.

CHAPTER THREE

"What do you think?"

"Your home is lovely."

"I suspected you'd like it." Vicar Bosworth pompously preened. "It has to be much grander than that school where you were teaching."

"Yes, it's much nicer."

Evangeline forced a smile, mustering every bit of fortitude she possessed so she'd appear composed and happy.

The rectory was a fine house, much larger than she'd anticipated. The rooms were a tad dark and drab though, the furnishings older and worn, the wallpaper peeling in the corners.

Don't be so picky! She could have ended up in many places that were much worse, such as a ditch or a hovel in the woods.

Because she was staying at Fox Run, she was viewing every detail through the wrong lens, comparing the rectory to Lord Run's mansion. And she was comparing Vicar Bosworth to Lord Run too—when she shouldn't. Such evaluations would only lead her down a very unsatisfactory road.

She and the vicar were in his front parlor. He'd just given her a tour of the residence and grounds. The church and cemetery were next. They'd stopped for tea before continuing on.

Their interactions were awkward, their conversation stilted and difficult, which was very odd for Evangeline. Typically, she was chatty and pleasant and liked to meet new people, but the vicar was quite grouchy and taciturn, and she hadn't figured out how to lure him into a better mood.

Whenever he thought she wouldn't notice, he'd surreptitiously study her. From his furious frowns, it was clear he didn't like her.

She sighed. An arranged marriage was always a dicey proposition, but what was a potential bride to do if her potential husband developed an immediate dislike? The prospect was aggravating in the extreme.

Perhaps it was her gray dress. The shade wasn't flattering on her. It washed out the color of her hair and skin so she looked wan and pale, so maybe he was worried she was sickly or feeble. She wanted to point out that she wasn't ailing, but she had no idea what topics were appropriate for their first encounter.

"You don't have a harpsichord or any other musical instruments," she said. "How do you pass the time in the evenings? Do you play or sing, Vicar Bosworth?"

"No, and I don't enjoy frivolity. Music is a distraction that diverts me from my higher pursuits." He made a waffling motion with his fingers. "The devil's handiwork and all that."

"Music is the devil's handiwork? Is that what you mean?"

"I assume you received my letter of introduction, Miss Etherton."

"Yes."

"Then you know I read Scripture in the evenings. I wouldn't care to have my contemplation interrupted by caterwauling."

"Yes, I understand how that would create problems for you." She concealed her dismay. If she couldn't play and sing to calm her mind, how would she carry on? "Thank you for writing to me. I actually wasn't aware that I'd been betrothed, and when I learned about it, the news was a shock. Your letter went a long way toward alleviating my concerns."

She forced another smile, thinking he might smile too, that he might admit he was nervous, but he didn't. He glowered at her.

"How was the betrothal a shock?" he asked.

"Miss Peabody, who owned the school, was gravely ill, and as her health failed, she had told me I would receive a bequest from her." She chuckled. "Silly me, I expected it to be monetary."

"Monetary?"

"Yes, it *was* money, but she used it as my dowry. She thought I should have a chance to marry and have a family of my own."

"I see."

"How about you? How did you meet Miss Peabody?"

"Lord Sidwell mentioned her to me. He knew I planned to take a bride this year." He puffed himself up. "I presume you've heard of Lord Sidwell? George Drake, of the Sidwell Drakes?"

"Yes, I've heard of him."

"We're cousins. He and I are *very* close."

"How lucky for you."

"So I'm sure you realize that—despite my lowly position in the church—I come from very elevated stock."

Evangeline fought to maintain a serene expression.

As far as she could tell, Vicar Bosworth wasn't close to the Drakes at all. He didn't seem to know that Aaron Drake had arrived at Fox Run. Nor had Lord Run shared any glowing comments about Vicar Bosworth. If memory served, Lord Run had described the vicar as being *all right*.

High praise indeed.

She didn't like conceit or pretentious behavior and couldn't bear the vicar's bragging. His mother's cousin had married another Drake cousin, so the connection was tenuous at best, but he'd boasted of the relationship a dozen times already. The more he harangued, the more irked she became.

It was as if he was trying to convince himself—rather than her—that he was important, which indicated a lack of self-esteem. What bride would want a husband lacking in confidence? Not her, certainly.

Stop it! she chided, and she assessed him, searching for some hint that there could be future affection between them, but there wasn't one. He was an effeminate fellow, his gestures and bodily movements lacking in manly vigor. But then if masculine qualities were missing, so too would be the anger and temper that some husbands were wont to display.

Still, she couldn't help but remember the talks she'd had as a girl with Rose and Amelia. They'd often discussed the handsome swains and dashing libertines they'd someday wed. Princes and dukes and pirates and highwaymen. None of those dreams had ever included a fussy, grumpy vicar.

Not for the first time, she wondered about Miss Peabody. While growing up under the older woman's caustic eye, Evangeline had struggled and suffered as she'd worked to tone down her natural exuberance and enthusiasm. According to Miss Peabody, nearly every trait Evangeline possessed was a bad one that had to be moderated and restrained.

Yet despite their differences, she'd always thought Miss Peabody had liked her—at least a little—but now she had to accept that Miss Peabody probably hadn't liked Evangeline at all.

Rose had been betrothed to a rich, landed gentleman and would be mistress of a huge estate. Amelia had been betrothed to Lord Run's brother, Lucas Drake. So Amelia would marry an earl's son, a viscount's brother. But with the same swipe of a pen, Miss Peabody had betrothed Evangeline to Vicar Bosworth, a poor relative of the Drakes and not a very pleasant or interesting one at that.

What was Evangeline to make of such a slight? Had Miss Peabody ever spoken to Vicar Bosworth? If so, what would have led her to believe Evangeline should be his wife?

The question boggled the mind.

What should she do? Vicar Bosworth had paid her coach fare to travel to Fox Run, and Evangeline had agreed to the match, had signed legal papers and everything. The dowry had been tendered, and from how Vicar Bosworth had preened over the new carriage he'd shown her in the barn, a substantial portion of the money had likely been spent.

Evangeline had nowhere to go, no family to take her in, and her two friends—Rose and Amelia—were off to their own weddings. Evangeline could hardly pop up on their doorsteps, begging their spouses for charity.

"Cousin Aaron has arrived."

"What?" she stammered, having been lost in her miserable reverie.

"My cousin is at Fox Run. He doesn't usually visit in the summer. Have you met him?"

"Yes, he introduced himself."

"He's invited me to supper."

"That's kind of him."

"*Kind*, yes, but definitely expected. I *am* the vicar in the community after all. I should be first on any guest list."

"Yes, absolutely."

"We may have to move you though."

She scowled. "What do you mean?"

"You are my fiancée, and with the banns just being called, it's over a month until our wedding. It's not appropriate for you to stay at the manor while Lord Run is in residence."

Her heart sank. She loved the beautiful house, her pretty bedchamber, and Lord Run fascinated her. He was so worldly and sophisticated.

He'd kissed her in the music room! He shouldn't have, and she shouldn't have let him, but it had occurred so fast there'd been no time to stop him.

It had left her all jumbled inside, and she'd tossed and turned all night, had staggered out of bed grumpy and confused. She'd wanted to track him down and demand an explanation. Considering that she was at Fox Run to wed his cousin, she'd behaved reprehensibly, but she didn't feel sorry or ashamed for having participated.

She peeked at the vicar, suffering from the strongest urge to blithely confess the indiscretion, so she wondered if the entire ordeal of marrying wasn't driving her a bit mad.

"Why would I have to leave Fox Run?" she asked. "It's a very large place. I doubt I'll ever see him."

"It's not appropriate, Miss Etherton!"

There was a sense of finality in his words that informed her she daren't argue the point.

"Whatever you think is best," she murmured, which she didn't believe at all.

"I'll speak with my cousin after the meal. We'll decide what's to be done with you."

"I'm sure you'll come up with a fine plan."

"Of course I will. Where you are concerned, I shall always guide you on the proper path."

She took a deep breath, recognizing that she was about at the end of being able to keep a smile on her face.

There was nothing timid or humble about her character, and if the vicar viewed her as a meek mouse, in constant need of his supervision and direction, there were some very grueling years ahead for both of them.

"Now then"—he dabbed at his lips with his napkin and stood—"I have a surprise for you."

"I love surprises. What is it?"

"It's time for you to meet Mother."

"I was hoping we'd be introduced."

"She'll live with us."

"Ah...she will?"

"She had one of her sick headaches today, so she's up in her room, but she's waiting for us."

"Is she ill often?"

"Not often."

"It will be nice to have an older woman on the premises." She was lying. She couldn't imagine a more horrid fate than living with his mother. "I'm an orphan myself, so I never had a mother of my own."

"The two of you will get on famously."

"I'm certain we will."

She stood and took his arm, holding tight so she wouldn't be tempted to run out the front door when they passed by it on the way to the stairs.

"What did you think of her, Mother?"

"She seems awfully...pretty."

"Yes, she's very pretty."

Gertrude Bosworth glared at her son and complained, "You know my opinion about pretty girls, Ignatius."

"Yes, Mother."

"They don't make good wives. They're too set on themselves. They're always gazing in the mirror, and they demand to be showered with baubles and fancy clothes."

Ignatius snorted. "If she expects me to keep her in expensive petticoats, she'll be disappointed. I have better things to do with my money than spoil my wife."

"I've taught you well." Gertrude nodded her approval.

They were in her sitting room. It was the only suite in the house, so she'd claimed it for herself. Ignatius was a bachelor and a dutiful child, so he didn't mind. He understood that his mother's wishes came first.

Miss Etherton was finally gone, and Gertrude and Ignatius could breathe a sigh of relief. Lord Sidwell had insisted Miss Etherton would be a fine match for Ignatius, and that ghastly Miss Peabody had insisted the same. Gertrude had let them convince her.

Yet Gertrude had been nervous. Ignatius needed just the right sort of bride, one who could be polite and subservient to Gertrude, but who still had the confidence to carry out her responsibilities as a vicar's wife.

It was a position of high visibility and prestige that required a special person. Was that person Miss Etherton?

"What else did you notice?" Ignatius asked.

"She appeared quite vivacious."

"She's extremely vivacious."

"She's probably constantly smiling and cheery, even when the situation calls for circumspection."

"She received a stellar education. That much was clear from her mannerisms and speech. She must have been coached in etiquette and decorum."

"I suppose."

"I found her to be pleasant."

"You're the one who has to live with her."

"So do you, Mother."

"Yes, well, it's more important that *you* like her."

"I must admit she worries me," Ignatius mused.

"Why?"

"She's been employed for years, so she'll have had a taste of independence. It might be difficult for her to be ruled by her husband."

"It's the reason I detest this modern age," Gertrude said. "A woman who earns her own income loses any sense of her lowly place in the world."

"I agree. It's madness for a female to work. It skews the balance of the universe. But she'll *do*, Mother, don't you think?"

"I imagine she will."

Ignatius grinned, but it was grim and ghoulish. He'd never been handsome, was plain and gaunt. In that, he took after his father.

Gertrude had been the beauty in the family, and her stable life had left her plump from affluence. She was short and rounded, her once-dark hair a silvery gray, but at least she had her hair.

Ignatius had very little remaining, and his baldness added to his morbid countenance. If he'd sought employment as an undertaker, no one would have been surprised.

Instead, he'd followed in his father's footsteps. Gertrude's husband had been a vicar who'd always been assigned to very wealthy parishes.

Ignatius had proved himself an adept student, so it was only natural that he join the clergy too. The decision had turned out to be excellent—for Gertrude. After her husband had died, she'd moved in with Ignatius, so she'd continued on in the types of vicarages where she was most comfortable.

Her sole regret was that he had to marry. She was perfectly content with it being just the two of them. Yet a man needed a wife, and he was already forty. They couldn't keep putting it off.

When the subject was initially broached with Lord Sidwell, Miss Etherton had seemed an ideal candidate. She had no option but to wed, and with her having no alternative, she'd bend over backward to fit in, to please Gertrude. She would be grateful for the chance to be a bride.

And if she wasn't? Well, Gertrude knew how to handle that kind of girl.

"So...we'll go forward with her?" Ignatius asked.

"Yes, we'll go forward."

"Thank you, Mother."

He'd spent most of the dowry, even treating Gertrude to a new fur-lined cape. If Miss Etherton had been horrid, and Ignatius had wanted to reject her, they couldn't have returned the money.

"There's one thing I forgot to mention," Ignatius said.

"What is it?"

"Cousin Aaron is here."

Gertrude scowled. "At Fox Run?"

"I guess he showed up yesterday with some friends."

"Drat it."

She'd been eager to impress Miss Etherton, so she'd convinced the housekeeper to let Miss Etherton stay at the manor. After all, the place was big as a castle. Who would notice or care if she was on the premises?

Gertrude had lied and claimed she'd gotten permission from Aaron, but she wouldn't have dared to request such a favor from him, so his arrival certainly presented a conundrum. How would she explain herself?

"Is he aware that Miss Etherton is at the manor?"

"He is."

"Is he aware that I arranged it?"

"He must be."

"Is he angry? Do we know?"

"I don't believe he's upset. He's invited us to supper this evening."

"Supper! Well!"

"It's been awhile since we dined out."

Ignatius had been at his post for eight months, Lord Sidwell having helped him to secure the position.

In the beginning, they'd socialized regularly, but the invites had swiftly dwindled. Anymore, their acquaintances rarely thought to include them. It was a frustrating development she didn't understand and had no idea how to repair.

"Who else will be there?" she asked.

"I expect it will be his London companions and Miss Etherton, but other than that group, it will probably be various neighbors."

She nodded, then stood and shooed him out.

"Leave me be, Ignatius, and send up my maid. I must decide what to wear."

"Whatever you pick, Mother, you'll be smashing."

"I know."

It was much too warm for her fur-lined cape, but Ignatius was generous about keeping her in fine clothes. She'd find something suitable.

"Where is he?"

"George said he went to Fox Run."

"Fox Run? Are you serious?"

Priscilla Cummings frowned at her mother, Claudia. They were at home in their front parlor. Claudia had just returned from an unsuccessful visit to Lord Sidwell.

"How could Aaron go?" Priscilla seethed. "Our wedding is in six weeks!"

"You needn't remind me of how rapidly your wedding is approaching, Priscilla."

Priscilla was Aaron's fiancée. She was eighteen, and he was thirty. They'd been engaged for an entire year, the months dragging by with excruciating slowness. But now, as they neared the end, matters were speeding up. There were parties and balls and banquets. Priscilla was to be feted everywhere, but suddenly and without warning, Aaron had vanished.

It had taken them a few days to realize he was missing. There had been a small dustup between Aaron and her mother, having to do with Lucas's betrothal to his ghastly fiancée, Amelia Hubbard. Some might even say that Claudia had schemed against Lucas, trying to prevent his marriage to Miss Hubbard.

Of course the person spewing those falsehoods was a renowned liar and trollop named Nanette Nipton. She was an unsavory doxy, but somehow, she'd persuaded Aaron that her story was true, and he blamed Claudia.

Aaron was the most predictable man in the world. He was even tempered and polite to a fault. She and her mother had been so certain he'd get over his fit of pique. After all, Lucas's infatuation with Miss Hubbard was hardly worth a huge quarrel. But Aaron hadn't come slinking back to apologize as Claudia and Priscilla had been positive he would.

Finally, Claudia had gone to speak with Lord Sidwell, only to discover that Aaron had sneaked off.

The next time Priscilla saw him, he'd definitely be informed as to how hideously he was treating her.

"Did Lord Sidwell give a reason for Aaron's departure?" Priscilla asked.

"No." Claudia shrugged. "He insisted he wasn't aware that Aaron had left, that he'd just learned of Aaron's absence shortly before I arrived."

"Obviously, Aaron is still angry about your shenanigans with Mrs. Nipton."

Claudia scoffed. "Angry? At me? Over a slattern like Nanette Nipton? Don't be ridiculous. Everyone agrees that she's lying, and you must stop proclaiming that she and I had an arrangement about Lucas. We most assuredly did *not!*"

Priscilla knew all about Claudia's plot with Mrs. Nipton, but while Claudia told herself that people believed her over Mrs. Nipton, they didn't. Claudia liked to envision herself as being very popular, but Priscilla had hung around in retiring rooms and heard plenty of gossip.

Claudia wasn't the society darling she presumed herself to be.

"What is Aaron thinking?" Priscilla fumed. "How could he trot off like that?"

"With a man, who can guess? As far as I'm concerned, they're all insane."

"But not Aaron! He'd never intentionally embarrass me."

"If that's what you suppose, it's clear I haven't prepared you for your role as a wife."

"What do you mean?"

"A husband will act however he pleases. He will come and go with no regard to your schedule or needs. He will humiliate you whenever the mood strikes him. He'll have mistresses and gamble away your money and thoroughly shame himself." Claudia flashed an annoying smirk. "And as a wife, you have to sit there and take it without complaint."

"Honestly, Mother. That may have been your experience with

Father"—Priscilla's father had been dead for years, and by all accounts, her parents' marriage bitterly unhappy—"but Aaron is different. He knows what I expect of him, and he'll conduct himself accordingly."

Claudia rolled her eyes. "I foresee decades of heartache in your future."

"You were a milksop who let Father walk all over you, but *I* am not you. I stand up for myself. Aaron wouldn't dare behave badly toward me."

"Aaron wouldn't? He's flitted off to Fox Run, hasn't he?" Claudia chuckled nastily. "What an immature little dunce you are."

"I appreciate your glowing words of support," Priscilla sarcastically said.

"You're welcome."

They glared, and for a moment, it seemed they might bicker, which they never did. They were very much alike and almost always in full accord. If they were currently out of sorts, it was Aaron's fault. He was making them cantankerous.

Priscilla was the first to back away. "How shall I handle this situation, Mother? How can I force him to come home?"

"There's not much you can do. He will remain at Fox Run until he's ready to return."

"But how will I explain his absence? I'll be a laughingstock."

"Yes, you will be."

"People will titter behind their fans. They'll spread awful rumors and say he's having second thoughts."

"Is he?" Claudia raised a caustic, perfectly plucked brow.

"Absolutely not," Priscilla huffed.

"Then there's nothing to worry about, is there?"

"No."

Yet Priscilla was unnerved. Her mother was thirty-eight, and she was staring at Priscilla as if she knew secrets Priscilla didn't know, as if she was privy to wisdom that only older women could ever attain.

"If Aaron isn't here in a week," Priscilla tersely stated, "I shall travel to Fox Run and bring him back."

"*You* will travel to Fox Run? I really don't believe you should."

"Well, I'm not about to let this humiliation continue."

"Let's give it two weeks. Perhaps he'll come to his senses without your having to make a fool of yourself by showing up there unannounced."

"Why would I be making a fool of myself? I'm Aaron's betrothed and about to be his bride. Once we're wed, Fox Run will be my home. He should be happy to see me there, no matter the circumstances."

"You may think that all you like, Priscilla, but I wouldn't barge in without alerting him to your planned arrival."

"Why not?"

"As I said, with men, you can't predict their behavior. If you bluster in to Fox Run, there's no telling what you might discover." Claudia pushed herself to her feet. "Trust me, darling, there are some things a woman is better off *not* knowing."

Her mother swept out, leaving Priscilla to fuss and fret and wonder what the devil she meant.

CHAPTER FOUR

"Miss Etherton!"
"Yes?"

Evangeline spun around to find Florella Bernard approaching.

Lord Run's servants had quickly put together a very large supper party, with dozens of neighbors invited. The meal was over, guests scattered through the various parlors to socialize and mingle. Some were playing cards, some were talking. Evangeline had naturally gravitated to the music room where a neighbor's daughter was playing the harpsichord. Evangeline could barely restrain herself from marching over and joining in.

Luckily, Evangeline hadn't yet had to converse with Miss Bernard. During the meal they'd been seated at opposite ends of the table, but now Miss Bernard was barreling down on Evangeline, evidently intent on rehashing their prior encounter.

Evangeline's cheeks flushed bright red. It was an annoying physical condition she couldn't prevent. Whenever she was embarrassed or flummoxed, her skin gave her away.

"Hello, Miss Bernard."

"Oh, you must call me Florella. Everyone does."

"Thank you," Evangeline said, but she didn't imagine she would and didn't extend the same courtesy.

In her sheltered world, people didn't use their Christian names, except on very familiar acquaintance. But then, since Evangeline had seen Miss Bernard removing her clothes, maybe they were already at that spot.

Her flush deepened as she recollected that Miss Bernard was Bryce Blair's…*mistress*. They were a strange and decadent pair, and Evangeline wondered what the other guests would say if they knew the truth.

Evangeline wanted to shun them, but was confused about what her feelings should be. Lord Run was great chums with Mr. Blair and wasn't bothered by Miss Bernard's loose morals. If he wasn't concerned, was it any of Evangeline's business?

"Let me apologize to you," Miss Bernard quietly beseeched.

"There's no need," Evangeline said. "I was spying when I shouldn't have been, and I have no right to protest what goes on under Lord Run's roof."

"I would hate to have you think poorly of me."

"I don't," Evangeline lied.

She hadn't precisely settled on an opinion. Miss Bernard was a contradiction in terms. She was a famous actress and doxy, which should have indicated coarse character, but she had very gracious manners, was extremely charming, and had carried on a pithy conversation at the dining table. Only Evangeline had been aware of her more sordid propensities.

How could so many disparate traits be encapsulated in one woman?

"Aaron tells me you'll be at Fox Run while we're here," Miss Bernard said.

"Well, I'm not sure. The vicar doesn't believe it's appropriate for me to remain now that Lord Run is in residence."

"Nonsense. Of course you'll stay, and I hope we'll be friends. I hope you can overlook our little…difficulty."

"There was no real harm done," Evangeline told her, for she was a kind person and didn't like to denigrate or hold grudges.

"Aaron also tells me that you're quite an accomplished singer."

"Lord Run said that?" Evangeline was secretly delighted that they'd discussed her.

"Yes, he was bowled over by you. My maid was too. Apparently, the whole house is agog."

"I can't imagine why."

"Will you sing for us this evening? These rural parties can get so dreary."

"I don't know if I should."

Evangeline glanced over at Vicar Bosworth. He and his mother were seated together on a love seat. There was an empty chair next to the vicar, and Evangeline probably should have joined them, but she couldn't bear the notion.

In their meeting earlier in the day, Widow Bosworth had been positively horrid, her dislike of Evangeline practically oozing from every pore.

Oh, what was she to do? She wished there was an older and wiser female who could advise her. Should she refuse the match? *Could* she refuse it? Could she say they were completely wrong for one another? Was that a valid reason to cry off?

She had no idea and was new in the community. If she breathed a word about her concerns, gossip would eventually find its way to the vicar and his mother, which would make the situation even more awful.

"If you don't sing tonight," Miss Bernard said, "then you must swear you'll sing for me tomorrow."

"I will."

That might have been the end of it but, suddenly, Lord Run entered the room, with several people following him in. He clapped his hands to get everyone's attention.

"I have a treat for you," he announced. "My home has been graced with an amazing talent. I'm planning to prevail on her to entertain all of you."

It took Evangeline a moment to realize he was talking about *her*. She was peering around, trying to see who would step forward, when she noticed him grinning.

"Me?" she gasped.

"Yes, you. You can sing for the servants. Surely you can sing for my guests."

There were general murmurs of *yes* and *please*.

Evangeline wasn't certain how to reply. Again, she peeked over at the vicar and his mother. They were whispering and scowling.

She was wearing her good violet dress, and she'd found a matching peacock feather in the yard. It was stuck in her hair so—in light of her having donned stylish gown and feather—she'd likely pushed the boundaries as far as she could with the Bosworths for one evening.

"Maybe I shouldn't, Lord Run," she mumbled.

"Don't be silly."

He clasped her arm and led her to the corner where there was a harpsichord and a pianoforte. He gestured to the two instruments.

"Which do you prefer?" Evangeline was anxiously assessing them when he said, "Actually, I have a better idea. How about if we have Bryce play the piano, and *you* simply sing. That way, you can more easily dazzle us."

"Mr. Blair plays the piano?"

"Not as well as you, but he can probably stumble through." Lord Run stared over at his friend. "Can't you Bryce?"

Mr. Blair bustled forward, and he was smiling at Evangeline. "I'll try my best, but from how Aaron has been gushing about you, I doubt I'm proficient enough."

"You'll be fine," Evangeline insisted, deciding to agree.

And why shouldn't she? Lord Run was her host, and he was begging her to proceed. Mr. Blair was already seated on the piano bench and gazing at her expectantly. If she refused, she'd seem like a spoiled fusspot.

The vicar might be upset, but perhaps—once he heard her—

he'd let her bring music into his quiet, dreary home. He'd be happier for it. She was sure he would be.

"Sit down in the front row, Lord Run," she said. "I'd be honored to sing for you and your guests." She turned to Mr. Blair and asked, "How did you learn to play? Did you study with a teacher?"

"I always knew how. It just came naturally to me."

"To me as well."

"We both have a gift for music."

"Let's hope we can confirm Lord Run's opinion that everyone will be dazzled."

He laughed, and they had a quick conference where they discovered they had the same favorite songs.

As she spun away from him, he winked and, for the briefest instant, her breath caught in her chest. He looked so much like her—with his blue eyes and blond hair—and for some reason the similarities disturbed her.

Her ears were ringing, a wave of vertigo rocking her, and she frowned, trying to figure out why she was suffering such a strange reaction. But he nodded encouragingly, and as the introductory chords sounded, she straightened and faced the crowd.

Her disorientation faded, and she tumbled into the song, singing for Lord Run who thought she was wonderful. Singing for Miss Bernard who'd heard she was grand. Singing for Mr. Blair whom she knew to be very dissolute, but who seemed to be very kind. Singing for Lord Run's guests so they would be pleased. And she sang for herself because she loved it and was flattered to have been asked.

When she finished, the audience clapped and clapped and demanded she continue. She ended up performing ten pieces, which was all she and Mr. Blair could manage together. Mr. Blair was the first to rush up, and he squeezed her hand.

"Marvelous, Miss Etherton. Simply marvelous. Thank you for permitting me to accompany you."

"You were quite amazing yourself, Mr. Blair."

He winked again, the gesture jogging a distant memory that made her feel dizzy and bewildered. But before she could reflect on it, others hurried up. Miss Bernard hugged her but was swiftly shoved out of the way so neighbors could introduce themselves and shower Evangeline with praise.

People exclaimed their delight that she had arrived to wed the vicar, how she would enliven the parish with her pretty charm, with her merry nature. They kept repeating how lucky Ignatius Bosworth was to have settled on her.

Gradually, the crowd thinned, and she turned to find the vicar standing next to her. As opposed to everyone else who'd been cordial and excited, he was his usual, stilted self. If he had any opinion about her recital, it was meticulously concealed.

"Would you care to walk in the garden, Miss Etherton?" he said. "You must be overheated."

She could think of nothing more horrid, but couldn't decline. Guests were furtively watching them, judging them as a couple, and no hint of her dislike could show.

She focused her smile on the vicar. "Yes, it is hot in here. I would love to walk outside."

She took his arm, and they meandered through the rooms, chatting with parishioners as they passed. They received many congratulations, many questions as to how the engagement had come about. Evangeline didn't have answers to their queries, so she let the vicar offer all the replies.

She studied him during each exchange, and he was awkward with everyone—so it wasn't just her. He possessed an odd temperament for someone who'd decided to be a vicar. His profession would constantly push him into contact with others who were in dire situations. Funerals. Unexpected deaths. Grave illnesses. He didn't have a sympathetic manner, but perhaps that was why he'd chosen her to be his wife.

She genuinely liked people, and in their marriage she would deliver the qualities he lacked.

Finally, they escaped onto the rear verandah. The garden paths were lit with lanterns that made the space appear enchanted; it might have been a prince's castle in a fairytale.

They went down the stairs and strolled along, not speaking, when she noticed someone was behind them. She glanced back to see his mother. Evangeline wanted to scowl with exasperation, but managed to restrain herself.

"Hello, Mrs. Bosworth," Evangeline said, but the woman merely nodded and didn't respond.

"I asked Mother to accompany us," the vicar explained. "As we're not yet wed, we shouldn't be alone in the garden."

"I've been on my own for many years, Vicar, and we are betrothed. I doubt anyone would mind if we were alone."

"*I* would mind," he sternly said. "I have a reputation in the community to uphold."

"Yes, of course."

"I regularly preach about immorality. It would hardly be appropriate for me to exhibit unseemly conduct."

"I understand."

Suddenly, she felt as if she was choking, as if she was in Miss Peabody's office and about to be lectured for an infraction. It dawned on her that—in a way—Miss Peabody had picked an exact copy of herself to be Evangeline's fiancé.

When Miss Peabody had been dying, she'd written that letter to Evangeline where she'd insisted Evangeline needed the guidance and restrictions that marriage to the vicar would bring. She'd insisted it would tamp down Evangeline's normal ebullience.

Apparently, Evangeline had escaped the school only to wed a male version of Miss Peabody! The notion was so depressing!

They arrived at a dark spot in the garden, and they were away from the house where there was no one to overhear. The vicar stopped and pulled away from Evangeline.

"I must speak with you about your behavior," he said.

"My behavior?"

"Your singing."

He pronounced the word *singing* as if it was an epithet, as if she'd been cursing and stripping off her clothes in front of Lord Run's guests.

"What about it?" Evangeline inquired.

"You are not to flaunt yourself ever again. I can't imagine what sorts of liberties you were allowed by Miss Peabody, but they won't be tolerated by me."

"It was just singing, Vicar Bosworth. I was the music and theatrics teacher at the school. Performance has been my whole life."

"It wasn't *just* singing, and you know it, Miss Etherton. You enjoy making a spectacle of yourself. You enjoyed how others were watching."

"Lord Run asked it of me. It would have been rude to refuse."

"I will mention the incident to him."

"Please don't. It would embarrass me."

"Well, *I* am already embarrassed, Miss Etherton. By you!"

"Everyone said I was very good. Why would you be embarrassed?"

"You deliberately sought attention, and you relished the applause. You are overly proud, Miss Etherton, and vanity is a great sin."

"I wasn't being proud or vain," she claimed, though she absolutely had been.

"You can't act so outrageously. It does not bode well for how you envision your role as my wife. You need to come to grips with how your situation will be reduced."

"How will my situation be reduced?"

"I will not permit public displays by you, and if you insist on it, there will be consequences. You must learn this lesson right from the start."

What did he mean? Would he beat her? Would he send her to bed without supper? Perhaps he'd simply lock her in a room with his mother and that would be a torment beyond imagining.

She glanced over at a glowering Widow Bosworth. Had it been her idea to scold Evangeline? Or had the vicar thought of it on his own? Had Mrs. Bosworth trotted along, gleeful at the prospect of seeing Evangeline chastised?

A wave of fury bubbled up inside Evangeline, and anything might have happened, but—luckily—Lord Run blustered up.

"Miss Etherton, there you are! I've been searching everywhere." He was smiling, happy, but as he noted their dour faces, he staggered to a halt. "What's wrong?"

"Nothing," Evangeline mumbled, as the vicar said, "Miss Etherton and I were discussing a personal matter."

"What personal matter?" Lord Run demanded.

Mrs. Bosworth piped up. "It's a trifle, Cousin Aaron, and naught with which you need concern yourself."

Lord Run glared at her, at the vicar. "Miss Etherton is a guest in my home. If it concerns her, it concerns me."

Vicar Bosworth straightened his shoulders and announced, "If you must know, I'm upset by her singing in public. As she's just being introduced to the parish as my fiancée, it wasn't a fitting reflection of the type of relationship we'll want to exhibit to the community."

"*I* asked her," Lord Run reminded the vicar.

Mrs. Bosworth responded with, "Ignatius was flattered by your request, but he simply feels that she should have obtained his permission before she proceeded."

Lord Run frowned. "Miss Etherton is not a child, Gertrude. I hardly think she should be treated like one." He turned his incensed gaze on the vicar. "Speak for yourself, Cousin Iggy, without your mother speaking for you. *I* presumed on Miss Etherton's good nature, and she graciously obliged me, so why are you standing here in my garden berating her?"

The vicar's cheeks flushed with rage. Lord Run was enraged, too, and Widow Bosworth matched them in ire.

Evangeline was more mortified than she'd ever been.

While she was delighted that Lord Run had come to her defense, she couldn't imagine how it would benefit her in the future. She had to figure out how to maneuver through her life with the Bosworths, and Lord Run could never be part of the solution. In fact, his interfering as her champion would only make the situation worse.

"Would you excuse me?" she muttered.

She slipped away without waiting for a reply from any of them.

She raced to the house, sneaked in a rear door, and skedaddled to her room, where she would hide for the rest of the evening. She'd experienced her first party at Fox Run, and in light of how hideously it had ended, Vicar Bosworth would likely get his wish. She was quite sure she'd never attend one again.

※　　※　　※　　※

Aaron stared at Ignatius. They were in Aaron's library, with Iggy swilling down liquor now that they were away from his parishioners and he could act true to form. He was a miser who rarely purchased his own liquor. He liked to drink in private—but have someone else pay for it.

It was just the two of them, Gertrude having tried to slither in too, but Aaron had shut the door in her face. No doubt she was lurking in the hall and peeking in the keyhole. She was more overbearing than any mother who'd ever lived, and she wouldn't like Aaron to have a conversation with Iggy to which she wasn't privy.

Iggy was an awkward fellow, and Aaron didn't know him very well. Or like him very much. When Gertrude had come begging—not Iggy, but Gertrude—for Aaron to intervene so Iggy would be appointed vicar at Fox Run, Aaron hadn't been overly opposed. Iggy was family after all. Distant family, but still family.

Aaron wasn't religious himself and didn't care who held the reins at the church in the village. As far as he was concerned, one vicar wasn't much different from another. He wasn't at Fox Run enough that it would ever affect him, but he felt sorry for the parishioners.

In times of trouble when they turned to their preacher for solace, it would be hard to receive any from Cousin Iggy. He wasn't very sympathetic.

"How are you finding Fox Run?" Aaron asked him.

"It's been excellent."

"You moved into the vicarage with no difficulty?"

"No, none."

"You're now sufficiently settled that you can afford to marry."

"Yes."

"Then things have definitely improved for you since you arrived."

"It's all been good."

"Tell me about Miss Etherton."

"What about her?" Iggy was disconcerted by the question, as if Miss Etherton was his dirty little secret.

"The two of you are an odd match."

"Mother says all couples seem oddly matched at first. She says it takes a bit of time and acquaintance to grow familiar."

Aaron's father constantly said the same about Aaron's engagement to Priscilla. Aaron was having major second thoughts, when in reality, there was no reason to back out. He'd traveled to Fox Run to get his head on straight, to remember why he was marrying: for Priscilla's money and property.

"If you and Miss Etherton don't become better suited," Aaron pressed, "what then?"

"Why wouldn't we become better suited? By attaching herself to me, she's taking a huge step up in the world. She understands that."

"Does she?"

"Absolutely."

Aaron recalled her expression when he'd stumbled on them in the garden. She'd appeared ready to pound Iggy into the grass, and it had been Aaron's exact sentiment.

"How is she taking a step *up* by attaching herself to you?" Aaron inquired.

"She's an orphan with no family or connections, so she's always been alone. She's actually been...working." Iggy spat the word *working* as if he'd just accused her of prostitution.

"Working at what endeavor?"

"She was a schoolteacher."

"Really? How strange."

"Why?"

"I've crossed paths with a few other teachers recently. There is a swarm of them out on the marriage market this summer."

His newly discovered cousin, Rose Ralston, was one of them, and Amelia Hubbard was the other. Hopefully, if Lucas had played his cards right, she was about to be Aaron's sister-in-law.

"If Miss Etherton is such a lowly individual," Aaron asked, "why did you select her?"

"She had a fine dowry, and of course, your father recommended her to me."

"My father suggested her?"

"Yes. We couldn't disappoint the old fellow by refusing her. Not when he'd taken such an interest in my future."

Aaron bit down a guffaw. His father was the worst person to pick a spouse for any man. He'd betrothed Lucas a dozen times, to one horrid girl after another. Only Miss Hubbard had been worth the bother.

As for Aaron, his father had demanded Aaron wed by age thirty. Aaron had consented, but when he couldn't decide on any of the available candidates, his father had simply betrothed him to Priscilla without seeking Aaron's opinion. And look how that mess had turned out! It was a disaster all the way around.

"I must admit that I'm rather exasperated with you, Iggy."

"Then I most humbly apologize," the obsequious toad insisted. "How have I vexed you?"

"This is my home, I'm hosting a party, and Miss Etherton is my guest."

"And *my* fiancée."

"That's as may be, but I won't put up with you scolding her."

"She's very independent, and she's been on her own for years. She doesn't comprehend what her role will be as my wife."

"So you were merely instructing her?"

"Yes."

Aaron rolled his eyes. "I will be here for a fortnight or so. While I'm in residence, you will not quarrel with her."

"I'm in complete agreement, and I'm making plans for her to move out."

At the news, Aaron was taken aback. "Move her?"

"Mother says it's not appropriate for her to be at the manor while you and Mr. Blair are on the premises."

"But Miss Bernard is here too, as well as my housekeeper and a dozen housemaids."

"Mother is worried about appearances. It's very important that Miss Etherton establish herself in the community in just the right way."

"It would damage her reputation to stay at Fox Run for a few weeks?"

Iggy had caught himself in a trap. If he said *yes,* he'd be insulting Aaron. If he said *no,* there was no reason for her to be moved.

Aaron couldn't bear to imagine Miss Etherton living somewhere else. He would be at Fox Run for only a very short interval, then he had to head to London and the responsibilities awaiting him there. Namely his fast-approaching wedding.

In the meantime, he was at Fox Run, and Miss Etherton was too. He suffered an incredible amount of pleasure from knowing he could come down to breakfast and find her in his dining room.

The entire house was brighter and merrier because she was in it, and he wasn't about to have her leave. Iggy and his mother be damned!

"Mother and I feel it would be best if she left."

"No," Aaron firmly stated.

"No?"

"She'll remain at Fox Run."

"I don't think that's wise."

"And I don't give a rat's ass what you think."

Iggy gasped with offense. "Honestly, Cousin Aaron, there's no need to be vulgar."

"No, there's not, so let me be clear. She's staying. Don't argue with me about it."

Iggy was about to pitch a fit like the spoiled child he'd always been, but ultimately, he dipped his head in defeat. "All right."

"While she's here, she will be welcome to behave however she likes. She can sing or dance or drink wine or ride my horses or chat with neighbors of whom you disapprove. It will be none of your business how she acts."

"I see," Iggy grumbled.

"You will not chastise or scold her for any conduct she undertakes, most specifically those that I have asked her to perform."

"I understand."

"If you can't mind your manners, you and your mother won't be invited to Fox Run ever again. You can sit in the rectory and pout about how unfair I'm being."

Two slashes of red marred Iggy's cheeks. He leapt to his feet. "Will that be all, Cousin Aaron?"

"For now. But if you aggravate me in the future, you'll definitely hear about it."

Iggy spun to go, but Aaron stood and beat him to the door. He yanked it open, and as he'd suspected, Gertrude had been peeking through the keyhole. She stumbled into the room, struggling to muster her aplomb, to not look like a fool.

"Cousin Aaron," she sputtered, "I was... about to knock."

"Were you?"

"I was wondering if Iggy could return to the party. There are guests leaving and they want to say goodbye."

Aaron simply glared at her until she shut up. Once she was quiet, he said, "My housekeeper informs me that you took it upon yourself to ensconce Miss Etherton at Fox Run."

"Well...ah...I didn't suppose you'd care. It is a big house, and you've always been so accommodating to me."

"I *do* care—very much. Not that Miss Etherton is here, but that you felt free to extend the offer on my behalf. You will not presume again, Cousin Gertrude. I've instructed the housekeeper to check with me first from now on. She's not to believe you on any topic."

"Fine," she fumed. "Be that way—if you must."

She grabbed Iggy's arm, and they stomped out.

CHAPTER FIVE

Aaron crept down the hall, feeling like a burglar in his own home.

The guests were gone, the servants in bed. He'd been downstairs having a brandy with Bryce, but it hadn't calmed him or improved his mood. Their conversation kept meandering back to Miss Etherton, and he'd struggled mightily not to display too much interest.

Bryce was a gambler and ne'er-do-well, and in light of Aaron's elevated position, it was odd that they were friends. But they'd attended school together as boys and had never lost their connection.

Bryce was the sort of fellow Aaron might have become if he hadn't been his father's heir. Aaron took his responsibilities seriously—to study, to learn the workings of their vast estates, to understand his role. Because of that burden, his life had been a tedious slog.

In many ways, Bryce was Aaron's exact opposite. He'd been an orphan and charity case at school, his tuition paid by a kindly benefactor. He rarely mentioned his past and claimed not to remember his parents, though Aaron wasn't sure if that was true.

Yet without the encumbrance of familial obligation, Bryce was free to live how he chose. There were no expectations to meet, no grumbling father to complain about his conduct. Bryce could gamble and carouse without worrying that anyone would notice or chastise.

He occasionally supplemented his income by performing on the stage. His plunge into theatrics was further evidence that Aaron should have cut ties long ago, but Bryce reminded Aaron of Lucas, and in Aaron's stilted, boring world, he needed more people like Bryce in it, not less.

Bryce had surrounded himself with actors and other performers, so he'd been particularly delighted by Miss Etherton, and the more they'd talked about her, the more determined Aaron had grown.

He absolutely could not allow her to marry his cousin. The match was a grand folly in the making, and Aaron was desperate to quash it. He could imagine nothing more horrid than beautiful, charming Evangeline Etherton wed to Ignatius Bosworth. It seemed a crime against the natural order, and the universe was pushing Aaron to intervene.

He arrived at her door and, without pausing to reconsider, he knocked.

Was she still up? He hoped she was. After Iggy had scolded her in the garden, she'd hurried into the house and hadn't reappeared. Clearly, Iggy's behavior had upset her, so she'd be more inclined to listen to Aaron. She had to refuse the match or agree to delay until they could come up with a more viable plan.

"Miss Etherton?" he murmured. "Miss Etherton? Evangeline?"

He pressed his ear to the wood and was debating his next move, when she moaned as if she was in distress.

"No, no..." she was saying.

Without hesitating, he spun the knob and stepped in, terrified over what he might find, but she was asleep in a chair by the fire and in the throes of a nightmare.

"No, no..." she said again. "Don't go! Don't leave me with them!"

He walked over and knelt in front of her. He clasped her arm and shook it.

"Evangeline, wake up."

"No!"

"Evangeline!"

She jumped to consciousness, lashing out with a fist at an unseen foe, so she nearly clocked Aaron on the jaw. He lurched back, and she barely missed him.

Gradually, her senses returned, her gaze focused, and she asked, "Lord...Run? What is it? What's wrong?"

"You were having a bad dream. I was passing by in the hall when I heard you cry out."

She was distraught, her cheeks pale, her hands trembling. There was a bottle of brandy on a table in the corner, and he went over and poured her a glass.

"Have a sip," he said. "It will calm you."

"Thank you."

He held it out, and she downed several swallows. Ultimately, she mumbled, "I hate that dream."

"Do you have it often?"

"Not often. When I'm stressed or weary, it comes to haunt me. The details are so real, I think it's probably an event that actually occurred, but I don't recollect."

He pulled up a chair and sat, positioning it closely enough that their knees were touching, their feet and legs tangled.

"What is it about?" he inquired.

"I'm very tiny, and I'm down at the docks. Maybe in London? I'm not certain where it is. There are some boys with me—they might be my brothers. We're being separated. I have to go away with someone, and I don't want to. I want to stay with them."

"You don't remember if you have brothers?"

"No."

"How many are there?"

She thought and thought, then said, "Three? There's always one for sure, and he's the oldest, but there might be others. Sometimes they're present and sometimes not. The oldest one claims I shouldn't be afraid, that he'll find me."

"Then what happens?"

"Then...I wake up. I guess the ending must be so heart wrenching that I can't bear to know what it is."

"Or perhaps you know the ending. Perhaps he was a child and wasn't able to come for you."

"Oh, don't say it! It would be too depressing." She forced a smile. "It's most likely just an orphan's fantasy due to my desire to have a family."

"Please don't tell me you grew up in an orphanage."

"No, in a boarding school."

"Thank heaven for that."

"Yes, my life has been all right—for all I don't recall the beginning of it. In my first memories, I'm four or so, and I'm at school."

"But safe and sound?"

"Yes, always safe and sound there."

She drank down the rest of the liquor, and it visibly relaxed her. As she placed the glass on a nearby table, he studied her.

In the fading firelight, she looked young and pretty and very, very alone. From the moment they'd met she'd fascinated him and that fascination appeared to be increasing at an alarming rate.

She was exhibiting a brave front, but he suspected that if he hadn't blustered in, she'd be weeping in anguish. Were her memories that ragged?

He wasn't the sort of person who comforted others. If he'd been asked to describe himself, he'd have said aloof, detached, cold, and stern. But suddenly, he was anxious to comfort *her*.

Acting on instinct, he didn't allow better sense to prevail. He drew her onto his lap, dragging her from her chair and onto his own. He spread his legs and balanced her on his thigh. She tried to push away, but he snuggled her down so she was nestled to his chest.

He caressed a soothing hand up and down her back, and he was surprised to discover that he liked it very much. Maybe he wasn't such an ogre after all. Maybe, deep down, there was a glimmer of humanity lurking beneath the stuffy, pretentious façade he showed to the world.

He'd had his share of romantic entanglements, but he wasn't a warm or cuddly fellow. He viewed his carnal relationships as commercial transactions: money paid for services rendered. There'd been no tender encounters, no quiet interludes in the dark of night, so he hadn't realized that affection could be so pleasant. The interval was emotionally charged, but in a way he enjoyed very much.

Eventually, she straightened and gazed at him. Her lush, ruby lips were only an inch from his own, and he couldn't help but kiss her. He just managed to touch his mouth to hers when she gave him a hard shove and jumped to her feet.

"No, no, no," she scolded. "We're not doing this. I can't."

"Yes, you can."

He grabbed her wrist, but she jerked away and stomped across the room. She pulled the door open and hovered next to it, as if—should he say or do the wrong thing—she would run out into the hall.

"What is it you want from me?" she inquired. "I don't know."

"This is the second time you've come in here. I'm your guest. I should be safe in your home."

"Safe—with me? You're mad if you assume so."

"If you can't leave me alone, then I agree with Vicar Bosworth. I need to stay somewhere else until my wedding."

"No."

"I'm not a chattel, and I'm not a slave. We're barely acquainted, and you have no authority over me. It's none of your business if I depart."

"And who does have authority? My cousin?"

"He would think so."

"He's an idiot."

She didn't respond to his insult. Obviously, she'd have liked to, but what would be the point? Unless or until the betrothal was severed, she was engaged to Iggy, and the notion aggravated Aaron beyond his limit.

"You can't marry him," Aaron insisted.

"Easy for you to say."

"You can't. I won't let you."

"*You* won't let me?" She snorted with disgust. "Would you go? I appreciate your checking on me, but I can't have you barging in."

"It's my bloody house," he crudely snapped. "I can behave however I wish."

"My betrothal is difficult enough for me. I can't have you making it worse."

"How am I making it worse?"

"You seem to want something from me, but whatever it is, I can't give it to you."

Did he want something? He thought he probably did. He was so happy when he was with her, so optimistic and hopeful, as if a remarkable future could transpire between them. But he wouldn't tell her that. Such maudlin drivel was completely foreign to his character, and he wasn't about to provide any hint of how deeply she affected him.

"Iggy is all wrong for you," Aaron said.

"So? In my experience, husbands and wives are never compatible. I expect my marriage to him will be very typical."

"Why would you agree to the match?"

"Because I didn't have any choice! Why do you suppose? It's not as if I have a hundred friends and family members lined up with other options. Should I have refused him? Would I be better off living in a ditch?"

"He claims you had a *fine* dowry. Why didn't you use it to pick someone more suited to your personality?"

"It wasn't up to me. I simply did as I was told."

"Pardon me, but you don't seem all that submissive. Why blithely consent?"

She scoffed and shook her head. "We're not all rich and lucky like you. Some of us—*me* in particular—are just scrambling to get by."

"Is that how you'll view your marriage? As just getting by?"

"Yes. What else is there for a woman in my position?"

When he found her to be so magnificent, the prospect of her being abused by her spouse was extremely wrenching. He couldn't bear to imagine her in a bad situation.

"Let me help you," he said.

"How could you?"

That was a question for the ages, wasn't it? What assistance was he prepared to bestow?

With his own wedding swiftly approaching, he couldn't take her to London. Nor could he leave her at Fox Run. He and Priscilla were moving to Fox Run after the wedding was over. He could hardly arrive with Priscilla and have Miss Etherton greet them in the driveway. There would be no way to explain her presence to his wife.

Iggy had mentioned that she'd been a schoolteacher, and Aaron didn't know why the post had ended. She could probably return to that dreary existence, but he couldn't picture her toiling away at such a dull endeavor. She was like a brilliant comet streaking across the sky. She ought to be in London on the stage, but he'd cut off his tongue before he'd put that idea in her mind.

If she flitted off to London, she'd wind up like Florella, with an empty purse, loose morals, and every libertine in the city begging her for indecent favors.

He pushed himself to his feet and marched over to her. She watched him warily, as if he was a rabid dog that might bite. And, he had to admit, he wasn't sure himself what he might do.

For months, he'd been raging and out of sorts. He'd traveled to Fox Run to ease his stress, to come to grips with his engagement, but since he'd met her, he was more dissatisfied than ever.

He truly thought he'd meant to storm out, but once he was next to her, he couldn't walk on by. He reached over and shut the door so they were sequestered again. She huffed out a frustrated breath.

"We can't be in here like this," she insisted.

"As I said, Evangeline, it's my house. I can act how I please."

"Well, I can't! What if a servant saw us? What if he told the vicar and—"

Before she could finish her sentence, he swooped in and kissed her.

He slid an arm around her waist and held her close so the entire front of her delicious, voluptuous torso was crushed to his own. The sensation was so stirring that his knees nearly buckled.

For a brief second, she shoved at his chest, but he wasn't about to release her. Ever since their fleeting kiss in the music room, he'd been dying to do it again, to do it more fully and completely so, hopefully, he would tamp down some of the lust she induced in him. But the embrace provided no indication that his ardor might be lessened. If anything, it was immediately pitched to a new and frightening level.

His hands roamed over her body, tracing her shoulders, her back. His fingers went to her spectacular blond hair, and he plucked out the combs, the blond mass falling down in an intoxicating wave. He riffled through it, the feel of the soft strands rattling him, goading him to take the kiss farther than it should ever go.

Ultimately, he began massaging her buttocks, pulling her loins to his own, and it was a limit she wouldn't allow him to cross. She yanked away, murmuring, "No, no, I can't."

Her pleading tone stopped him, and they stood in silent

misery, their foreheads pressed together, their breathing labored as if they'd run a long race.

He'd never been so titillated, and he yearned to pick her up, to carry her into the bedchamber and try things with her he'd never previously considered with a female. It was a wild and feral urge that was almost beyond his control, and—should he give it free rein—it would ignite a spark and incinerate them both.

He gazed down at her. She looked rumpled and adorable, and he was so smitten by her.

Before he'd left London, he'd told his father that he wouldn't marry Priscilla, that he planned to cry off. Lord Sidwell had counseled that it was simply bachelor's jitters, and as a cure, he'd suggested Aaron meet a nice girl and have a fling to work off some of his discontentment.

Aaron had scoffed at the notion, but why had he? Why not have an affair? What was preventing him?

Her wedding was in a month, and his was in six weeks. Neither of them was eager to proceed. Why not misbehave for a short interval before duty and obligation rendered many onerous challenges?

Aaron could stay at Fox Run for the month, could have thirty whole days with Evangeline! Why shouldn't they seize the opportunity? Who would ever know? And if no one knew, where was the harm? He would never tell Priscilla, and Evangeline need never confess to Iggy. It was the ideal solution.

"I'm going to ask you a question," he said, "and you have to say *yes*. Don't you dare refuse. I couldn't bear it."

"What is it?"

"I want us to have an affair."

"What? No, absolutely not."

"Evangeline..."

"Don't call me by my Christian name. It's not right."

"We can have an entire month together." He grabbed her by the shoulders and gave her a slight shake. "We can loaf and play and please ourselves."

"No!"

"It will be a secret we'd take to our graves."

"You're mad," she chided, "and you insult me by mentioning it."

"Why?"

"There's no benefit for me to participate. No benefit at all, and if the vicar found out—which he would—my chance to marry would be destroyed."

"Then be my mistress. Tell my cousin to sod off, and I'll move you to London and buy you a cozy little house. I'll fill it with a staff of fawning servants and attire you in the prettiest clothes. I could be with you all the time."

Aaron was shocked he'd tendered the scandalous proposal. He hadn't meant to; it had just slipped out. But once voiced, he rippled with excitement. He would bring her to the city—quietly and discreetly of course—and he'd tuck her away in a private love nest. It wouldn't matter that he had to wed Priscilla, because he'd have Evangeline.

It was perfect! Perfect!

"Your mistress?" she said, scowling.

"Yes, we could be so happy."

"I repeat, you're mad. And you have to go."

"No, no, Evangeline, you're not listening to me."

"I'm listening." She nodded with derision. "Believe me, I heard every word, and I'm embarrassed for both of us."

"Why?"

"You presume I'm the type who would...who might...who would like to..."

Apparently, his request was so offensive she couldn't verbalize her upset.

"There's a physical attraction between us," he said.

"So what? We're not animals. We don't have to act on it."

"We could have the most wonderful liaison."

"Why would you suppose it is what I seek or covet?"

He couldn't fathom her reticence, not when he was so thrilled by the idea. How could he see the advantages so clearly, and she see only disadvantages? He was desperate to persuade her it was for the best.

"I'm very rich, Evangeline, and I can be extremely generous."

"Bully for you."

"Think about your future. Think about your life at the vicarage with my cousin. Then try to picture yourself in London with me. We'd attend the theater, and we'd have fascinating friends. I'd dress you in gowns and jewels. You'd want for nothing."

"You actually assume I'm pining away for gowns and jewels? You actually assume that's the sort of person I am?"

"You're so beautiful, Evangeline. Let me pamper you. Let me make you mine."

She jerked open the door and stepped into the hall without checking first to ensure no servant was walking by. It was late, so it was unlikely, but her brazenness yanked him back to his senses and forced him to recognize that she was correct. He'd gone temporarily insane. It was the sole explanation.

What had come over him? Why had he offered such a ridiculous, untenable proposal?

He was getting married in a few weeks, and though he wasn't the most moral man, he liked to imagine that—at least at the beginning—he might be faithful and loyal. What would it say about his character if he took a mistress right before he took a bride?

The answer to that question was too awful to contemplate.

They stared and stared, and finally she said, "I'll pretend none of this ever happened."

"Fine."

"You're leaving now, and I'm locking my door. I realize this is your house, but you are *not* to visit me again. Do you understand?"

He considered arguing just because he could be contrary and obstinate, but sanity was gradually sinking in. He'd been behaving like a lunatic and was mortified.

"I apologize," he said. "I won't stop by again. I promise."

She didn't reply, didn't smile, didn't indicate any heightened feeling. Had she none? How could he be brimming with affection and she be completely indifferent?

She simply waited, then waited some more, until it dawned on him that she was *waiting* for him to depart.

He walked out and kept on down the hall, and when her door closed, when the key spun in the lock, he didn't glance back.

CHAPTER SIX

Evangeline sat at the harpsichord in the music room at Fox Run. It was very late, and she was smarter now, so she didn't touch the keys. She was afraid she'd attract an audience.

For the prior four days, ever since Lord Run had kissed her in her bedchamber, she'd been a ghost in the house. She'd sneak down early to breakfast, then flit back to her room and hide all morning. She spent the afternoons with Vicar Bosworth, calling on neighbors and being introduced to important parishioners.

When she returned to the manor, she'd creep inside, would rush upstairs and have a supper tray delivered. The evenings were long and dreary and, occasionally, she heard laughter and singing wafting by, as if Lord Run was entertaining. Those were the most difficult hours, as she yearned to go down and join in the merriment.

She was a very social person, not prone to moping or solitude, so she was being particularly reserved. Yet it was necessary to restrain herself. Lord Run had an uncanny ability to coax her to flagrant immoral behavior, and the only deterrence she could devise was complete avoidance.

So far, it had been working well. She hadn't seen him again, and he hadn't bothered her.

Her awkwardness around the vicar was gradually waning, and Evangeline was starting to realize why Miss Peabody had betrothed her to him. Though the area was prosperous, there was suffering too, but he wasn't concerned about the less fortunate.

Evangeline could make a difference, could perform good deeds and help others who hadn't had her advantages in life. Marriage to Vicar Bosworth wouldn't bring her joy or devotion—or even much in the way of companionship—but happiness was fleeting and could be illusory.

Instead, she would settle for contentment, and in the longer scheme of things, that was a higher pursuit, a higher goal.

Why then, was she so miserable?

In her palm, she clasped a miniature statue that had always

been hers. It was a goddess—she'd never learned which one—and carved out of ivory. The initials *AB* were written on the bottom in dark ink, but they had faded over the years. In her first memories, she'd had it with her, and she thought it might be a significant item from her past, often wondering if it had been her mother's.

She always carried it, and when she looked at it, she felt calmer and more in control. She placed it on the box of the instrument, and she stared at it, sensing as she constantly did that it was sending her a message. Unfortunately, she could never decipher what it was.

She traced a finger across the grooved lines of the carving, curious about the artist, why it had been made, why she had it.

"Tell me what to do," she murmured, but of course she received no reply.

She'd asked Vicar Bosworth if there'd been any progress on removing her from the manor, but Lord Run had refused to allow it so, apparently, that ended the matter.

For the moment she was trapped, but she had to leave. And in the future, when Lord Run was in residence, she had to ensure she never bumped into him.

Though she hated to admit it about herself, she'd sinned with her body *and* her mind. By kissing Lord Run as she had, she'd betrayed Vicar Bosworth, and she ought to confess her indiscretion to him, but she was too cowardly.

During any part of the torrid embrace, she could have stopped it, but she hadn't. She'd been eager to keep on to a conclusion she couldn't describe, but that she certainly seemed to crave. All these days later, she was raw and jumbled on the inside, as if invisible fires had been ignited and needed to be extinguished.

Lord Run had begged her to have an affair, to be his mistress. While she'd assumed herself insulted by the request, on further reflection, she was surprised to discover that she wasn't actually that opposed.

He intrigued her in ways she hadn't known she could be by a man. She was a very passionate individual, but under Miss Peabody's stern rules, she'd had to tamp down her wilder impulses. Lord Run lured them to the fore. He made her feel she could give them free rein, that she could—in his presence—be the person she was meant to be. She wouldn't have to conceal her true nature.

Her desire to grab that more reckless, more carefree existence was so potent she could almost taste it.

She glanced up, and to her dismay, Lord Run was watching her from over by the door. She wanted to tell him to go away. She wanted to tell him to *never* go away. She wanted to ask him if he was sorry for their kiss. She wanted to tell him she hoped he *wasn't* sorry for their kiss.

For all her sheltered upbringing, she was very intelligent and pragmatic. She recognized that women got themselves into trouble with scoundrels. She'd heard the horror stories as to how easily a rogue could wear down virtuous impulses, but Evangeline had believed fallen women to be imprudent and weak of character.

Now, all of a sudden, she understood how physical attraction could spur a female to perilous conduct. She was on a very dangerous ledge, desperately keen to do whatever he suggested.

"Hello," he quietly murmured as he came over to her.

"Hello."

"I thought you might be down here."

"You know me well. Musical instruments seem to call my name."

He pointed to her goddess statue. "That's a pretty carving."

"Yes, it is."

He reached for it, but she snatched it away and stuck it in her pocket. Though her anxiety was silly, she kept the statue secreted away, so most people weren't aware she had it. It was her good luck charm, her talisman for protection, to ward off evil.

She suspected she'd once been told to never let go of it, to never lose it. Or maybe it was simply an orphan's attachment that didn't indicate anything at all.

At her odd, grasping behavior, he scowled.

"I apologize," she said, "but it's a special memento."

"It's all right. I merely wanted to look at the details."

She shrugged, trying not to appear foolish. "I've just always had it. It might have been my mother's, but I'm not sure."

"Then by all means, you should keep it close."

"I always do."

Their stilted conversation stumbled to a halt. They stared and stared, a thousand questions rocking her. She'd like to ask why he'd come downstairs, if he'd been searching for her, but they couldn't be in the same room, not for a single second. The minute she saw him, she was eager to race to ruin. It was a disastrous urge that couldn't be acted on.

"You've been hiding from me," he said.

"I figured I should."

"You don't have to. I'm an adult, and you were very clear that I should leave you alone."

I don't want you to leave me alone, she nearly wailed.

"How are things with my cousin?" he inquired. "I'm told the

two of you have been socializing in the afternoons."

"We have."

"Is the situation getting any better for you?"

"Yes," she lied.

"Are you being honest with me?"

She frowned. "Why wouldn't I be honest?"

"I warned him to be kind to you. If he's not, I'll talk to him."

The notion that he'd intervened on her behalf again, that he was determined to be her champion, was inordinately thrilling.

"I don't need your assistance," she insisted. "He and I will be fine."

Dubious and unconvinced, he nodded, and she held herself very still, her gaze level and calm. She was being pelted with such intense yearning that she could barely keep from leaping off the bench and throwing herself into his arms. Could he feel the pressure building between them?

"I've decided I should return to London," he abruptly announced.

The news was extremely distressing, and she gripped the edge of the bench so she'd remain firmly planted on it.

"Why would you?" she asked. "I hope it's not because of me."

"Of course it's because of you," he baldly admitted, and he sounded angry.

"If my presence is disturbing you, I'm quite content to depart. Simply inform the vicar that you no longer mind, and he'll find me other lodging."

"No. You can stay here."

"But it's ridiculous to let yourself be chased away by me. I'm insignificant to your daily routines, and as I've proven, I can keep out of your way."

"I don't want you to keep out of my way. That's the problem."

Giddy elation rocked her, but she fought to conceal her reaction. She couldn't be glad about his interest, couldn't be delighted by what it indicated.

"About the other night..." His voice trailed off.

"What about it?"

"I'm not sorry. You're probably expecting me to apologize, but I won't."

"There's no need to apologize."

"Why is that?" He glared at her, daring her to respond. "You can say it, Evangeline. Why is there no need?"

She shook her head. "It doesn't matter."

"It matters to me."

"It couldn't possibly."

"It does."

He was overwhelming her with his greater size and imposing nature. Just by his standing so near, she was completely befuddled. She was a very lonely, very ordinary female. How was she to ignore what was occurring? How was she to fend it off?

"Tell me you feel it," he said.

"I won't."

He gestured to her, then himself. "Then tell me you don't feel it. Tell me it's not happening."

"There's nothing happening."

"Liar."

"I'm not lying."

"You are, and you shouldn't try it with me. With me, your face is an open book."

"Fine, then. Here's the truth, and it's all I'll say about it."

"Fine. What is it?"

"It's as if sparks ignite when we're together. I don't understand it."

"Neither do I."

"It confuses me."

"Me too."

"You're much too sophisticated, and I'm much too naïve."

"You are," he agreed.

"Separation seems the only solution."

"I concur, which is why I'm leaving for London in the morning."

Don't go! she yearned to plead, but for once, she kept her mouth shut.

"I think it's probably for the best," she resolutely replied.

"I don't."

"Why?"

"If I never see you again, I'm certain I'll be abandoning something remarkable."

She smiled. "If that's what you suppose, then your imagination is running wild."

"My imagination is working perfectly. I can *imagine* all sorts of indecent scenarios, and you're front and center in every one."

Her heart raced with a pulsating flutter, but she paid it no heed. "I don't have an indecent bone in my body, Lord Run."

"Don't you?"

"No."

"You're wrong, Evangeline. In fact, I suspect *every* bone in your body might just be pining away for what I can give you."

"And what is that?"

"I have to show you. If I don't, I'll always regret it."

Being obstinate and demanding as he rarely was, Aaron lifted her off the bench. She didn't protest being manhandled—not exactly—so he simply told himself she was amenable.

She'd rattled loose an intriguing facet of his character. He'd previously viewed himself as being passively restrained, happy to go along and get along. Apparently, he'd never wanted anything as much as he wanted her, and on this occasion, he wasn't about to be denied.

As he crushed his mouth to hers, as he swept her into a stirring kiss, he felt as if he was floating outside himself, as if he was watching some other hapless fellow behave precisely as he shouldn't.

He'd informed her that he was departing for London, and he meant it. His bags were packed, and he'd left instructions with the housekeeper. Bryce and Florella were staying for another week or two, but Aaron was riding off at dawn.

For four torturous days and nights, he'd been fretting over what to do about her. He'd traveled to the country to escape the pressures in London, to take a break from the burden of being engaged to Priscilla. Yet his brief sojourn had provided no haven at all.

He'd tried to avoid Evangeline, but he was infatuated beyond all reason or sense. Finally, he'd been forced to deal with the madness she'd induced. He *had* to leave, but a tiny and insistent voice in his head kept telling him not to go without a goodbye.

There was a sofa behind them, the back of it facing the door so if anyone walked by, they couldn't be observed from the hall. He spun them and laid her on it. He followed her down and stretched out on top of her, trapping her so she couldn't squirm away.

He hadn't ceased kissing her, and he wasn't sure he ever would. The sparks they generated had inflamed him, seemingly to the point of no return, and he couldn't decide what he was planning. He wanted to strip off her clothes, to see her naked, to lick and nibble and taste and never stop.

His hands were everywhere, in her hair, on her shoulders and arms, each stroke of his palms arousing him to a higher level. He rolled them so she was wedged to the back of the sofa. She was wearing one of her functional gray gowns, the buttons easy to manipulate through the buttonholes.

He opened the front and slid a hand inside, quickly finding that—it being very late—she'd shed corset and chemise, so he encountered bare skin, then a perfect breast. He massaged it, pinching the nipple between finger and thumb. She moaned against his lips, and snuggled herself to him more tightly, as if she couldn't get enough of what he was doing to her.

At least he told himself that was what was happening. It was entirely possible she'd like him to desist, but he was too consumed by lust to notice.

He pushed down her dress, then abandoned her mouth to blaze a trail down her neck, her chest, until he reached her bosom. He sucked a pert nipple into his mouth, laving it, biting it.

He shifted to the other breast, to the other nipple, giving it the same potent attention, then he wandered back and forth, back and forth.

Eventually, she whispered, "Lord Run, please. We can't keep on."

"I'm desperate to know you like this, Evangeline."

"But it's so wrong."

"No, it's not. When there is such an attraction between us, it can only be very, very right."

"Spoken like a true libertine."

"I am a libertine. I can't deny it."

"Well, I'm not loose. *And* I'm about to be married."

So am I, he nearly admitted, but didn't. His pending wedding was a distasteful reality, and when he was with Evangeline he hated to think about negative topics. Besides, his life with Priscilla had no connection to Evangeline. The two worlds didn't intersect. Why mention his engagement? There was no point.

She looked beautiful and conflicted, and she was stirring his protective instincts. He was on the verge of begging her to travel to London with him so he could shower her with the boons he'd previously promised. Yet he'd tendered the offer, and she'd refused it. He wouldn't behave so foolishly ever again.

"Everyone's in bed," he soothed. "There's no one to know what we're doing."

"*I* know."

"As do I, but with my leaving in the morning, this is our last chance to be together. We shouldn't squander it."

"You're pressuring me horridly."

"Am I?"

"Yes."

"Tell me to stop then," he said. "Tell me, and I will."

She groaned with dismay. "I can't tell you. You overwhelm me. You goad me into making bad choices."

"Good. Now hush."

He was kissing her again, caressing her breasts. She was a very sexual creature, and he was able to swiftly draw her into the spiral of pleasure. Gradually, he tugged up the hem of her skirt, baring her calves, her knees. She didn't seem to notice, or if she did, she didn't slap him away.

He arrived at the vee of her thighs, and he slid a finger inside her, then another. She was already so stimulated from his ministrations that it took no further effort to pitch her into a strident orgasm.

They'd been whispering, shielding their voices to avoid detection but, suddenly, she cried out. He covered her lips with his, capturing the sound, swallowing it until slowly, languidly, she floated down and landed—exhausted and exhilarated—in his arms.

"Oh, Lord Run," she murmured, "what was that? Was that passion?"

"Yes, and quite a stunning example of it too."

"Am I still a...a..."

"Yes, yes, you're fine."

He gazed at her, and her innocent blue eyes were troubled and confused. He should have felt guilty, should have felt like the cad he was, but he was suffering no remorse at all. He'd betrayed his cousin. So what? He'd betrayed his fiancée. So what? He'd goaded Evangeline into conduct she'd never intended. So what?

He was Aaron Drake, Viscount Run, master of his life and the people in it. Rules no longer applied to him.

"Don't be sad," he told her.

"I'm not."

"And don't you dare be sorry we did this."

"I'm not sorry exactly. I'm just...just..." She blew out a heavy breath. "I can't describe what I am."

"It was simply kissing, Evangeline."

"It was more than that, Lord Run, and you know it."

"Call me Aaron."

"I can't, and you mustn't call me Evangeline. I'm afraid you'll forget and use my Christian name when you shouldn't."

"I won't forget."

A frown creased her brow, and he wished he could alleviate her concerns, that he could make her understand there was no reason to worry. Their behavior was a trifle, a lark. In his sordid world, it was practically expected. It was silly to fuss over it.

"Why are you so upset?" he asked.

"I should confess to my fiancé. He should be apprised so he can decide if he still wants me."

"Don't be ridiculous. You're not *confessing* to anyone. You haven't done anything wrong."

"I have! I'm not like you and your friends. I'm extremely disturbed by all this."

"You haven't had the experiences that I've had, so you must listen to me. We're adults and we're very attracted to each other.

We acted on it. That's all it is. We've harmed no one. There's no sin or damnation involved."

"Have you tried this with other women?"

His cheeks flushed with chagrin. "Yes."

"Many times?"

"Not...many. Some."

"So...I'm not abnormal."

"No, you're very, very normal."

Despite his reassurances, she was pulling down her skirt, covering her legs. She was reeling, struggling to convince herself he was telling the truth, that their conduct was perfectly acceptable. Her distress rattled him, reminding him of how innocent she was, of how dissolute he could be.

He'd forged ahead when he shouldn't have, and he might have happily spent the night explaining their situation, showing her even more salacious misdeeds. But furtive footsteps sounded in the hall, then giggles. They froze as Bryce and Florella sneaked by, likely off to the kitchen for a snack or perhaps to the lake to flit about naked in the cool water.

Evangeline's eyes were wide with silent alarm, and he visually urged her not to be afraid. They huddled down, hidden from view, until Bryce and Florella vanished and the house quieted again.

Appearing angry and terrified, she crawled over him and slid to the floor with a muted thump. He rolled to face her, and they were nose to nose.

"You are so dangerous to me," she said.

"I don't mean to be."

"Can you imagine what would have happened if they'd entered this room?"

"They didn't."

"You're trotting off to London tomorrow, but I'll still be here. If I had wrecked my chance with Vicar Bosworth, what would I have done?"

He might have told her that Bryce and Florella wouldn't have been shocked, wouldn't have cared that she was with Aaron, but he didn't suppose he should.

She was buttoning her dress, scooping up the combs he'd yanked from her hair. He felt a hard object under his hip and dug around to find that her goddess statue had fallen out of her pocket. He held it out to her, and she grabbed it.

"I've never acted this way before," she said.

"I realize that."

"I'm not loose or easy. Please don't think I am."

"You're *not* loose. I could never think that about you."

"And if you return to Fox Run someday, how will we get on? I'll be a wife, but you'll know what sort of trollop I am deep down."

The word *wife* agitated him, but he ignored the bubble of anguish that rose in his chest. "Don't worry about the future. I came in here tonight because I couldn't bear to leave without seeing you one last time."

"I would hate to have squandered your good opinion."

"You couldn't."

"I'm so glad to hear you say so." She breathed a sigh of relief.

"I thought it would be remarkable to dally with you, and I couldn't go without learning for sure."

She chuckled miserably. "It's still wrong though—no matter how you view it. We shouldn't have proceeded."

"But we did, and it's over, and I won't have you fretting about it."

For an eternity, she hesitated, then ultimately said, "All right, I won't."

"I'll never tell anyone what occurred," he promised.

"Neither will I."

"But I'll always secretly be very, very happy that we were together like this."

"I'll always be happy too."

He pulled her to him and stole a final, quick kiss. She allowed the briefest touch of her lips to his, then she leapt to her feet, and ran out. The echo of her strides faded down the hall so swiftly she might not have ever been there at all.

CHAPTER SEVEN

"Have you always been an actress?"

"Yes, ever since I was a girl."

"How did you begin?"

"A group of traveling players came through our village. I was allowed to attend their performance, and I was so enchanted by it that I ran away with them."

"You ran away?"

Evangeline gaped at Florella Bernard.

Often in Evangeline's younger years, she'd wondered if she shouldn't run away to London to pursue a life on the stage. She'd wanted to sing and dance and perform—it had been a nearly uncontrollable obsession—but Miss Peabody had frowned on her displays of talent.

Evangeline had chafed and fumed and battled Miss Peabody, but she'd never have been courageous enough to flee. And of course, there'd been frequent horror stories about what happened to naïve women in the city. The tales had served as a warning not to contemplate such a rash act.

She'd swallowed down her worst impulses, had settled for a world of students and school, of learning, then teaching.

But that old dream still resonated. She felt there was a more exciting destiny awaiting her out on the horizon, and she'd missed the turn that would have led her to it.

"Did you ever see your parents again?" Evangeline asked. "What did they think?"

"I was an orphan in a very squalid orphanage," Miss Bernard confided. "There was no one to care much if I vanished. It was one less mouth to feed."

"I'm certain that's not true. Someone must have missed you."

"During that period, I was changing from girl to woman. If I *was* missed, it was for reasons we probably shouldn't mention."

"I won't even ask what you mean."

Evangeline's cheeks flushed bright red, and Miss Bernard laughed.

"I've shocked you. I'm sorry. I'm so used to being around scoundrels like Bryce that I forget there are normal people who are easily offended."

"I'm not offended," Evangeline said. "I'm merely surprised by such a frank admission. I'm accustomed to more reticence in my conversations."

"And I'm fully prepared to blurt out my entire sordid biography without hesitation." Miss Bernard laughed again. "The owner at the orphanage had taken a particular interest in me, and with my being so pretty, it was hard to hide from him. I decided it was silly to stay and be molested, so I left."

"How old were you?" Evangeline inquired.

"Thirteen? I've never been sure of my age or my birthday."

"That's so young. You were very brave."

"Or very foolish. I guess it depends on your point of view. I had a knack for acting, and I reinvented myself. Paltry, pathetic Flora Smith became Florella Bernard." She pronounced her stage name in a dramatic way. "The rest—as they say—is history."

"Are you successful? I apologize, but I'm not familiar with the London theater."

"It's all right. I wouldn't expect you to have heard of me."

"Are you able to earn a living?"

"Most of the time. Occasionally, I supplement it by liaisons with men like Bryce." Evangeline's cheeks grew even redder, and Miss Bernard looked chagrinned. "I've shocked you again."

Evangeline knew she should end the discussion. Miss Bernard's habits were not anything a potential vicar's wife should learn. But Evangeline was so intrigued by Miss Bernard, by her ready acceptance of what any decent female would deem to be grossly immoral conduct.

"No, no, I'm not shocked," Evangeline insisted. "I'm fascinated. There are such awful stories about the scandalous types who are drawn to the theater, but you seem very normal to me."

"Yes, we're all very normal—except perhaps in some of our personal relationships."

"Yes, except for that."

They smiled, Evangeline realizing that a friendship was forming. Considering the circumstances when they'd met, it was odd to fathom, but Evangeline found herself liking Miss Bernard more and more.

Part of it was due to the fact that they were roughly the same age and enjoyed many of the same pursuits. But also part of it was that Lord Run had left, and she was rambling around the large house, feeling lost and out of sorts. Her afternoon socializing with Vicar Bosworth didn't relieve the tedium.

Evangeline had just suffered through a dreary visit to the vicarage, much of it spent in awkward conversation with Widow Bosworth. On arriving home, Miss Bernard had been loafing in a downstairs parlor. When she'd suggested a walk in the garden, Evangeline had instantly agreed to accompany her.

They'd been together for over an hour and were headed back to the manor. Their chat had shown they actually had quite a bit in common. They were both orphans. They'd grown up in the care of people who hadn't liked them very much and who had viewed them as difficult. They had a similar love of performing and relished an audience's applause.

"I don't see my position with Bryce as being much different from yours," Miss Bernard said.

Evangeline scowled. "What do you mean?"

"You're marrying for fiscal stability, and I've attached myself to a man for the same reason."

"Don't you worry about the moral implications?"

"The moral implications of what?"

"Ah...well...of living in sin."

"I'm not religious, Evangeline, so no, I don't worry about it. If it's a choice between moral misbehavior and starvation, I'll take the moral misbehavior any day. I've been hungry, and I've had a full belly. I'd rather have the full belly."

"I've never been hungry," Evangeline told her.

"That makes your decisions easier."

"Have you a genuine affection for Mr. Blair?"

"I suppose you could call it affection."

"Then how do you explain your dalliance with Lord Run?"

"He's much richer than Bryce."

It was such a cold, pragmatic reply, and Evangeline was confused by it. How could money be all that mattered in picking a man?

"His wealth is what's important to you?"

"No, he has an air of mystery that's intriguing too. Bryce is all sunny temperament and happy moments. With him, what you see is what you get. With Aaron Drake—should he be roused into a reaction—I can't guess what sort of explosion might occur."

"I can't imagine Lord Run exploding." Evangeline was lying. She could absolutely imagine it.

"Plus, he's handsome as the devil. Bryce is handsome too, make no mistake. But Aaron is *rich* and handsome. When his fortune is factored in, there's no comparison."

"Mr. Blair isn't bothered by your interest in Lord Run?"

"Bryce is aware that I'm a mercenary." Miss Bernard smirked. "It's part of my charm."

Evangeline wanted to steer them further onto the topic of Aaron Drake. Miss Bernard had known him forever, and Evangeline suspected she could discover a great deal of exciting information.

Yet it was hard to probe for personal details, and in the end, she probably shouldn't. She was mourning his absence, but she couldn't breathe a word of her upset. She felt as if she was carrying a heavy secret that might ultimately choke her to death.

"If your financial situation wasn't dire on occasion," Evangeline inquired, "would you have involved yourself with Mr. Blair."

"No doubt I would have. He's delicious, don't you think?"

"Delicious? Can a man be delicious?"

"Yes, and he's also good in the..." Miss Bernard's voice trailed off. "Never mind."

"Tell me. What is he good at?"

Miss Bernard hemmed and hawed, then said, "Let's just say he pleases me in many ways we oughtn't to discuss."

It dawned on Evangeline that the reference was to intimacies, and her flaming cheeks returned. "You're an excellent companion for me, Miss Bernard."

"Why is that?"

"I've lived a very sheltered life and have a small circle of acquaintances. I can already see—in my role as vicar's wife—that my horizons will expand enormously. You're training me to listen to any kind of wild tale and to accept it with equanimity."

"From how your cheeks are blushing, you're not all that composed."

"I'm working at it."

Miss Bernard took Evangeline's arm. They were at the stairs that led up onto the verandah, and they climbed them together.

"I believe we're becoming friends, Miss Etherton."

"I believe we are too."

"But we'd better keep my past to ourselves. We won't mention any of it to your betrothed."

"Gad, no," Evangeline said. "If he knew you were an actress, he'd have an apoplexy."

"We wouldn't want to injure the poor fellow."

"No, we shouldn't. If he perished, I'd be in a jam."

"Why is that?" Miss Bernard asked.

"I came here because the school where I was teaching had closed. If the marriage doesn't occur, I have nowhere to go."

"That puts you in a tight spot, doesn't it?"

"Yes, a very tight spot."

"Will you wed the vicar though? Are you certain you should?"

Miss Bernard studied Evangeline, looking shrewd and wise and more worldly than Evangeline could ever dream of being.

"I have to. It's not as if I have any other options."

"You two are an odd match."

"Every bride and groom are an odd match."

"Too true, but this quiet, boring life at Fox Run"—Miss Bernard gestured to the picturesque park and deserted woods—"might prove stifling for you."

"I'll have many duties as a vicar's wife." Evangeline's heart fluttered with dismay, but she ignored her reaction. "I'll be so busy I won't notice the quiet or the empty spaces."

"I'm sure you'll be fine."

"Yes, I'm sure I will be."

For a lengthy moment, Miss Bernard hesitated and, obviously, she wanted to expound, perhaps to warn Evangeline or advise her to beware.

In the end, no counsel was offered, and what purpose would it have served anyway? As Miss Bernard had stated earlier, Evangeline was doing what all women did by marrying. She was protecting herself in the only available way.

"Let's go in, shall we?" Miss Bernard said. "We'll find that rascal, Bryce, and head to the music room. We'll make him play the pianoforte so you can sing for me."

"I would love that."

"Marvelous." Miss Bernard beamed. "I'll have my own private concert, and I promise to be the most receptive audience you shall ever have."

They swept inside, calling for Mr. Blair to entertain them.

"How long have you known Lord Run?"

"Twenty years? More?"

Evangeline smiled. She was in the garden again, with Mr. Blair this time. Another day had passed since Lord Run left for London.

The previous evening, after hours of singing, she, Mr. Blair, and Miss Bernard had played cards and read by the fire. Then Mr. Blair and Miss Bernard had acted out several scenes from a romantic theatrical they'd seen in London. They were both very talented, and Evangeline had enjoyed herself immensely.

"When did you first meet him?" she asked.

"At school. He was the rich, entitled son of an earl, and I was a charity case. I figured—in light of my low social standing—he'd be a perfect chum."

"You were how old? Six?"

"Yes, and I already had a fairly clear picture of how the world worked. I glommed on to Aaron immediately, and he was kind enough to let me dance around in his orbit."

Evangeline laughed, but didn't peer up at him. If she stared directly into his blue eyes—eyes that were an exact replica of her own—she suffered the strange vertigo that had been plaguing her ever since they'd been introduced. She didn't know why it transpired, but she couldn't stop it, so her glances were fleeting and casual.

"What was he like as a boy?"

"Stuffy. Tedious. A horrid bore and very posh snob. Much as he is today."

Evangeline laughed even harder. "Posh and horrid?"

"Trust me, he's a veritable compilation of dull traits. I've tried to turn him into a more jolly fellow, but I've nearly given up. The poor sap doesn't have a merry bone in his body."

"You're awfully caustic for someone who claims to be his friend."

"Just stating the facts, Miss Etherton. Besides, Aaron is fully aware of how dreary he can be. He'd be the first to admit it."

She was obsessing about Lord Run, but couldn't help it. He was the most handsome, sophisticated man she'd ever met. She kept telling herself that—after he was gone for a while—her interest would wane. Wouldn't it?

"Why is he so dreary?" she asked.

"Oh, it's his father, Lord Sidwell."

"What's wrong with his father?"

Evangeline had heard plenty of gossip about Lord Sidwell from Rose, who was his niece, but she couldn't resist hearing more. She was hungry for information about the Drake family. Her appetite appeared to be insatiable.

"The earl is a pretentious, pompous buffoon," Mr. Blair explained. "He's always been exhaustively demanding of Aaron, and Aaron is overly accommodating. He can't bear to quarrel, so he does whatever his father requests."

"And that makes him dreary?"

"Yes, and he has a younger brother, Lucas, who is his complete opposite. Lucas was always in trouble, always vexing their father to the point of apoplexy, and the more Lucas enraged Lord Sidwell, the more Aaron tried to keep the peace."

"Where was his mother in all this?"

"She died when he was tiny, so he and Lucas grew up at Lord Sidwell's mercy. The earl was quite a strict taskmaster. Aaron struggled with it, but Lucas couldn't have cared less."

Evangeline absorbed the news, fascinated beyond measure. A cruel, stern father. A wastrel brother. Boys with no mother. It sounded like a plot out of a novel.

"Well, I must confess, Mr. Blair, that I don't find Lord Run to be stuffy or tedious at all."

"You don't? You're likely the only person in history to say so."

"Ever since I arrived at Fox Run, he's been very gracious."

"Yes, he can be charming—when he tries. He's showing you his good side."

"Shouldn't we all do that?"

"Yes, but when our bad side is the one that rules us, wouldn't it be better to apprise others right up front?"

"Perhaps."

They were walking back to the house, their leisurely stroll at an end. Evangeline was about to begin her hours of socializing with the vicar, and she needed to spend a few minutes in her room, adjusting her attitude and calming herself so she had the fortitude to endure it.

Luckily, she now had two friends at the manor, and if her visit became too mind-numbingly vile, she would concentrate on the pleasant evening she would have later with Mr. Blair and Miss Bernard once she returned.

"What about you, Mr. Blair?" she asked. "You mentioned you were a charity case at school. Where are you from? Who is your family?"

"I'm an orphan, Miss Etherton. My tuition was paid by a benefactor in the community. I was never told who it was."

"That's my story exactly," she said. "I know nothing of my past. How about you?"

"I remember it very well. My mother was a notorious actress and singer."

"Was she? Is that where you get all your talent?"

"I should hope so." He tugged on his vest, looking funny and pompous.

"And your father?"

"Oh, he was a very high-born fellow and much too grand for my mother." He laughed, but there was a tinge of sadness in it. "She was a devilish vixen, or so I heard. She lured unsuspecting men to their doom."

"More than one?"

"Hundreds! Thousands!" he sarcastically, dramatically exclaimed.

She peeked up at him and, suddenly, the vertigo was back with a vengeance. There was a ringing in her ears, and it increased. She felt physically ill as if she might swoon—when she'd never swooned in her life.

"Miss Etherton?" He shook her arm. "Are you all right?"

"Yes, yes, I'm...I'm fine." She yanked her gaze from his. "I had an odd moment."

"You were a million miles away, as if you'd floated off somewhere."

Struggling for composure, she forced a chuckle. "Your story resonated with me. I wonder if my past holds similar secrets."

"We orphans all like to believe we had aristocratic fathers, don't we?"

"Yes, I like to imagine that's the case."

"We wouldn't have any other kind. When we can make up the identity of our father, who wants a farmer when they can have a duke?"

She dared to peek at him again, and it occurred to her that she wouldn't be surprised if his father was a duke, or even a prince. With his golden blond hair and striking blue eyes, he was very magnetic, very dashing. Surely he had a famous sire.

Movement on the verandah caught her attention, and she glanced up to find that the vicar had arrived early. In his black hat and coat, he looked like an undertaker, like the bearer of bad tidings, like Death having sneaked up to suck out her soul.

Her merry disposition vanished in an instant. Mr. Blair noticed her change of mood, and he peered up and saw the vicar too.

"He's not very happy," Mr. Blair said, "but then he never is. If he smiled, his face would crack."

"He's a stickler for the proprieties. He won't like that I've been in the garden with you."

"Don't you hate religious cretins?"

It was a question she didn't dare answer. Her reasons for being at Fox Run were mixed and complicated. If there were negative aspects to the arrangement, how could it signify? Every facet of life had negative and positive aspects. She had to focus on the positives and—after sufficient time had passed—there would be so many positives, she wouldn't recall there had ever been negatives.

"I'd better be going," she said. "If I make him wait, he'll be irritated."

She tried to turn away, but Mr. Blair was clutching her arm and wouldn't release it. He appeared concerned and worried, which was very sweet, but very pointless. He had no ability to help her, so why fret over it?

"Miss Etherton, I don't know you very well, but may I say something that's very rude and very blunt but that needs to be said?"

"Of course, Mr. Blair."

"Must you marry him? Isn't there another path you could take?"

"I can't see one."

"You two seem so wrong for each other."

"I doubt any bride and groom are compatible in the beginning. We'll grow to like each other. I'm certain of it."

He stared intently, and she braced for more of the same, but instead, he inquired, "Have we met before?"

"Why would you ask that?"

"You look so familiar to me."

"You look familiar too, but I'm good with faces. I'd have remembered you."

The ringing in her ears exploded to a loud din, and she pulled away, feeling so dizzy that—if she didn't—she might collapse to the ground. Why did he rattle her so completely? She liked him so much. Why would he induce such a peculiar reaction?

She stuck her hand in her pocket, reaching for her goddess statue, running her fingers over and over it until she started to calm down.

"I have to go," she mumbled, and she hurried to the verandah, mustering her composure on the way. She greeted the vicar as cordially as she could manage. "I'm sorry I'm not ready. I wasn't expecting you for an hour."

"Obviously." He glowered at her, then his stern glare wafted out into the garden to Mr. Blair. Mr. Blair had no shame, and he grinned and waved.

Mr. Blair's impertinence enraged the vicar. "What are you doing with him?"

"Walking."

"Walking?" He snorted with disbelief.

"Would you like some tea?" she asked, refusing to feel guilty. "We could invite Mr. Blair and Miss Bernard to join us. They're very nice. You'd enjoy chatting with them."

"Have you been...socializing?"

"Yes. We're all staying here as Lord Run's guests. Why wouldn't I socialize?"

"They're not suitable companions for you."

"Oh, for pity's sake," she fumed with more ire than she'd meant to display. "They're Lord Run's friends. He and Mr. Blair have known each other since they were boys."

"What about that doxy, Florella Bernard?"

Miss Bernard definitely had some low character traits, but Evangeline would never admit it. "She's not a doxy, and what about her? She's a guest too."

"She traveled to the country—alone—with Mr. Blair." He

practically hissed the accusation.

"So? Lord Run was with them, as was her maid, and she's an adult. She's fully capable of deciding how to get where she has to go."

"Her behavior is not appropriate, and the fact that you seem to think it is worries me greatly. What am I to make of it, Miss Etherton?"

She studied his harsh features, his angry countenance. He was frowning so ferociously, almost as if he hated her, and it was so depressing to suppose that he might.

What bride could begin a marriage this way? Here at the start, couldn't he at least pretend fondness? Weariness swept over her— as did a grim realization.

She couldn't wed him. She didn't care what Miss Peabody had arranged, didn't care what Miss Peabody thought was best. Miss Peabody had always been horrid to Evangeline, had never understood Evangeline or known what she needed.

Yes, Miss Peabody had given a valid explanation as to why her plan was good for Evangeline, but why was Miss Peabody's opinion the correct one? Why would Evangeline follow it when the entire betrothal was awful?

She had to devise a different future. That much was patently clear. She would write to Rose and Amelia. They were starting new lives, and Evangeline had convinced herself she shouldn't bother them, that she shouldn't seek their help. But why shouldn't she? If *they* were in trouble, she'd jump to assist. The three of them were like sisters.

Perhaps with all the changes they were experiencing, they might have come across a situation for Evangeline. Perhaps they'd encountered someone who could offer lodging or employment, and she was happy to return to working. She liked to be busy, and she *would* find something that didn't involve a hideous marriage to Vicar Bosworth.

She would continue to play the part of the devoted fiancée, but she would spend every second strategizing. As soon as she could, she would cry off, and she doubted Vicar Bosworth would mind. He liked her no better than he had the very first day, and certainly, his mother would celebrate.

"You seem upset," she said.

"I'm not upset," he replied, but he was so furious, he was shaking.

"I'm not well this afternoon," she lied. "Maybe you should make your social calls without me."

"Without you?" he scoffed. "You think being indisposed is reason to postpone our community obligations? No, Miss

Etherton, in my family we keep our appointments."

"I understand," she murmured, hoping she looked sufficiently contrite.

"You were perfectly hale during your walk with Mr. Blair, so don't act as if you're under the weather now."

"I merely assumed you might wish to proceed without me."

"It would likely be preferable, but we shall go together." He bent down so they were nose to nose. "Get your bonnet and be quick about it!"

She nearly told him then and there that she was through. She nearly, crudely, told him to sod off, but she was generally a courteous and affable person.

She stepped away, putting a bit of space between them. "I'll just be a minute. Let's meet in the front foyer."

"Yes, let's do," he snapped.

As she spun away, she noted Mr. Blair was scowling at them, his consternation evident. He'd watched her being scolded as if she was a recalcitrant child, and it was galling to have him witness her humiliation.

She went inside, wondering if she'd ever come back out.

CHAPTER EIGHT

"Smile, Priscilla."

"Why should I?"

"Because we're about to be announced, and every person in the room will stare at us."

Aaron had been home for three taxing days, tending to business and hiding from everyone. He'd tried to force himself over to Priscilla's house, but hadn't been able to make himself go.

When he'd fled London two weeks earlier, he'd quarreled with Priscilla and her mother. They'd interfered in his brother's life, had schemed to stop Lucas's engagement to Amelia Hubbard, having determined that Miss Hubbard was too lowborn to be allowed to marry into the Drake family.

As if it was any of their business!

Aaron was quite a snob and didn't feel different classes should mingle, but he genuinely liked Miss Hubbard and she would be a wonderful wife for his brother—if Lucas could convince her to have him.

Claudia and Priscilla could choke on their indignation for all he cared.

He'd believed he was over his fit of pique, that he'd forgiven them for their meddling but, apparently, he hadn't. He hadn't visited Priscilla to announce his return. He hadn't sent a note.

Finally, someone—probably his father—had tattled and informed her that he was back. She and her mother had popped over at once, and they were all on their best behavior, pretending no rift had occurred.

He and Priscilla were marching into a formal ball, and as he'd just mentioned to her, their names were called. The crowd looked up, and Aaron exuded a calm, composed façade. He hated public scenes and wouldn't stand for a display of displeasure or anger.

"If you continue to scowl," he told Priscilla, "people will think we're fighting."

"You'd like that, wouldn't you," she spat, "to have rumors spreading?" But she was socially astute and she pasted on the smile he'd demanded.

They promenaded down the stairs, guests taking furtive glances, but the dancing had already begun, so attention was quickly diverted to the dancers. Aaron and Priscilla were forgotten, and he peered around, yearning to see his brother in the pulsating throng, but Lucas wasn't present.

Most likely, he was still up north at his friend James Talbot's wedding. Hopefully, Lucas would soon be participating in his own wedding to Miss Hubbard.

Aaron worried that he wouldn't hear if a ceremony was imminent. Lucas had treated Miss Hubbard so shoddily that he'd have a difficult time persuading her to be his bride. The Talbot wedding was being held very close to the Scottish border, and Miss Hubbard was a guest too. Lucas might simply elope with her to Gretna Green before she came to her senses.

If that happened, Aaron wouldn't have a chance to attend, and the notion was incredibly depressing. Lucas, for all his faults, was Aaron's favorite person in the world. Lucas was carefree and dashing and reckless in a way Aaron had never attempted to be. Aaron had always wished he had a bit of Lucas's panache and brave negligence, but Aaron had never possessed a single bad habit.

Their mother had been talented and flamboyant, and Lucas had inherited all her traits for music, charisma, and dramatic misadventure. Aaron, on the other hand, had been left with the traits from their father, so Aaron was stodgy and fussy and pompous. He was constantly vexed by his arrogant nature, but his routines were too ingrained and he couldn't seem to change.

He and Priscilla reached the ballroom floor, and they were besieged by acquaintances, the flow of the crowd separating them. Aaron didn't try to stay near her. She was whisked off by friends who, no doubt, would interrogate her over Aaron's explanation of his absence.

Unfortunately for the gossips, Priscilla wouldn't have any juicy answers. With Claudia and Priscilla tiptoeing around Aaron, there'd been no opportunity to bicker or accuse or justify. Priscilla had to be about to explode.

She had a temper and would eventually let loose on Aaron. It was interesting to him that she was so young—just eighteen—yet so sure of herself, so positive it was appropriate to speak her mind. If she had any idea how little her opinion mattered to him, she'd faint with shock.

He had his own temper, but it was tightly controlled and rarely exhibited. He'd spent too many years in his father's house, watching Lord Sidwell's rages and tantrums, and Aaron had grown up knowing he would never act so ludicrously.

So people assumed he was mild mannered, but he wasn't—as Priscilla would ultimately learn to her great regret.

He strolled out onto the rear verandah and waited for her, figuring she'd arrive with scant delay. She was nothing if not predictable. In a few minutes, he glanced over and saw her approaching.

"Let's walk in the garden," she said.

"Yes, let's do."

She took his arm, and they went down the stairs and proceeded down a lighted path. Rapidly, they were away from the party. It was a quiet night, the stars out, no clouds drifting by.

He thought about Fox Run, about Bryce and Florella being there with Evangeline. How lucky they were to be there with her, while he was in London and more miserable than he'd ever been. Did Evangeline miss him?

He missed *her*. It was silly and ridiculous, but he couldn't help it. She made him smile, made him happy. His father had advised him to have an affair, and what better female could he have found?

But of course, he'd run away. He was back where he belonged, being the dutiful son, the dutiful fiancé. How had he become so tedious and absurd? Why couldn't he be more like his rowdy, unruly brother? Would it kill him to misbehave? Would it kill him to enjoy himself?

His life had been a boring slog of burden and obligation. Why couldn't he reach for a more rewarding, more fulfilling existence?

They rounded a bend in the path, and Priscilla pulled away.

"I have something I should like to say," she announced.

With her white-blond hair and violet-colored eyes, she was very beautiful, but in an icy, poisonous way. She was very glum, as if she'd been sucking on sour pickles.

"What is it?" he asked.

"I apologize for what my mother did to Lucas."

"Thank you, but I rather imagine she should apologize herself."

"I'm expecting she will once she can catch you alone."

"I'll look forward to it."

"So...we can put this unpleasantness behind us."

"Certainly."

She studied him and frowned. "You don't appear to mean it."

"I mean it."

"My words don't seem to have made any difference. Are you still angry? You can't blame me for how Mother behaves."

"I don't," he claimed, but he absolutely blamed her.

She presumed she had the right to boss him, to meddle in his affairs, but it was his own fault. He was so averse to quarreling that he simply wouldn't. He'd let her run wild, but his trip to Fox Run had altered him.

He had to seize control of their relationship. She was a girl, not far removed from the schoolroom. Her days of nagging and complaining had to end. He couldn't continue in their current condition.

"If you're not upset," she fumed, "what's wrong then?"

"I'm not upset."

"Well...good." She stared, fiddled with her skirt, stared again. "Where were you the past two weeks?"

"At Fox Run."

"Why did you leave London?"

"You know why. I was sick of you and your mother."

She tsked with offense. "You don't have to snipe about it. We received your message loud and clear."

"Perhaps next time you'll think twice before involving yourself in nonsense."

"It wasn't *me* who schemed against Lucas. It was Mother. How many times must I tell you?"

"No more. I can't bear to discuss it any further."

She glowered, appearing less winsome by the second. His father had betrothed them for the size and scope of her dowry, but there had also been some benefit in her being fetching, with many people insisting she was the prettiest debutante to have come out in years.

But her snobbish qualities overrode her stellar looks, and with his father keeping most of the dowry—it belonged to the estate, not to Aaron—Aaron's bounty was to be the blushing bride. Yet as he watched her, he was recalling vivacious, flamboyant Evangeline.

In that comparison, Priscilla didn't stand a chance and, suddenly, Aaron's reward in the engagement—the beautiful bride—didn't seem like much of a reward at all.

"What were you doing for two whole weeks?" She hurled her question like an accusation.

Trifling with a houseguest in very inappropriate ways. My father thought I should.

"I was with Bryce." He left Florella out of the equation, for she was a doxy and not anyone with whom he could ever expect Priscilla to socialize.

"I might have known," she muttered.

"What's wrong with Bryce?"

"He's so beneath you, Aaron."

"It's not really any of your business, is it, Priscilla?"

"Not my business?" she huffed. "We're about to be married. How would it not be my *business* that you have unsavory companions?"

There was a bench directly behind her. He pointed to it.

"Sit down, Priscilla."

"I'd rather stand," she snottily retorted.

She glared at him, mulish, defiant, and he sighed with exasperation.

This conversation had been pending for ages, and in light of his usual tendency to avoid discord, he'd put it off for as long as he was able. But his patience had finally evaporated.

"Sit!" he said again.

He grabbed her arm and led her over to the bench. When she refused to oblige him, he increased the pressure on her arm and forced her down. The fact that he had to manhandle her, that she wouldn't comply simply because he'd asked, was galling and infuriating.

"Honestly, Aaron," she seethed, "there's no reason to be a bully."

No, there wasn't, but when she constantly enraged him, what was he to do?

"You had a few things to say to me," he snapped, "and now I have a few things to say to you."

"What are they? Get on with it."

"Priscilla, let me be very clear. Your days of *saying* things to me are over."

"I'm about to be your wife. My opinion ought to be the most vital one in your world."

"If that's what you suppose, then you have grossly miscalculated the relationship you shall have with me."

"I have no idea what you're talking about. You're acting so oddly, you could be a stranger."

"I *am* a stranger to you. You know nothing about me."

"I've known you since I was a little girl, and we've been engaged for a year. Of course we're close."

"No, we're not."

"You're being absurd, and I won't converse with you when you're in such a foul mood."

She started to rise, and he bellowed, "Sit down! And if you pry your bottom off that bench again before I'm through, I'll take a switch to you."

He'd never physically abused a woman in his life, had never threatened abuse either, but she'd pushed him beyond his limit. Apparently, his spurt of temper caught her attention. Aggrieved and offended, she plopped down.

"Speak your piece," she said, "and make it fast. I've heard about all I'll tolerate from you for one evening."

He assessed her, like a scientist examining a peculiar specimen he'd never previously encountered. She was very young, and he was a male, twelve years older and her superior in every way: size, station, wealth, reputation.

How had she mustered the temerity to be so brazen? Her mother had fostered this perception of magnificence, and Priscilla believed every story her mother had told her. Lord Sidwell could have picked any candidate for Aaron to wed, and the fact that he'd settled on Priscilla had only increased her elevated sense of importance.

Visions of their pending marriage swarmed in his mind. He saw decades of quarrels, of pointless bickering, of his patience stretched to breaking.

They'd have to live apart, would bump into each other at balls or parties. He'd have to travel to Fox Run occasionally to fornicate with her, to plant the heir the Sidwell title had to have. After she birthed that son, he'd have to plant another, and perhaps even a third after that. Then he'd be shed of her.

What a sad, ghastly life it would be!

"I'm normally a very calm person," he said, "so you have an erroneous impression about me."

"What impression is that?"

"You seem to think you can nag and complain and disrespect me."

"Well, if you insist on foolishly—"

"Shut your mouth, Priscilla. For once, just shut the hell up."

"You can't talk to me like that."

"Be silent!" he shouted. "You're laboring under the mistaken notion that we are equals. You assume that I give a rat's ass about you or this wedding or anything else."

"How dare you say that to me!"

"Yes, how dare I? I've listened to your harangue for twelve arduous months, and we are making some changes. As of right now, you will only ever address me in a manner that displays the regard I am due as your fiancé."

"I'd show you respect if you ever deserved it but, sometimes, you behave like an idiot. Look at that fiasco with your brother. Was I supposed to ignore it?"

"Yes, Priscilla, you should have ignored it. It was between me and my brother. Not me and you. Or you and him. I will have my own life. I will come and go and have my own friends and carry on however I please. I will *never* be any of your business."

She burst into tears, and he stoically watched her, wishing his father was present to witness the disaster he'd orchestrated by selecting her. Could they possibly have chosen a girl more juvenile and frivolous?

"You're ruining everything," she wailed.

"No, I'm merely establishing the rules as to how we'll proceed from this moment on. I will not waste another second dealing with your childish antics. You will grow up and act like an adult woman, as if you're mature enough to eventually become a countess, or I swear to God, we're through."

She gasped. "You'd cry off?"

"Yes."

"I'd be humiliated before the entire world."

He shrugged. "You certainly would be, so I suggest you don't aggravate me in the future."

There was no way he could back out of the marriage, but she didn't know that, so it was a good threat.

Her mother had already given Lord Sidwell a substantial portion of the dowry, but Lord Sidwell was a gambler and wastrel who had huge debts. He'd spent every pound as quickly as he'd received it. If Aaron walked away from the match, they'd have to repay the money, but there was no money.

He wasn't sure what might have happened, but her mother blustered up, probably sensing they shouldn't be alone, that calamity could arise.

"There you are," Claudia chirped. "I was wondering where you'd gotten off to."

She tried to pretend all was fine, but with how he and Priscilla were glaring, their discord couldn't be concealed.

"What is it?" Claudia hissed. "What's wrong now?"

"I've been explaining some things to your daughter," Aaron said.

"What things?" Claudia asked.

"He wants to cry off!" Priscilla bleated.

"Don't be ridiculous," Claudia scoffed. "No one is crying off. Lord Sidwell and I wouldn't consider it for an instant."

"He couldn't, could he, Mother?" Priscilla whined. "I'd be a laughingstock."

"You're worrying over nothing, Priscilla." Claudia turned her exasperated gaze to Aaron. "What's the problem, Aaron? Tell me what it is, and let's see if I can fix it."

"I was betrothed to your daughter without being consulted and against my better judgment." It was a terrible remark to voice in front of Priscilla, and he wasn't usually so crass, but he was suffering from a bout of temper the likes of which he'd never experienced prior.

"She's very young, Aaron," Claudia said. "When your father and I first discussed the engagement, I understood you might have reservations. I *still* understand them."

"Mother!" Priscilla huffed.

"For the past year," Aaron continued, "she has sassed and scorned and verbally abused me. She has prevailed on my good nature, ruined my calm demeanor, and enraged me beyond what I can abide."

"She can be horrid," Claudia agreed. "I admit it."

"Mother!" Priscilla protested again, but Claudia and Aaron ignored her.

"I am at the end of what I will allow," Aaron seethed. "She will decide here and now that she will conduct herself as is expected of the woman about to wed the Sidwell heir or I'm finished with her." He paused, shocked at his outburst. "What is it to be?"

"Of course she'll be the bride you expect." Claudia turned to Priscilla and ordered, "Priscilla, get down on your knees and apologize to Aaron."

"Apologize! For what? I've done nothing wrong."

"You see, Claudia?" Aaron fumed. "What am I to make of it?"

"I've spoiled her, Aaron," Claudia said. "I've let her run roughshod over me, so she assumes she can run roughshod over you too."

"Yes, she does," Aaron concurred, feeling ragged and undone, as if he might simply shatter into a thousand pieces, "and I would love to hear your advice—for I've had it with both of you."

"I don't blame you."

Claudia studied him, her concern visibly evident. She stomped over and yanked Priscilla off the bench and forced her to her knees.

"Tell him you didn't mean to be awful," Claudia demanded. "Beg his pardon. Humbly and sincerely. Do it, Priscilla."

Priscilla gnawed on her cheek, debated, delayed, then she folded her hands as if in prayer and dipped her head.

"I'm sorry, Aaron. I didn't realize I'd been upsetting you. I can be obstinate, and I'm blind to my faults. Please don't spurn me. If you cried off, I'd just die!"

It was a pretty speech, and she peeked up at him, not appearing contrite in the least, and he supposed it was all he'd ever receive from her. Words, not actions.

He nodded, accepting her apology, but he was sick with disgust. Aaron knew—no matter how Priscilla might currently grovel—their relationship would never improve.

Claudia lifted Priscilla to her feet as she told Aaron, "There now, that has to have mended a few fences. Hasn't it?"

"We'll see," he said. "I'm not optimistic."

"I'll spend the whole month with her, Aaron. I'll work on her temper and attitude."

You've had eighteen years! he wanted to complain, but what would be the point?

Instead, he replied with, "I appreciate it."

"I haven't prepared her to be a wife. I haven't explained her role or her true position, but I will."

"I'm exhausted, Claudia."

"There's no need to be. We've smoothed over your troubles, haven't we?"

He gaped at her, practically weak with fatigue. He *hated* bickering! It reminded him of his childhood, of listening to his father rant at Lucas, whip Lucas, shame and damage Lucas until he was an unruly miscreant who was beyond repair.

"Are we fine now?" Claudia nervously asked.

He took a deep breath, pulling back, reverting to form. "Yes, we're fine."

"There'll be no more talk about crying off?"

"No, there'll be no more such talk."

"And I'll get Priscilla squared away. I promise you. Next time you see her, you won't even recognize her. She'll be so changed, you'll think she's a new girl entirely."

Claudia flashed a tremulous smile, but he didn't return it. He didn't believe proper conduct was possible for Priscilla—despite how Claudia might guarantee it.

Claudia waved toward the house. "Why don't you head into the party? Find some of your friends and have a few stout brandies. You'll feel better."

"I'm sure that's precisely the cure for what ails me," he said.

He spun away and left.

Priscilla—thank God—hadn't uttered another comment. She simply stared, looking as if she'd like to throw something at him, but with Claudia standing there, she wouldn't dare.

He hurried inside, but didn't stop to socialize. He kept on through the ballroom, up the stairs, and out the front door, wondering where to go, wondering what to do.

CHAPTER NINE

Aaron stepped into the manor at Fox Run, stopped in his tracks by the strangest sound. Music. Vocal music, loud and merry and ringing off the rafters.

He paused and actually glanced around the foyer to be sure he was in the right residence, that he hadn't stumbled into the wrong house by mistake. He'd owned Fox Run for a decade, and it had always been a quiet, empty place. He'd certainly never encountered singing when he'd walked through the door.

It was late in the evening, and he hadn't been expected, so there were no servants to meet him in the foyer, but he didn't mind. He was just so relieved to be back.

After his fight with Priscilla and Claudia, he'd left London—again without a word to anyone—and had proceeded straight to the country.

The entire journey, he'd fretted about Priscilla until it had dawned on him that he wasn't a sentimental man. While once he'd naively thought he might like to marry for love and affection, he'd never valued maudlin traits. Why be upset over the fact that he possessed no tender feelings for Priscilla?

Many of his acquaintances had been wed for years and not a single one had ended up satisfied with his choice. Why should Aaron's marriage be any different?

He was putting too much emphasis on irrelevant details. He'd been fuming because Priscilla would never make him happy, but he couldn't care less if she made him happy. Priscilla was who she was, and Aaron was who *he* was. His father wanted the union, and Aaron would never defy Lord Sidwell in such an important decision. Lucas would, but Aaron wouldn't.

So why fuss over it? Why carry on until he felt ill with regret?

Evangeline was at Fox Run, and Aaron was getting married in a month. If he trifled with Evangeline for a bit, it would calm his raging upset, so it would benefit everyone involved. Particularly Priscilla.

Evangeline was the key. Evangeline would fix everything.

He'd already asked her if she'd have an affair, and she'd refused, but why take her word for it? He would simply wear her down and change her mind. And if he couldn't?

Then he'd have three weeks of flirtation and dalliance before his responsibilities drew him back to London.

The ruckus was coming from the music room. He went down the hall and peeked inside, smiling at the sight that greeted him.

Evangeline, Bryce, and Florella were rehearsing, with Evangeline at the piano, and Bryce and Florella singing a duet. Several of his servants were also participating. They were arrayed in a chorus behind Bryce and Florella and sounding quite grand. He hadn't known members of his staff were so talented!

Bryce kept forgetting the lyrics, which would cause them all to laugh and jest. They were a mixed group, but having a jovial time, and it occurred to him that he was so bloody glad to have Evangeline in the house. She'd brought this noise and gaiety with her, had enlivened his home, charmed his servants, and beguiled his friends.

How lucky he was to have her staying under his roof. In such a swift and remarkable way, she'd altered his whole world.

He had a vague recollection of this sort of raucous energy pulsating through the halls of Sidwell Manor when he'd been a little boy, when his mother had still been with them, but after she'd passed on, all the jollity had passed with her.

From that day forward, it had been an era of dreary tedium, of lonely, lost brothers maneuvering around a petulant father who'd lashed out when crossed. On watching Evangeline direct the ensemble, he realized how much he'd missed his mother's commotion and uproar. Who could have imagined it?

He loitered in the hall, in the shadows, not eager to bluster in and wreck their fun. He silently observed until, finally, they declared themselves finished. Bryce and Florella collapsed onto the sofa, the servants discreetly stepping away, trying to look unobtrusive now that their role in the chorus was ended.

Clapping enthusiastically, Aaron burst in. They all whipped around to learn who had arrived. The servants appeared sheepish, worried they might be in trouble. Bryce and Florella waved, beckoning him over. But it was Evangeline who riveted him, who told him he was right to have returned.

"Lord Run!" she said. "What a nice surprise!"

"Hello, hello." He included everyone, but it was all for her.

"What are you doing here?" Bryce asked.

"There were rumors of a fantastic musicale being presented in this part of the country, and I raced back to see it."

"It was all Evangeline's idea," Bryce said.

"I'm sure it was," Aaron agreed.

"We can't keep up with her."

Aaron grinned at Evangeline. "You've drafted my servants into your mischief again."

"After I heard them in the choir at church, I couldn't resist. Aren't they marvelous?"

"They're your devoted acolytes. If they're busy with your frivolous pursuits, how will they ever get their chores done?"

"Who cares about chores," she saucily retorted, "when they can spend time singing instead?"

"I demand my own private performance," he announced, and he marched over and pulled up a chair next to the pianoforte.

She glanced at her assembled troupe and asked, "What say all of you? Can you do it again for Lord Run?"

"You're a slave driver, Evangeline," Bryce protested, but he was already pushing himself to his feet.

"No rest for the weary," Florella chimed in as she rose too. "Or is it the wicked?"

"It's the wicked," Bryce said. "Definitely the wicked."

Evangeline urged the servants to stand behind Bryce and Florella. For a moment, they looked anxious, but she had such a clever way with people that she instantly put them at ease.

She played the introductory chords, and as Bryce began to sing, Aaron sat back to enjoy the show.

Three weeks, he mused to himself.

Four weeks to his wedding, which meant three weeks to dally with Evangeline at Fox Run. He would charm and woo her until she relented. If he was shrewd, if he was lucky, she just might shower him with everything he'd ever wanted.

Evangeline paced in her sitting room. She'd stare at the door, then pace, then stare at the door, but no matter how fervidly she tried to conjure Aaron Drake, he didn't appear.

She'd been positive he would.

When he'd entered the music room, she'd nearly shrieked with delight. She'd been that happy about his arrival. She knew she shouldn't be glad, that it was wrong and misguided and dangerous, but she couldn't help it.

It had been two hours since she'd left him in the parlor, drinking brandy with Bryce. Would he visit her? He had to! If he didn't, how would she bear it?

Suddenly, footsteps hurried down the hall. They were heavy, male, halting right outside. She ran over and jerked the door open.

"Lord Run!"

"Hello, Evangeline."

"Get in here before someone sees you."

She grabbed his wrist and yanked him inside. There was an eerie sense of destiny in the air, as if their futures had aligned, as if their paths had been leading them in one direction, but had abruptly pushed them in another. They'd never be able to go back to the route they'd previously pursued.

"Why are you at Fox Run?" she asked. "Tell me the truth."

"I will, but don't you dare gloat."

"Just say it."

"I missed you."

"I knew it," she cockily said.

"Come here."

He held out his arms, and she leapt into them. Then he was kissing her so forcefully she wondered if they'd ever stop. It was wild and feral, out of control, beyond what she could imagine or describe.

She'd known that adults kissed each other. *She* had been kissed before. She'd been kissed by *him* before, but none of it had prepared her for such an explosion of passion.

She felt as if he'd been away for years, as if he'd been lost and wandering and had finally found his way home. Issues of morality, of her engagement to his cousin, flew out the window. She simply didn't care about anything but this moment and this man and the undiluted elation he generated.

"Why did you stay downstairs so long?" she inquired when she could take a breath.

"Bryce wouldn't shut up. I couldn't escape."

"How could you make me wait?"

"I wanted you impatient and chafing with temper."

"I am chafing," she said. "I absolutely am."

He picked her up and spun them, and he proceeded into her bedchamber. As he dropped her onto the bed, as he followed her down, she was laughing, merry, content beyond measure, and she wouldn't spend a single second worrying about how she was sinning.

When he made her so happy, when the very air seemed to sizzle with their proximity, how could their conduct be wrong?

He rolled on top of her, and they were nose to nose, their bodies touching from foreheads to toes.

"I leave for a few days," he told her, "and I come back to find that you've charmed my friends and corrupted my servants."

"I enjoyed every minute of it too!"

"Should I scold you for your riotous behavior?"

"No. You should be grateful that I decided to liven up this

drafty old place."

"I am grateful, Miss Etherton."

"Are you really? Do you mean it?"

"Yes, I mean it."

"You're not upset, are you? That I took liberties? Especially with the servants."

"I didn't realize they could sing."

"I was at church on Sunday, and they were all in the choir. They were so good I couldn't believe it."

"You may press them into your service whenever you wish. They're all half in love with you—particularly the footmen. If I refused to let them cavort with you, I'd likely have a mutiny on my hands."

"You're being awfully kind."

"I'm not usually, but with all your energy flowing through the halls, you make me feel dull and stodgy."

"Stodgy? You? Never."

"I'm trying new things lately. I have to become more rambunctious so I'm more like you."

They chuckled, their banter dwindling to a halt. They were grinning, staring, and as Evangeline gazed into his blue eyes, it seemed as if her heart was swelling in her chest, as if it no longer fit between her ribs.

Fondness was burgeoning, beginning to grow. Where would it lead? Where would it end?

They were from completely different stations in life, and if she had any antecedents that would recommend her to him, she wasn't aware of what they might be. Miss Peabody had always claimed there was no evidence as to Evangeline's parents, so she had no history to indicate a relationship should form.

Despite how she was betraying the vicar and racing away from her betrothal, she was a very moral person. Lord Run had asked her to debase herself with an affair, which she would never consider. And societal restrictions would never allow them to marry.

But when he smiled at her like that...

Oh, my! What was she to think?

Was there another road they could travel together? What might it be? If he appeared so smitten after such scant acquaintance, what might transpire after a prolonged association? Might he eventually lower himself to wed her?

She didn't suppose it was possible, but why couldn't she hope for it? Why couldn't she set out to entice him, to win him?

Occasionally—not often, but occasionally—there were men of his rank who did the unexpected, who married the governess or the nanny or the poor cousin. They fell in love and couldn't help themselves.

Why couldn't that occur for Evangeline? Why shouldn't she shoot for the moon?

She'd always dreamed big dreams, but had never been in a position to chase after them. Yet she was an adult now, floating free from her past, and about to break her engagement to the vicar. She'd written to Rose and Amelia to ask their advice, to beg their assistance. As soon as she heard back and was certain she had someplace to go, she'd inform Vicar Bosworth of her decision.

Maybe, if she played her cards right, she wouldn't have to ever leave Fox Run. She wouldn't need rescue from Rose or Amelia. Why shouldn't Lord Run be the biggest dream of all?

"I'm so glad we met," he murmured.

"So am I."

"Doesn't it seem as if...ah..." He paused, his cheeks flushing with chagrin. "Oh, never mind."

"No, say it."

"Doesn't it seem as if there's some destiny at work between us? I rarely visit Fox Run, but I just happened to stop by when you were here. It's as if the universe intended for us to cross paths."

Hadn't she been thinking the very same? Yes, there was destiny at work. Where would it take them?

"I agree," she said. "I feel as if I was specifically brought to Fox Run by the unseen hand of Fate."

"I tried to depart so you'd be safe from my wicked ways."

"Your wicked *ways*?" She laughed, liking him more and more.

"Yes, my very wicked ways, but I couldn't stay away. You were a magnet, dragging me back."

"A very strong, very potent magnet. I obsessed over you every second while you were gone."

"Did you?" He beamed with pleasure. "It was almost as if you'd planted a message in my head, as if you were calling to me across the miles to jump on my horse and hurry to your side."

"I won't embarrass myself by confessing how often I sent you that precise message. When I looked up in the music room and you were standing there, I thought, there's a man who knows how to obey."

It was his turn to laugh. "You'll be the death of me."

"I sincerely hope not. I rather enjoy your company. I'd hate to have you perish before you can shower me with more of it."

"I'll try to hold on—just for you."

"Thank you."

Their banter died down again, and he started to kiss her. He was still stretched out on top of her, his large body pressing her down. With his greater size, he should have seemed heavy, but he didn't. She relished the solid feel of him, the weight of him. She couldn't get enough.

She kissed him back enthusiastically. He was touching her all over, driving her to a chaotic state of excitement, and she was doing the same to him. He'd previously shown her some of the decadence he could produce, and she was anxious to let him proceed, to let him create all those wild sensations again.

But she was sufficiently rational that she realized they shouldn't continue. He was disrobing her, unbuttoning her dress, baring her arms and shoulders.

She'd once told him she wasn't loose, that she wasn't easy, and if she wanted to coax him into a deeper relationship, she had to exhibit the moral traits of the virtuous person she'd always been.

She laid a hand on his, stilling his questing fingers.

"You're awful," she said. "You draw out the worst parts of my character so I'm eager to misbehave."

"Wonderful."

"But...I'm not going to."

"Why not? I've typically found that it's more fun to be naughty than to be nice."

"You're much too worldly for me. I can't carry on as you do."

"Does this mean I can't kiss you anymore?"

"Absolutely not. You can kiss me as frequently as you like."

"Praise be." He raised an arrogant brow. "And how about sneaking into your room late at night? Are you barring me?"

"No, again, Lord Run. You may visit whenever you like—so long as you're discreet and you mind your manners."

"You make it difficult to rein in my base tendencies, but I'll try my best."

"After we've been friends for a while, you won't have any base tendencies. I'll drum them out of you."

"Here's hoping."

There was such a passionate look in his eye that she thought he might declare elevated feelings, and she was on tenterhooks, her pulse racing with exhilaration to hear what they would be.

Yet what he said was, "When we're alone, would you call me Aaron? It wouldn't be appropriate when we're around the servants or the neighbors, but when we're by ourselves, it would probably be all right. What do you think?"

She was so disappointed by the query. Not because he wanted a more intimate mode of address, but because she'd been prepared for a different remark entirely.

He was waiting for her reply, and she smiled, desperate to bring them back to the light, teasing place where they'd been through the whole encounter.

"Yes, I would be happy to call you Aaron when we're alone, and you've already been calling me Evangeline, and now I give you my permission, you lucky dog."

He swooped in and stole a last kiss, then he slid away and stood. She missed him instantly and could barely keep from begging him to lie down again.

"I traveled all day." He was drooping, yawning. "I'm dead on my feet."

"Then head for your bed, you silly man."

"Unless you'd like to invite me to stay in yours?"

"No! I'm determined to show you that I am a virtuous young lady."

"I find virtue to be highly overrated."

"You do not."

"Since I met you, my attitudes are changing."

He swooped in again, palms on the mattress. He studied her, his beautiful blue eyes riveting, mesmerizing, then he took another quick kiss.

"Good night, Evangeline."

"Good night, Aaron."

At her use of his Christian name, he flashed a huge, beguiling smile.

"Join me for breakfast in the morning," he said. "At ten."

"I will."

"Do you ride?"

"Yes." Not very well, and not very often, but she wouldn't tell him that.

"We'll take a ride after we eat."

"I'd like that very much."

He dawdled, and they gaped like a pair of halfwits.

She braced, thinking he was about to address a vital topic that would send her soaring, but he didn't. He spun and left.

She listened to him go, feeling almost bereft as the door closed behind him.

What now? How would she maneuver their acquaintance with any aplomb? After such a fiery rendezvous, their future assignations would grow in heat and intensity. How would she survive them?

She couldn't imagine.

"Thank you for coming."

"Lord Run is in residence again, so I can only tarry for a minute."

Gertrude Bosworth stared at Mrs. Turner, a frumpy, dour

housemaid at Fox Run. They were in the parlor at the vicarage, Ignatius out for the afternoon. Mrs. Turner had stopped by unexpectedly, but then that's how her visits always occurred.

"What is it you have for me?" Gertrude snapped. "Make it quick, would you? You're not the only person in the world who's busy."

Mrs. Turner was employed at the manor. She was widowed, with her husband having previously been in charge of the stables. She loathed Aaron Drake because—toward the end of Mr. Turner's life—he was nearly fired for drinking on the job.

Mr. Turner had fallen to the ground right in front of Aaron's horse. Any other landlord would have rid himself of such a drunkard, but the negligent pair had managed to convince Aaron not to terminate the old sot.

In many ways, Aaron was a fool. He could be too kind and accommodating. He'd done the Turners an enormous favor, but Mrs. Turner had never forgiven Aaron for accusing her spouse of sloth and dereliction.

It proved the saying that no good deed went unpunished.

Mrs. Turner was very devout, and she didn't like Aaron's loose morals or his dissolute friends. She viewed it as beneath her dignity to serve a doxy or gambler.

She opened her bag and pulled out some letters, handing them to Gertrude.

"You told me to inform you if Miss Etherton wrote to anyone."

"My, my, what have we here?" Gertrude studied the letters, seeing they were addressed to two women named Rose Ralston and Amelia Hubbard. "Was this her only correspondence?"

"Yes."

"If there are any others penned, you'll bring them to me immediately."

"Yes, of course."

Gertrude might send them on after she read them. Or she might not. It depended on Miss Etherton's comments.

"What about the goings-on at the manor?" she asked Mrs. Turner. "You mentioned that my cousin has returned."

"Just in time too, although with his low habits, I don't know if it will make any difference."

"What do you mean?"

"Miss Etherton has been in a frenzy, with her singing and carrying on. She's tight as a knitted cap with those two friends of his, that Miss Bernard and Mr. Blair."

"They've been singing together?"

"Yes, and they've even invited a few of the servants to join them in their choruses. The blasted racket continues day and night. A body can't find a moment's peace."

Gertrude frowned. "She's fraternizing with the servants?"

"Yes. It's quite shocking. I never saw anything like it, and believe me, in *that* house, I've seen plenty."

"What does the housekeeper say about it? What about the butler?"

"They think it's humorous. They take time away from their chores to watch. I'm surprised any work gets finished at all."

"Miss Etherton is the instigator?"

"Yes."

"Well, I'm sure my cousin will put a stop to any misbehavior."

Mrs. Turner shrugged, being careful not to voice an untoward remark about Aaron. Mrs. Turner hated him and loved to tattle, but Aaron was family, and Gertrude wouldn't permit a servant to speak ill of him.

"I appreciate you coming by," Gertrude said.

"You're welcome."

"If there's more I should know, notify me at once."

"I will."

"I'm especially curious—now that my cousin is back—if he'll allow Miss Etherton to keep flaunting herself."

"I understand."

"We have to be certain she's suited to being a vicar's wife."

"She hasn't seemed to be so far," Mrs. Turner snidely stated.

"That's for me to judge, Mrs. Turner. Not you. Good day."

Mrs. Turner had been dismissed, but she hovered, hoping Gertrude might slip her a coin. Gertrude compensated her occasionally—if she felt the information provided was worthy of remuneration. Apparently, Mrs. Turner was starting to expect financial reward. By her demonstrating her greed and sense of entitlement, she'd ruined any chance of fiscal gain.

Gertrude raised a brow. "I trust you can show yourself out?"

Mrs. Turner scowled, then mumbled, "Yes, ma'am."

She slinked off, and Gertrude listened until the door shut, until she was sure she was alone, then she opened Miss Etherton's letters.

The messages were insulting and offensive. The little ingrate! She didn't wish to marry Ignatius! She claimed he was horrid to her, that he would be an awful husband. She begged her friends to send money so she could escape.

How dare she!

Gertrude was so upset she was glad she was sitting down. If she'd been standing, she might have collapsed with affront.

For several minutes, she dithered over the best plan of action. Should she tell Ignatius? Should she not? Should she wait and tell him later on? What were the benefits of waiting? What were the detriments? In whatever she chose, how could she damage Miss Etherton the most?

The young woman was very popular, had ingratiated herself everywhere, so they would have to tread carefully.

They couldn't simply toss her over. They'd have to run her off, but with their hands clean, their involvement hidden. Gertrude would have to orchestrate Miss Etherton's downfall to the last, most excruciating detail.

When she left, it had to be in disgrace so people would be relieved she was gone, and of course, Gertrude would have to conduct some research on the dowry. If Miss Etherton was deemed unfit for some reason, then Gertrude and Ignatius would keep the dowry. It was only fair, but as they'd already spent most of it, she had to be clear on her legal position.

In the meantime, a distant cousin had written that she had a daughter who needed a situation. Gertrude remembered the girl. She was a mousy, homely twit, but she was also obedient and obsequious and exactly the sort Gertrude had assumed they were getting when they'd agreed to Miss Etherton.

Perhaps she'd reply to her cousin's inquiry and have the daughter come for an extended visit. Gertrude had felt from the start that Miss Etherton wasn't the right woman to be Ignatius's bride. Obviously, they had to begin looking again.

There was a fire burning in the grate, and she went over to it.

"You begged your friends to help you, Miss Etherton," she murmured, "but I'm very sorry to report that they will never know you asked."

She threw the letters into the flames, watching as they dwindled to ashes. Then she returned to her desk and continued reviewing the household accounts.

CHAPTER TEN

"Aaron is gone?"

"Yes."

George Drake, Lord Sidwell, glared at Claudia Cummings. They were in his library, in his London town house. She'd blustered in without sending a card, without asking if he'd like to see her. If it had been up to him, he'd have refused an audience, but then she likely knew that to be the case, so she'd shown up unannounced.

In a few weeks, they would be in-laws, and the notion wasn't as pleasant as it had previously been. Claudia was a neighbor, and her deceased husband had been a boyhood chum of George's. Practically from the day Priscilla was born, he and her father had figured Aaron would marry her.

Yet when George had broached the subject with Claudia, she'd dithered for ages. The Sidwell title was only two generations old—a pittance in the history of British aristocratic families. Many people viewed George as an interloper to the peerage, snickering that his title wasn't very grand. Claudia had been wrangling for a fiancé who was higher on the social ladder.

But it had been a slow year for duke's and earl's sons. Ultimately, she'd been forced to agree to Aaron, pretending he had been her first choice all along.

"When did he leave?" she inquired.

"Saturday night. Or maybe Sunday morning. I'm not sure. He wasn't here when I came down to breakfast."

"That's after we were with him at the ball."

"Oh, that's right. He escorted you and Priscilla."

"Yes."

"I trust all was well between them?"

"Why wouldn't it have been?"

She glanced away, not able to hold his gaze, and he nearly snapped at her. She was a busybody who'd stirred plenty of trouble for him and his sons. What had she done now?

George had betrothed Aaron without seeking his opinion about

Priscilla. Aaron had accepted Priscilla with good grace, but lately he'd been chafing, having second thoughts. George had convinced him to continue on with Priscilla, and Aaron had promised he would, but he kept sneaking off—and the wedding was only weeks away. What was George to make of it?

He wasn't certain what was happening at Fox Run, but Bryce Blair and that slattern, Florella Bernard, were there with Aaron. Florella was likely entertaining both men, and if Claudia and Priscilla weren't careful, Aaron might never come back.

"I'll be frank, Claudia," George said.

"If you feel you must."

"I have friends everywhere, and they delight in tattling to me."

"If that's the case, perhaps you should get some new friends."

"That's as may be, but I've had several reports from the ball Saturday night."

"Have you?"

"I know they were fighting out in the garden."

"They weren't fighting," she insisted. "They were...having a disagreement."

"Apparently, it was sufficiently heated that Aaron stormed out and left town immediately after."

"If he left right after, it had naught to do with Priscilla."

"Seriously? You expect me to believe that?"

"I smoothed over their discord."

"What was causing it?"

"He merely wished she'd treat him in a more respectful manner."

George nodded. "Understandable."

"I promised him I'd spend this month working with Priscilla. Obviously, I haven't prepared her to be a bride."

George suspected it would take much more than a month to whip the girl into shape, but they didn't need to worry about it. There were many ways for a husband to deal with a disobedient wife. Before the pair marched down the aisle, George would apprise Aaron of all of them.

"So," George mused, "it sounds as if their argument was settled."

"It seemed to be, which is why I'm surprised that he's disappeared again."

She paused, waiting for George to provide an explanation for Aaron's absence, but George simply stared, not inclined to share information with her.

"Where is he?" she finally asked. "Is he back at Fox Run?"

"I have no idea," George lied.

"I hate to mention it, but he was quite vexed the other night.

He actually spoke of crying off, of jilting Priscilla." She gave a frilly laugh, as if the remark had been hurled in jest. "I told Priscilla he didn't mean it, but she's in a state."

She was desperate to be reassured, and George had to confess, he was a bit rattled himself. Aaron was extremely conflicted about the engagement, but George could hardly admit it to Claudia.

"Of course he didn't mean it," George scoffed. "He was just angry."

"He hasn't broached the subject with you?"

"No, and I wouldn't listen if he had. He's a dutiful son. He knows his role. I want this marriage, and he would never defy me."

"If he *is* at Fox Run—"

George cut her off. "As I said, Claudia, I have no idea where he is."

"Would it help if Priscilla and I visited him?" At George's shocked look, she hurriedly added, "I thought their relationship might improve if they spent time together in the country."

"Let me be very clear, Claudia."

"Yes, please."

"Whether Aaron is or isn't at Fox Run, a visit from you and Priscilla wouldn't be in anybody's best interest."

"What are you saying?"

"I'm not saying anything. I'm simply telling you to stay away from Fox Run."

"Will he return for the wedding?"

"Yes."

"Swear it to me," she demanded.

"I swear, so stop fretting. Everything will be fine."

They glared, and she was furious, dubious. Finally, she pushed to her feet.

"If you're lying to me," she fumed, "if he leaves her standing at the altar, I'll kill you."

"Always nice to see you too, Claudia," he jovially retorted. He waved to the door. "Now then, if you'll excuse me, I'm awfully busy today."

She spun and huffed out without another word.

"Come back to bed."

"You've worn me out for the afternoon, Florella."

"Good."

"Yes, you're earning your keep for a change."

Bryce was in his bedchamber at Fox Run. He was over by the window, naked, sipping a brandy and gazing out at the park.

Florella was on the bed, naked too, preening, trying to entice him to look over at her, to join her and start in again.

She enjoyed a frisky romp as well as any man, so she was a perfect lover. But as a mistress? She wouldn't win any medals.

She had expensive tastes, and he had a modest income, so it was a trial to find the money to keep her happy. Yet it humored him to brag that she was his, so he continued on with her—trollop that she was.

She had her own mind, her own friends, and even though they supposedly had an exclusive arrangement, she pretty much did what she liked.

If she crossed paths with a man who tickled her fancy, she'd trot off with him. If Bryce protested, she'd advise him that they could split if that's what he wanted. How was he to lord himself over such an independent woman?

She'd been on her own since she was very young, had always earned her own wages, so she had no concept of how a female should act with men. She certainly had no concept of being the inferior gender, of needing male counsel or guidance.

He chuckled to himself. He liked her. What could he say?

He often visited Fox Run with Aaron, but it was Florella's first time. They were maintaining the pretense of separate bedchambers, but their suites had an adjoining dressing room, so they probably weren't fooling any of the servants. They'd sneaked off for a tumble, but as typically happened, it had extended dramatically in both duration and intensity.

He was feeling content and sated.

"When do you have to be back in London?" he asked her.

"How about never? Let's remain here forever."

"You'd die of boredom in the country. I give you another week, and you'll be begging me to return to the city."

"Ah, you know me well. I love all this luxury though. I can't get used to it."

"Neither can I."

"I like Aaron, but his kind takes this opulence for granted. It aggravates me."

By his *kind,* she meant the upper classes. She and Bryce flitted around on the edge of that wealthy group, welcomed as friends and mistresses, but never fully accepted. "At least he doesn't throw his position in our face every two seconds," Bryce said.

"Thank God."

They might have hurled more condescending comments about Aaron, but Aaron had always been loyal and considerate, and Bryce wouldn't denigrate the man in his own home.

"Why is he at Fox Run again?" she asked. "He left, then hurried back."

"I think he's fretting about his wedding. He's a bachelor, and the notion of a leg-shackle is terrifying. It would be to *me*."

"And his fiancée is horrid, yes? What's her name? Priscilla?"

"Yes."

"I don't know her."

"Lucky you."

"I feel sorry for him."

"So do I."

"Is she disgustingly rich? That would make it partially worth it."

"Yes, she is disgustingly rich."

"And pretty?"

"If you like ice maidens."

Florella laughed her sexy, sultry laugh. "Now I'm dying to meet her so I can decide if you're telling the truth."

"You scandalous hussy," he teased. "You could never be introduced to such a paragon of virtue."

"Well, if she stumbles into a box at the theater some night, you have to point her out to me."

"I will."

He stared across the park, and far out on the road, he noticed Aaron riding with Evangeline. They'd been gone for hours, having departed after breakfast. Bryce had assumed it would be a short jaunt around the estate but, apparently, they hadn't been in any rush to finish.

They started up the lane that led to the manor. Their horses were walking at a snail's pace, and they were leaned toward one another, chatting intently, their heads pressed close.

Aaron was so focused on Evangeline that Bryce wouldn't have been surprised if he'd grabbed her and pulled her onto his lap. He looked that besotted, and his visible interest was extremely disturbing. Bryce had known Aaron since they were five, and Aaron had never gazed at a woman as he was gazing at Evangeline.

There was a tangible spark shooting between them that would have been evident to anyone who'd seen them passing by. Bryce hoped they hadn't ridden through the village or—heaven forbid— by the vicarage.

"Damn," he muttered.

"What?" Florella asked.

"It's nothing."

He continued to watch, as they neared, as they skirted the house and kept on to the stable. Gradually, they moved out of sight, and he was frozen in place, studying the spot where they'd been.

Now he understood why Aaron had fled Fox Run so abruptly, why he'd returned without warning. It had nothing to do with Priscilla and everything to do with Evangeline.

Over the past week, Bryce had spent an enormous amount of time with Evangeline, and he liked her very, very much. While she was funny and ebullient and charismatic, she was also very naïve. Did she grasp what was occurring with Aaron? Did she recognize the strident affection that was blossoming?

She was a very moral, very decent person, and she'd come to Fox Run to marry Ignatius Bosworth. She wouldn't engage in a flirtation with Aaron unless she'd decided not to wed the vicar, unless she'd begun to suppose a different, better ending had presented itself.

Most clearly of all, she wouldn't involve herself with Aaron if he'd told her about his betrothal so, obviously, he hadn't. How far had matters progressed? Had Aaron seduced Evangeline? Or was it still on the horizon?

Bryce was disgusted and worried and anxious to determine his role in the debacle. Of a certainty, he was wishing he hadn't glanced out the window! He'd have been perfectly content to not know, to not see.

What did he owe to Aaron? They were friends, Bryce was a guest in his home, and Aaron would expect complete discretion from Bryce. But Bryce adored Evangeline and she had no one to look out for her. If Aaron interfered in her betrothal to the vicar, especially if she reneged, anticipating a commitment from Aaron, she'd be destroyed.

Bryce had no connection to her at all—except for a few days of pleasant acquaintance. Should he warn her to be careful? Should he tell her about Aaron and Priscilla? Had he a duty to Evangeline? Or had he a larger, more pressing duty to Aaron to be silent, to keep his secrets?

He had no idea, and on such short notice, couldn't figure it out.

"Why are you scowling?" Florella asked from over on the bed.

"Aaron and Evangeline are back from their ride."

"Their arrival is making you scowl?"

"No. It's making me realize we don't have time for another tumble."

She raised a tempting brow. "Who says we don't have time?"

She caressed a hand over her breast, and it was all the invitation he required.

"How was my sermon?"

"Your...sermon?"

Vicar Bosworth frowned at Evangeline. She'd been woolgathering, and he'd caught her out.

"My sermon, Miss Etherton! At least pretend to listen to me. It's infuriating to talk to you when it's obvious you couldn't care less."

"I apologize," Evangeline said. "I was...ah...thinking about my friends I mentioned. Rose and Amelia?"

"Yes, I recall them. Weren't they your fellow teachers?"

"Yes. I've been writing to them, but I haven't received a single reply. It's worrying me. I hope they're all right."

"Why wouldn't they be?"

"They were traveling to new situations—as was I. I'd simply like to be assured of their safe arrival."

She didn't understand why they hadn't answered. They should have been settled by now, unless some disaster had occurred—as it was occurring with Evangeline.

She refused to believe they wouldn't help her, so she could only assume they hadn't gotten her letters, that they weren't aware of her plight. The minute she returned to Fox Run, she'd write them again. And she'd keep on writing until she heard back. With Aaron at Fox Run, matters were escalating, and Evangeline was desperate.

She had to cry off from her engagement, had to make plans for herself, but she wasn't certain how to do that. She'd like to contact Mr. Thumberton, Miss Peabody's attorney, who had first informed Evangeline about the betrothal. Unfortunately, she didn't know his address, and even if she did, she wasn't sure there was time to mail a letter to him in London, no time to wait for his response.

Her wedding was winging toward her with the speed of a runaway carriage. If she truly intended to stop it, she had to act. At once. But she was paralyzed and couldn't force herself to take the necessary steps.

She was terrified to speak the words aloud to the vicar for it would set in motion a chain of events that couldn't be reversed, and she had so many questions about what her decision would entail.

Could she cry off? Was it allowed in her circumstances? When a dowry had been paid and contracts signed, was it an option? If she announced she wouldn't proceed, merely to learn that she legally had to, she'd have made an enemy of the vicar and his mother. How would they all live together afterward?

She and Aaron were growing incredibly close, and every second she was on pins and needles, expecting him to tell her to back out, that he would keep her for himself. Yet to her great consternation, no declaration was uttered.

She was so miserable! She was so confused!

"About my sermon," he said again. "What did you think?"

His sermon had been boring and much too strident for Evangeline's tastes. People didn't like to be scolded, and sermons ought to be uplifting. Still, she knew without a doubt that she could only ever praise him.

"It was good. Everyone seemed to enjoy it."

"It wasn't too long?"

"No," she lied. Congregants had been fidgeting and dozing off by the end. How could he have failed to notice?

They were in front of the church, the last parishioners having trickled out. She and the vicar had stood as a couple, thanking them for coming. His mother had invited Evangeline to the vicarage to have Sunday dinner. A few neighbors had been invited too, as well as Widow Bosworth's very plain, very shy female relative. Apparently, the girl was staying with the Bosworths for several weeks.

Even with other guests being present to provide a buffer, Evangeline envisioned the entire gathering like going to the blacksmith to have a tooth pulled.

Speak up, Evangeline! Tell him you're crying off!

But she simply couldn't.

Momentarily, she considered talking to Aaron, but she was scared to risk it. He'd only been apprised of a tiny bit of her history, so he didn't realize that she'd met his brother, Lucas, that Lucas was engaged to Evangeline's friend, the lowly schoolteacher, Amelia Hubbard. He didn't realize that his cousin, Rose Ralston, was her other friend.

The Drake family had behaved very badly toward Rose, and whenever their kinship was mentioned, Rose had never had a kind word to say about any of them.

If Evangeline told Aaron who she was, that her friend was the cousin his family had always despised, she couldn't guess what his opinion would be. She was afraid it would underscore their disparate positions, making it less likely that he would ever view her for a more important role in his life.

What to do? What to do?

The vicar took her arm, and as they walked out to the lane, a carriage rounded the bend. Quickly, she noted that it was Aaron. He reined in right beside them. She was so delighted she could barely keep herself from rushing over and climbing in. It seemed wrong that she was standing with the vicar rather than sitting with Aaron.

"Miss Etherton!" He smiled at her and nodded at the vicar. "Cousin Iggy."

He hadn't attended Sunday services, and the vicar—with a definite scold in his tone—said, "We missed you at church this morning."

"You know me, Iggy. I'm not a religious man."

"You should be."

"I'm not, and your sermons are a tad dry for my taste. I can't drag myself out of bed for them."

The vicar bristled. "That was uncalled for."

"Yes, it was." Aaron turned to Evangeline again. "I'm on my way back to the manor. Would you like a ride?"

More than anything in the world, Evangeline wanted to abandon the vicar and go off with Aaron. But it would cause a huge scene out in the middle of the road where any passerby could see. When she finally mustered her courage, she and the vicar needed to be in a quiet room, with the doors closed.

As she debated her reply, the vicar cut off any chance for a different conclusion.

"She's joining us for Sunday dinner at the vicarage," he said.

Evangeline assumed Aaron would argue the point and claim she was expected for dinner at Fox Run, but he simply grinned. "Well, then, I won't keep you. I'm sure Gertrude would have a fit if you were late."

He clicked the reins and his horse trotted off. As he went by, Evangeline thought he winked at her, but she wasn't positive.

Did he ever reflect on her situation? She felt so intimately connected to him, but on his end, it appeared that he liked her but not *too* much. How could that be? If she brought up the possibility of breaking her engagement, how would he react? What if she provided an opening for him to declare himself, only to discover that a continuing association—other than an illicit one—hadn't ever crossed his mind?

She was so disconcerted over her predicament, over her choices and how to implement them, that she was dizzy and nauseous. She was holding the vicar's arm, and he took off at such a brisk pace that she stumbled after him.

"Vicar, please, slow down."

At her plaintive request, he halted, struggling for calm. The vicarage was next to the church, and they were almost at the gate. Very likely, some of their guests had already arrived. He shouldn't be seen in a state of high dudgeon just before they entered the house.

"My apologies, Miss Etherton."

"It's all right. Why are you upset?"

"I realize it's bad form to denigrate one's kin, but I loathe that man."

"Lord Run?"

"Yes. He's much above me in station, but he relishes any opportunity to insult me."

"I didn't find him to be belligerent."

"Don't defend him to me!"

"I'm sorry. I thought he was merely trying to be funny."

"You would," he muttered.

"Perhaps he was embarrassed to have missed church. Most people would have no idea how to explain their absence to a pastor."

"Be silent, Miss Etherton."

He stared up at the sky, rubbing the bridge of his nose, as if she was a great trial, a heavy weight to be born.

Ultimately, he glared at her. "I've been very patient with you, but before we go in, there's a topic I must address."

"What is it?"

"You were seen riding with my cousin the other morning. Alone."

"So?"

"Don't let it happen again."

Evangeline was absolutely in the wrong and had no excuse for her conduct. She was sinning grievously, betraying him in her heart and her mind. Still, she said, "Why are you so angry about it? It was entirely innocent. Lord Run asked me if I liked to ride, and I haven't had the chance in ages. When I admitted as much, he insisted on giving me a tour of the neighborhood."

His cheeks flashed bright red, an indication of his fury she was witnessing more and more often. "I don't want to hear ever again that you were with him."

"You're being ridiculous."

He leaned down so they were nose to nose, and he hissed, "Never again, Miss Etherton! Do you understand me?"

He straightened and waited for her reaction. Was she to weep? To grovel? To plead for mercy?

Tell him! Tell him now! she urged herself, but she didn't know how. She was such a coward!

Instead, she murmured, "Yes, I understand."

"Good, and when we go inside, I expect you to behave."

"To behave?"

"Yes. No singing or laughing or drawing attention to yourself. I won't have it. Not with the mood I'm in."

She gnawed on her cheek, took a deep breath and let it out. "It might be better if I proceed on to Fox Run. You're vexed with me, and I don't wish to—"

"You would leave and humiliate me in front of my company? In front of Mother?"

"No, I'm simply certain you'd be happier if I departed."

"Get inside, Miss Etherton. Now!"

"No, really, I think I should—"

"Get inside!" he shouted.

He pointed to the door, appearing so enraged, she worried he might strike her. She nearly told him to sod off, to have his bloody dinner without her, but she glanced over to see a guest peeking out the window. Had he observed their quarrel?

Evangeline was mortified.

It was an elderly parishioner who liked Evangeline very much. He looked sympathetic, looked protective and kind. He waved and smiled encouragingly, motioning her to join him.

Evangeline hovered, debated, then pushed through the gate and went in.

CHAPTER ELEVEN

"Play me another."

"I'm running out of songs."

Aaron sipped his brandy and smiled at Evangeline.

"Then start again at the top of your repertoire."

"You are insatiable, Lord Run."

"Guilty as charged, Miss Etherton."

They were in the music room, and it was very late. The door was closed, a single candle burning. They were being very quiet, not wanting anyone to hear them, not wanting any interruptions as Aaron enjoyed his private concert.

With each passing minute, he was more obsessed with her, and his fixation seemed dangerous. He couldn't focus, couldn't complete his chores or even engage in conversation. He could only think about her, worry about her, wonder how he could keep her in his life.

He was certain his fascination was being spurred by an overwhelming need to fornicate with her. If they rolled around on a mattress a few times, he was positive his interest would wane. With previous lovers, it had always faded quickly, and no doubt an affair with her would prove no different from any of the others.

He figured he could easily persuade her to carnal conduct. She'd grown so attached, her adoration so evident, that he could persuade her to do whatever he asked.

And then what?

The question rocked him constantly.

He wasn't about to cry off from his engagement. No matter how tempting it was, he wasn't his brother. He hadn't his brother's lack of morals or probity. He'd sworn to his father and to Priscilla, both by signing the marital contracts and by verbally proposing to her.

He would follow through on that pledge.

Yet what about Evangeline? Where did that leave him with regard to her?

He hadn't mentioned his betrothal, but if she learned of it, he had no doubt his relationship with her would be instantly severed. It would have to be shortly anyway—when she wed Iggy. She would never countenance adultery, and he was amazed she was willing to flirt so brazenly with Aaron. He supposed it was a mark of his ability to lure her to misbehavior.

He couldn't abide the notion of her as Iggy's bride. The very idea made him nauseous, and he incessantly debated whether he should talk her out of it. But what would become of her? She'd once advised him that marriage to Iggy was her only option. She'd declined the opportunity to be Aaron's mistress, so if he convinced her to spurn Iggy, what would happen?

He couldn't begin to guess.

She was sitting on the bench at the harpsichord, and he was seated on a nearby sofa. She'd been performing for over an hour, but she didn't look exhausted and likely could keep on until dawn. It was also obvious that she liked performing for *him,* that she would keep on forever if he requested it.

"Come here," he said.

"I thought you'd never ask."

She slid off the bench and snuggled herself on his lap.

"That's better." He sighed with contentment. "You were much too far away."

"You seem sad tonight," she told him.

"I do?"

"Yes, and right in the middle of my singing too. What's a girl to think?"

"She should think I'm *not* sad."

"Liar," she murmured. "What's wrong? You can tell me whatever it is."

Oh, if only he could!

I'm engaged to be married and my wedding is in three weeks.

"I like you very much," he said. "I simply wish things were different."

"What things? That I was rich and from a top-lofty family?"

He chuckled and shrugged. "It would fix a few problems."

"What problems are those?"

He gazed into her beautiful blue eyes, anxious to unburden himself, but he didn't dare. As each day raced by and he managed to omit Priscilla from the conversation, he was climbing out onto a limb with Evangeline.

If she was apprised of his betrothal, she'd be crushed and furious. But then she'd learn of it very soon when he left for London and came back a married man. Which was worse? To be informed at once? Or to hear servants' gossip?

He was so smart, but such a coward. How had he landed

himself in such a quagmire?

"Your station doesn't concern me," he said. "I haven't been fretting over it."

She studied him, then to his great surprise, she said, "Should I wed the vicar?"

He held himself very still, eager to formulate the correct comment, to not let his enormous affection or enormous ego get in the way of his response.

"Why are you asking? Are you having second thoughts?"

"Yes. He and I are incredibly mismatched."

"I agree."

"I've tried to deny it, and I've even denied it to *you*, but I have to start being honest with myself. I should back out, but I'm so conflicted."

"Why?"

"My circumstances are the same as they've always been. If I cry off, I'm afraid about what will happen to me. I've written to two old friends, seeking their assistance, but they haven't replied."

"That's too bad."

"If I had any other option, I'd take it."

She paused, clearly waiting for him to jump in and say *yes, there was an option, that he was the answer to her prayers.* But with his marriage so near, he was in no position to help her.

Despite his concerted efforts at wearing her down, she wasn't interested in an indecent liaison, and as to Priscilla, Aaron would have plenty of trouble with her as his wife. He wouldn't deliberately exacerbate the situation by supporting Evangeline financially. He barely knew her, and there was no justification for it.

For an eternity, she watched him, and finally her smile faded. She'd bravely furnished him with a chance to declare himself, but by his silence, he informed her she'd been rejected.

"If I back out of the engagement," she asked, "could I stay at Fox Run?"

"At Fox Run?"

His panic must have been evident because she hastily said, "Just until I can make contact with my friends? There's been some problem with my correspondence. After I hear from them, I'm positive I'll have somewhere to go."

She waited again, on tenterhooks for his affirmative reply, but he couldn't give it.

Tell her! a voice was loudly urging. *Tell her everything!* But he simply couldn't.

Once the words were uttered, they couldn't be retracted. She'd be shocked and hurt. Very likely, she'd storm out and would never speak to him again, and the notion of their affair abruptly ending was too wrenching to contemplate.

Wasn't he a cad and a bounder! Wasn't he a despicable libertine!

She shook her head. "Listen to me! Prevailing on you—after all you've done for me already! I usually have better manners."

She was saving him from himself, and he felt awful, like the blackguard he was.

"I'm sorry." Without meaning it, he added, "Of course you could stay at Fox Run for a bit."

"There's no need for you to offer. I'm being a pest."

"No, no, I just have a lot on my mind. I have some…issues in London that are plaguing me. I'll get them sorted out. And you're *not* prevailing on me. I'm happy to help you."

But she didn't believe him, and he'd squandered his opportunity to be truthful, to be a friend. His entire relationship with her was wrapped up in lies and deceptions. Maybe he wasn't the decent fellow he'd assumed himself to be.

He should have been down on one knee, apologizing, proposing marriage, begging her to have him, but instead he was focused on how he'd foolishly promised she could stay at Fox Run for a while—when she absolutely couldn't stay.

"I hate that you're so distressed," she said.

"I'm not."

"You're the worst liar, even worse than me."

"My life is…complicated."

"Am I making it more complicated?"

"No!"

She squirmed away and stood. "I should head to bed."

"I don't want you to go up yet."

"I have to."

"No, play a few more songs for me. Sing for me again."

She stared at him, looking shrewd and wise and much older than he generally considered her to be.

"I have to raise a difficult topic with you," she said, "but please don't take it the wrong way."

"I won't."

"I've been so happy since I came to Fox Run."

"I'm glad."

"I was nervous at first. I was engaged to the vicar without my ever having met him. It was scary."

"You've been very brave about it."

"Right away, I realized the match was a mistake, and I need to cry off." She searched his eyes for a reaction. "But can I? If the dowry was already paid, can I refuse to proceed?"

"I'm guessing you can. It causes a bit of a kerfuffle, but it happens."

"How do I refuse? I have so many questions about it."

"Such as?"

"Do I just tell the vicar? Would that end it? Can he decline to let me end it? Does he have a choice? If it's simply my own decision, must I have legal papers drawn up to make it binding?"

"I have no idea. You should probably talk to an attorney."

"I don't have any funds to consult with an attorney."

He yearned to invite her to travel to London with him, to speak with his solicitor, Mr. Thumberton. Yet if Aaron involved himself in severing the betrothal, when that betrothal was to his own cousin and when Aaron's own father had apparently arranged it, it would open a massive can of worms.

Betrothals could be dissolved, but it was very rare. There would be unceasing gossip as to his role in the debacle. Was he prepared to wade into such a morass?

He felt as if he was walking across a field of broken glass in his bare feet and every step was a bad one. He couldn't bear to envision her wed to his cousin, but when his motives toward her were so dastardly, he couldn't give her the wrong impression or raise false hopes.

"I have to know your opinion about something else," she continued.

"Just say it, Evangeline."

"Well...ah..." She halted, blushed furiously. "I've rehearsed this a hundred times, but it's so much more difficult than I imagined."

He was still sitting, and she was standing, and he took her hand and tried to pull her onto his lap again. But she yanked away and moved back so there was more space separating them.

"When you touch me, it confuses me," she said.

"Good, I like you confused."

"Be silent and let me get through this."

"Go ahead."

"You wouldn't ever...that is...you wouldn't ever think of marrying me yourself, would you?"

It was such a daring, unexpected query. A woman never proposed to the man—at least not in his stilted world where weddings involved huge transfers of wealth and were often contracted when a babe was in the cradle.

"You're putting me in a tough position," he said.

"I don't mean to. I like you so much, and I've built up these wild scenarios about you."

He smiled. "Not too wild, I hope."

"When we're isolated here in the manor, I forget myself."

"Me too."

"I start to picture a future for us, but you don't see it occurring, do you? I'm a trifle? It's fun and games?"

"Oh, Evangeline..."

He might have expounded, but any comment would crush her, and she held up a palm, stopping whatever remark would have followed.

"It's all right," she said. "I had to be sure."

"You're asking such hard questions."

"They're not hard, and I'm not a child. You can be honest with me. I had a very sheltered upbringing, so I've had no experience maneuvering through such a muddle. I'm not certain what's allowed or forbidden for me to discuss with you."

"I understand."

"And recently I heard stories about a nobleman's son who wed a commoner. She had no antecedents to recommend her."

She gazed at him with a tormented expression. She'd just described his brother's exact marital circumstance. Was she referring to Lucas?

Lucas was marrying Miss Hubbard, but Lucas's situation was totally different from Aaron's. Lucas had no title to inherit, no earl's line to continue with his sons, no pressure to marry as high as he was able. Lucas could pick whomever he wished, but Aaron couldn't. It was simply the law of the universe in which he lived.

"Occasionally, a man will wed beneath his station," he mumbled.

"But you couldn't see it happening to *you*?"

"Well..."

"I've embarrassed you, haven't I? I'm sorry to blurt out what's vexing me, but there's no way to tiptoe around the edges of this. You'd never consider me as a bride, would you?"

He couldn't tell the truth. Instead, he said, "I asked you this before—crudely and boorishly—but we'd just met, so let me ask it again. Would you come to London with me?"

"To be your what?"

"You know what. To be my mistress."

She gave a soft, miserable laugh. "No, I could never do that."

They stared, and a terrible wave of sadness swept over him. They might have had a bright future. It would have been so extraordinary, he'd have braved Priscilla's wrath and society's censure merely to pursue it.

It hovered there, like a tangible object, but he couldn't grab onto it.

"It would be grand to have you as my mistress," he insisted, and it would be grand—on *his* end. For her, it would be ruination, coupled with some financial support until he grew tired of her and moved on. "Many women would deem themselves lucky to be allied with a rich fellow like me."

"Only a *rich* fellow like you would view it that way," she countered.

Chastised, he nodded. "You're correct."

The light that seemed to glow around her was dimming, the joy she emanated gradually waning.

"I had previously claimed that I hate to prevail on you."

"Stop feeling as if you've been a burden. You haven't been."

"I'd like to leave Fox Run."

"Leave! Isn't that a bit drastic?"

"My friend who I've been writing to about my predicament? I haven't received a reply, but I thought it might be best to simply go to her. She'd help me."

"It might be best," he tepidly agreed, rattled by her announcement.

"Could you loan me a few pounds so I could purchase a ticket on the mail coach?"

"On the mail coach?" he asked like a dunce—as if he'd never heard of the vehicle.

"I'll pay you back as soon as I can."

"It's not that," he scoffed. "It's just...you're making rash decisions."

"Rash? How are they rash?"

"You wish to depart and travel across the countryside alone. It's happening too fast. Let's slow down and think for a minute."

"I've been thinking about nothing else since I arrived."

"I can be with you at Fox Run for two more weeks before I have to return to London. I want you here with me."

"I can't be."

"Why can't you?" he snapped more hotly than necessary. "Is it because of our relationship? That should be the reason we both stay."

"Well, I know how I feel about *you*," she stated, "but I'm not exactly sure any of my sentiment is reciprocated."

"What is that supposed to mean?" Suddenly, his temper was flaring, when there was no basis for it to be.

If she left, she'd be doing him an enormous favor. For the price of a ticket on the mail coach, his problem would be solved. Why not hand her the money?

"You said it yourself, Aaron," she kindly chided. "You would never marry me, and the only role you could see me filling would be as your mistress."

"We could be happy that way."

"*You* could be happy that way. I never could be."

They glared, silently fighting, which was idiotic and pointless. There was naught to fight about. She had no place in his life and was eager to depart. He should let her.

Why then, was he experiencing such crushing alarm at the prospect of her going?

"This is ridiculous," she ultimately muttered. "Why are we quarreling?"

"I don't know."

"Will you give me the money? It's fine if you'd rather not."

"It's not the money," he claimed.

"What is it then?"

"I don't want you to leave."

"So? What purpose would be served by my tarrying a moment longer?"

"We could have two more weeks together!" Why couldn't he make her understand?

"Doing what?"

"What we've been doing. Singing and riding and dining. It's been so enjoyable."

"Yes, it has—like a relaxing, entertaining holiday. I'll always remember it. I'll always be grateful that I had the chance to visit your home."

It was such a final comment, as if she already had a foot out the door.

"What about your engagement?" he asked.

"What about it?"

"You have to end it, and it will take some time and effort. You can stay while you wrap things up."

"I can't stay. Every minute I spend with you is a betrayal of your cousin."

"Don't be absurd."

"It is! Don't deny it. I'm being consumed by guilt."

"I'm not. Besides, if you're crying off, how can our relationship matter to him? It's none of his business."

"He was kind to bring me here, and my decision will cause hard feelings all around. It will upset the community and upset the vicar and his mother. It will be better for everyone concerned if it's handled from a distance."

"I'll help you—if you remain with me."

"You can't be involved in it."

"I suppose not," he grumbled. She was right again, of course. He couldn't have his name bandied within a hundred miles of the debacle.

"As I wade through it, I need to be surrounded by friends. I need their support and advice."

"When would you tell my cousin?" he inquired.

"Tomorrow morning."

"Tomorrow!"

"Yes, and I'd like to leave immediately after. The mail coach comes by at noon. I'd like to be on it."

He felt as if she was already walking away, and once she did, he'd never again enter his dining room to see her seated at the breakfast table. He'd never stand in the foyer and hear her piano music drifting down the hall. He'd never gaze across the parlor at a party and proudly watch her as she charmed his neighbors and enchanted his friends.

Though it was horrid, he let an image of Priscilla float in the air between them. He'd never previously given much thought to Priscilla being at Fox Run, to Priscilla supervising the servants and running the household.

He tried to picture her in the manor, making his home the easy, merry place Evangeline had turned it into. He tried to picture the servants looking at Priscilla with the adoration they showered on Evangeline.

Yet Priscilla wasn't Evangeline and would never behave like Evangeline.

With Priscilla in residence, it would be as dreary as it had always been, but accompanied by bickering and strife, by accusations and blame. With Priscilla in residence, Aaron might never visit Fox Run.

Evangeline had arrived at a decision—to sever her engagement—and she was prepared to follow through. Why couldn't he do the same?

A separation from Priscilla would create a huge mess, would stir controversy and bring fiscal catastrophe. But why would he blithely carry on when the marriage was so wrong? Why was he allowing his father to pressure him? Why couldn't he seize what he craved for once?

"No," he murmured.

"What?"

"No. You're not crying off tomorrow, and you're not leaving in the morning."

"I have to," she insisted. "It's the only way to save myself."

"No," he said more firmly, and he pushed himself to his feet and marched over to her. "You're not proceeding until I have time to figure out a better conclusion."

"You'd never wed me, and so long as that is your opinion, there is no *better* conclusion for us."

"There has to be. I just have to find it."

"It's pointless, Aaron."

"No, not pointless. Don't say that."

He dipped down and kissed her. He'd been putting it off all night, but he didn't want to control himself, didn't want to stay away from her. He wanted to be so soundly connected that there could never be an inch of space between them.

For a brief second, she tried to pull away, but their physical attraction was too strong. She moaned with despair, then leaned into him, her arms wrapping around his waist.

His tongue was in her mouth, his hands in her hair. Her body was pressed to his, but he simply couldn't get her near enough. Short of fornication, he couldn't truly have her in the fashion he desperately desired. But he wasn't so sufficiently corrupted that he'd deflower her on the sofa in his parlor. If she deserved anything from him, she deserved that.

He kissed her forever, for hours perhaps; he couldn't guess how long it lasted. He couldn't bear to release her, feeling that if he did, she might vanish right before his eyes.

He held her and caressed her and pleased himself, captivated by how she fit against him, how she responded to his slightest move, his slightest touch. She was perfect for him, but he'd convinced himself he couldn't have her.

Why couldn't she be his? He would cast caution to the wind, would tell his father to sod off, would tell Priscilla it was over. He wasn't concerned about the morass it would cause, about ruined reputations or legal suits for breach of contract.

He thought he might be in love with Evangeline, that he might be pitifully, completely, wildly in love. And if a man couldn't marry for love, why marry at all?

Gradually, he slowed and drew away.

"I have to ride to London tomorrow," he told her.

"Why?"

"I have to take care of some family issues."

"What issues?"

"It's some old trouble."

"All right."

"While I'm gone," he said, "I want you to promise me you won't talk to my cousin. Don't leave. Just...wait."

She was clutching his shirt, seeming weak, as if the least poof of wind would knock her to the floor. Finally, she repeated, "All right."

"I'll fix everything while I'm there."

"I have no idea what that means."

"I'll explain once I'm back."

She was dubious, skeptical. "Tell me I'll be fine, that there will be a good ending for me. Tell me it will involve you."

"It will, but you have to be here when I return."

Her shoulders sagged as if with defeat. "I will be. I promise."

"We'll work this out, Evangeline, I swear it to you."

"Here's hoping." She spun and ran for the stairs.

CHAPTER TWELVE

"How was your journey?"

"Invigorating. Calming."

"Good. You look better than you have in ages."

Aaron stared at his father, wishing they were in the country at Sidwell Manor, but earlier in the summer, his father had come to town. He hadn't left, which was exhausting and expensive. Lord Sidwell felt entitled to behave as most gentlemen of his station behaved. He gambled and caroused and bought costly horses, art, clothes, and jewelry he didn't need.

He constantly chastised Lucas for his reckless fiscal habits, but Lord Sidwell wasn't any different—especially with regard to his gambling—but the family couldn't afford it. The Sidwell estate couldn't afford it. Aaron couldn't afford it. If his father dropped dead that instant, the debts would pass to Aaron.

In his own life, Fox Run was prosperous, and he was careful about his finances. As a boy, he'd had excellent tutors and had learned his lessons well. He didn't throw his money away, and he'd drown himself in the ocean before he'd enter a gambling house.

Claudia had paid a substantial portion of the dowry to Lord Sidwell, and he'd squandered most of it. If he was still in town, he was likely borrowing against future monies Claudia was obligated to tender after the wedding. Every penny Lord Sidwell frittered away made it harder for Aaron to reach the resolution with Priscilla he was desperate to achieve.

They were in his father's library, with guests about to arrive for supper. It was the first quiet moment they'd had since Aaron had returned to London.

"Have you been at Fox Run the whole time?" Lord Sidwell asked.

"Yes."

"Getting the place ready for your bride, are you?"

"Not really. It's in fine condition. It doesn't need alterations."

"Every bride makes changes."

"I don't want anything changed. I like it just how it is."

"We can have this discussion again in a few months, and we'll see how matters stand."

"What's that supposed to mean?"

"Wives generally get their way with household affairs. On the husband's end, it's typically not worth fussing over. I suggest you set up an account for her and tell her how much she can spend. Otherwise, she'll bankrupt you before Christmas."

"I'll keep that in mind."

Lord Sidwell was seated at his desk, Aaron in the chair across. They were having a brandy, trying to pretend the conversation wasn't awkward and strained. Lord Sidwell was difficult to like, and Aaron didn't like him very much—mostly because of his horrid reprimands of Lucas when they were children.

Aaron had been the perfect and adored son, while Lucas had been wild and unruly and constantly—viciously—punished. Aaron suffered great guilt over their disparate treatment, and his relationship with his brother was rocky because of it.

Still, Aaron was courteous and civil to Lord Sidwell. Their family was very small, without a hoard of aunties and uncles and just a scattering of distant cousins such as Gertrude and Iggy Bosworth. Mostly, it was Aaron, Lucas, and his father, and if Aaron didn't have his father and his brother in his life, who would he have? Priscilla and Claudia?

"Have you heard from Lucas?" he asked his father.

"Don't mention your brother to me."

Lord Sidwell and Lucas were fighting again, with Lord Sidwell having proclaimed Lucas to be disowned and disinherited. The usual threats.

Aaron rolled his eyes. "Have you heard from him!"

"Yes."

"You received a letter?"

"Yes."

"Has he found Miss Hubbard? Has he proposed?"

"He found her, and I believe she agreed to have him. Poor girl."

"Are they married? Have they eloped across the border? What?"

"I'm not his social secretary, Aaron. I have neither the desire nor the need to be apprised of his plans."

"If they didn't elope, are they coming to London to wed here? Or are they hoping to wed at Sidwell Manor?"

"He will *not* wed at Sidwell Manor. He's not welcome there, and he knows my feelings about it."

"You're being ridiculous," Aaron scolded. "You've been trying to marry him off for eight years, and he's finally done as you've been demanding. I like Miss Hubbard, and she'll be good for him. If they wish to have the ceremony at Sidwell, then of course they will. I won't let you refuse to host a celebration for them."

"I won't spend a farthing on it," his father petulantly snapped.

"Then *I* will. If you're determined to behave like a fool, you'll only be hurting Miss Hubbard. I'm sure Lucas couldn't care less where he marries."

"Precisely."

"So if they ask to use Sidwell Manor, it will be because Miss Hubbard would like to honor you by holding it there."

"Oh," Lord Sidwell grumbled, the notion obviously not having occurred to him.

Aaron thought Miss Hubbard would be a breath of fresh air for the family, that she was exactly the sort of kind, considerate person they should have in their midst. And she was madly in love with Lucas.

Aaron had once watched Miss Hubbard and Lucas together, had observed their visible affection, and he'd wondered how it would feel to have a woman gaze at *him* like that someday. Well, it had happened, and he could definitely say it was remarkable. It certainly trumped Priscilla's cool, detached disinterest.

"Speaking of weddings"—Aaron had to force himself to address the difficult topic—"I need to talk to you about mine."

"Three weeks away, hm? Coming at you with lightning speed."

"Yes, it's coming much too quickly."

"You seem much more resigned than the last time we discussed it." His father flashed a sly grin. "You must have taken my advice. I heard Florella Bernard was with you at Fox Run."

His father's comment raised a dozen questions, and Aaron could hardly decide which to address first. He chose Florella.

"How did you know Florella traveled with me?"

"An acquaintance mentioned it. People delight in apprising me of you and your brother's antics." His father grinned again. "Since you appear much more *relaxed,* I assume you enjoyed her in all the ways I suggested."

His father had told Aaron to have a fling before the wedding. Initially, Aaron had been offended by the idea. But, apparently, he hadn't been as offended as he'd believed himself to be. Hadn't he raced to Fox Run and acted just as his father had directed him to act?

"I haven't been consorting with Florella."

"You needn't lie about it, Aaron. We're both adults. You don't have to hide your indiscretions from me. I'm usually informed about them anyway."

"Bryce was with me too. He brought her."

"So? Doxies are notorious for sharing their favors."

"I didn't share *favors* or anything else with her."

"Say what you will," his father smugly replied. "I can see from your demeanor that *someone* relieved your stress."

"It wasn't Florella."

Aaron's tone was suddenly very solemn, very serious, and in the embarrassed silence that followed, Lord Sidwell mused, "There was a woman at Fox Run?"

"There was."

"I'm so glad. With how your mood has altered, she must have been amazing."

"She was. She *is*."

"She *is*? Are you setting her up as your mistress? Good for you. It will ease your transition from bachelor to husband."

"I'm not setting her up as my mistress."

"What then?" Lord Sidwell pondered the situation, then gasped. "Don't tell me she's a housemaid at Fox Run. That could be a bit dicey once Priscilla moves in."

"No, she's not a housemaid."

"But she's still at Fox Run? I hate to sound like an old fusspot, but is that wise?"

Aaron chuckled miserably. "No, there's nothing wise about it at all."

"You have to secret her away. I'm all for a man doing as he likes in his private affairs, but a wife has a way of sniffing out an indiscretion. The woman's proximity could get you and Priscilla off to a rocky start."

"We're already off to a rocky start."

"You'll figure out how to carry on, but a paramour on the premises won't help."

"I don't want to simply *carry on*. I want much more than that in my life."

"What do you mean?"

Aaron felt as if he was on a cliff and racing toward the edge. He hurled himself over, falling free, curious as to where and how he would land.

"I've decided to cry off."

"What?"

"I won't marry Priscilla."

His father stared and stared, then banged a palm against his ear. "There must be some problem with my hearing. I could have sworn you said you were crying off."

"Your hearing is fine. You know precisely what I said."

"Aaron, the wedding is in three weeks! It's been coming for an entire year."

"I'm aware of how long it's been coming. I lived through every blasted day of the engagement."

"And now—here at the very end—you think you can just change your mind?"

"Yes."

"You act as if we're dithering over how much sugar you'd like in your tea."

"I realize how serious this is. Don't lecture me."

"Don't lecture you? Don't lecture you?" Lord Sidwell's voice and temper were rising. "You'll be lucky if I don't lock you in an asylum for this."

"There's no need to threaten or bellow. I intend to discuss this quietly and rationally, or I won't discuss it at all. I'm asking you how to handle the dissolution with a minimum of fuss and bother. If you refuse to advise me, I shall ride back to Fox Run, and I won't return, which will leave you to clean up the mess on your own."

"He calls it a *fuss!*" his father muttered to himself. "A fuss!"

Lord Sidwell gaped at Aaron. He looked thunderstruck and more enraged than Aaron had ever seen him, and considering how Lucas had vexed their father over the years, that was really saying something.

"What the hell has come over you?" his father demanded.

"I don't wish to marry Priscilla."

"So? You never wished to."

"I've...met someone else. I wish to marry her instead."

"Someone else?" His father's face was such a violent shade of red that he appeared on the verge of collapse. "Is it this woman at Fox Run?"

"Yes."

"You've been acquainted with her...what? All of two weeks?"

"Actually, it's more like three weeks."

Crudely, his father sneered, "You've been fucking some trollop for three weeks and—"

Incensed at the slur to Evangeline's character, Aaron huffed, "She's not a trollop, and I haven't been fornicating with her."

His father ignored Aaron's comment. "You feel this makes her qualified to eventually be Countess of Sidwell? Because you've known her for twenty-one days? Please tell me you haven't lost your bloody mind."

When his father put it like that, Aaron's declaration sounded patently ridiculous.

At Fox Run, Evangeline had charmed him, and with their being sequestered in the country, it had seemed perfectly logical that Aaron shuck off all that he was and all he'd ever been. He'd convinced himself that he could blithely ruin several lives—most particularly his own—merely to satisfy his quest to be happy.

But as his father had mentioned, he hardly knew Evangeline. He was such a self-centered oaf that he'd scarcely quizzed her about her background. She'd once told him she was an orphan and had no details regarding her history or family. She could be anyone! She could come from any inferior place!

Aaron believed in the British system. The lower classes shouldn't mingle with the upper ones. There were reasons people were separated, that lines shouldn't be crossed, but when he was in Evangeline's company, she was like a sorceress. He forgot the rules and restrictions by which he'd been raised, by which he'd always thrived and succeeded. She was just so amazing.

When he was with her, it was difficult not to love her. And he *did* love her. Wildly and heedlessly. But so what?

He was pragmatic, sensible, and prudent. He'd never been governed by his emotions, had never let sentiment guide him. He assessed a situation, evaluated the pros and cons, then proceeded in the most cautious and rational fashion.

He'd never previously been in love. Was that the problem? Was romantic attachment driving him insane?

He yearned to be happy, but it wasn't a factor that mattered in choosing a bride. Wealth, property, and position were what mattered. Evangeline could never be his wife. She'd be an ideal mistress though, and Aaron had asked her, but she'd refused. Since she'd declined the only function available in his life, why had he assumed she could become more than what was allowed?

Yet he couldn't give up on her. He'd promised her they could be together, and he'd meant it.

Yes, happiness was fleeting and illusory. Yes, passion faded, but he simply *liked* her so much and wanted to be with her, to be with her forever. What was the answer for them?

"Who is she?" Lord Sidwell reined in his temper. "Is it anyone I know?"

"I'm not sure if you've met her, but you were responsible for bringing her to Fox Run."

"Me? How?"

"She's engaged to Cousin Iggy."

His father's brows shot up. "She's Iggy's fiancée?"

"Yes."

"Let me get this straight. You'd like to cry off from Priscilla, and this woman would cry off from Iggy? You'd destroy two families, then ride off into the sunset?"

"It wouldn't be like that," Aaron tried to claim.

"It would be exactly like that," Lord Sidwell hissed. "My God,

Aaron, what is wrong with you?"

"I'm in a terrible state, Father. I feel half mad with indecision."

"What's her name?"

"Evangeline Etherton."

"Ah, yes," his father said. "Are you aware of where I found this stellar specimen of womanhood?"

"No, where?"

"You haven't bothered to inquire? You're ready to push her into line to be our next countess, and you didn't think you should find out?"

"It all happened so fast."

"She taught at that stupid school with Miss Hubbard."

"No..." Aaron breathed.

"Yes," his father replied. "She boarded there as a girl, and she was a teacher later on."

"She told me she'd been a teacher."

"But she's an orphan, Aaron, and there is no information as to her antecedents. Her mother could have been a whore in a brothel."

Aaron bristled with affront. "Don't insult her."

"I'm not. I'm simply trying to jar you into viewing this rationally. We don't know her history, and we can't *ever* know. How could you—for even a single second—consider her as your countess?"

"She's wonderful, Father." Aaron felt as if he was begging.

"I'm sure she is, Aaron. If she's charmed you so thoroughly, and in such a short period of time, she must be magnificent, but it doesn't signify. It can't signify."

"You had no qualms about betrothing her to Iggy."

"Well, of course not. Iggy has naught to recommend him but the post at the church we helped him to secure. And Gertrude was looking for a tepid mouse who would let Gertrude continue to run the household. With Miss Etherton having no kin, she was a perfect bride for him—and his mother."

"Even if there might be whoring in her past?" Aaron caustically spat.

"I shouldn't have been so crude about her. She probably has a connection to a wealthy family—someone always paid her tuition—but she'd have been some fellow's by-blow. Very likely, it was a younger son who tumbled a housemaid. You understand how these affairs are handled. She couldn't be abandoned alongside the road, so she was sent to Miss Peabody."

"She's good enough for Iggy but not for me?"

"Exactly, and if you weren't behaving like a lunatic, you'd

realize I'm right."

"You permitted Lucas to marry a teacher from that school. In fact, you absolutely insisted on it."

It was the weakest argument Aaron could have raised, and it made him sound frivolous and immature.

"You're correct. I picked Miss Hubbard for him, but Lucas isn't you. Lucas isn't in line to inherit an earldom. He isn't in line to become a peer of the realm, and besides, Miss Hubbard's father was a French count."

"A French count?" Aaron scoffed. "Seriously?" "Yes. Her mother wasn't that lofty, but her father definitely was. She has a very elevated background, so she's appropriate for Lucas. But *you* aren't Lucas, and you know you're not. Honestly, Aaron, get a grip on yourself."

Aaron took a deep breath, trying to deduce why his scheme had seemed so logical at Fox Run, but why it seemed so absurd now. He might have been a child and his father dissuading him from having a piece of candy he'd desperately wanted to taste. Yet he wasn't a child, and he hadn't known Evangeline for twenty-one days.

He'd spent part of that interval in London, so the actual count was more like fifteen days. Why had he rushed to London and spewed drivel to his father about Evangeline? As his father had pointed out, Aaron belonged in an asylum.

Evangeline had to be his mistress. He had to convince her to agree. He could set her up in a house in London, and he'd draft a contract with her, would offer her a small pension so she'd be fiscally secure in the future after he tired of her and they went their separate ways.

It was the only path he could pursue with her, and as to Priscilla...

If Aaron wished to create a huge catastrophe, he could refuse to wed Priscilla, but then he'd have to select another girl just like her. But if he jilted Priscilla, what other father—after such an outrage—would give Aaron his daughter?

Aaron would be branded a cad and a liar. He'd be dragged through the courts for breach of contract. He hadn't inquired as to how much of the dowry Lord Sidwell had frittered away, but Aaron would be bankrupted paying it back.

As he contemplated the quagmire, he was ill with regret.

"What is Miss Etherton's opinion of your approaching wedding?"

His father's question yanked him out of his despicable reverie.

"I haven't told her," Aaron muttered.

"Why not?"

"She's a very moral person. She wouldn't understand how I could have developed an affection for her when I'm about to marry someone else."

"When were you planning to tell her about it? Or were you going to simply waltz into the front foyer with Priscilla and introduce them?"

"I hadn't thought it through. I'm so confused."

"Here is what I need you to do, Aaron," he father firmly, stoically said.

"What?"

"I want you to return to Fox Run and seduce Miss Etherton."

"Father!" Aaron scolded. "I won't talk about it."

"She's fascinated you, so avail yourself of her many charms. Have that fling I encouraged you to have. Get her out of your system before this eats you alive."

"I can't decide how to proceed."

"Aaron...son...listen to me."

"I'm listening, I'm listening."

"Passion fades. Romance fades. You're a man. You enjoy the chase, the hunt, but once you corner your quarry, your infatuation will wane." Aaron must have looked as if he'd argue the point, for his father added, "You know this is true."

"I suppose."

"Let Miss Etherton thrill and tantalize you. Dine on her attributes. Feast until you are sated, but then I'm begging you, I'm pleading with you! Send her away so you can come home and wed Priscilla."

"I'm not sure I can, Father. You might finally be asking too much of me."

"I'm not, Aaron. I'm only asking what I've always asked, that you be a dutiful, loyal son. Please!"

His father had never begged Aaron for anything, and Aaron had never refused to do his father's bidding. His father—for all his rants and foibles—had Aaron's best interests at heart. Aaron realized that fact, which was why he'd never rebelled as Lucas had.

"If you would treat Priscilla so hideously," his father softly said, "what will become of us? We'll be shunned. We'll be ostracized. I couldn't bear it. Could you?"

The query rang out with an exhausting resonance, and Aaron winced.

At Fox Run, his choices had seemed so simple. He'd told himself he could tot off with Evangeline, but there were so many unconsidered aspects to such treacherous behavior. He was stupidly, foolishly in love, so he'd pretended none of those other aspects mattered, but they did.

And with his father staring, pleading, Aaron was at the end of his rope.

"I have to go," he mumbled.

He pushed up from his chair and practically ran from the room.

"Aaron!" his father called. "Are you heading to Fox Run? Where will you be?"

Aaron ignored Lord Sidwell and kept on.

"Might I have a private word with you?"

"If you must."

Claudia glared at George, thinking she'd be delighted if he staggered out to the garden and drowned in the fountain.

Family difficulties were escalating. Aaron had left again, and Priscilla was in a wretched state, constantly asking if she was about to be jilted.

Claudia had no answers for her daughter. She wished she'd never given George the time of day when he'd suggested the betrothal. She wished she could get on a fast ship, sail away, and never come back.

She couldn't imagine that a man as sensible and amiable as Aaron would cry off, but if he did, Claudia would buy a gun. A very large, very deadly gun. She'd use it to murder George Drake, then Aaron Drake. As she was dragged to the gallows, she'd climb the stairs with a smile on her face.

They were at a supper party, with Claudia not having known George would be present too. She'd been avoiding him, determined they wouldn't cross paths until the night before the wedding when they were jointly hosting a lavish fete for the happy couple.

Happy couple, bah!

She was so disgusted, she nearly spat on the floor.

The meal was over, the guests mingling. George motioned to a quiet hallway, and she walked down it with him and followed him into an empty salon. He closed the door, and she watched as he went over to the sideboard and poured himself a whiskey.

When he poured her one too, she braced, recognizing that—whatever he was about to say—it would be very, very bad.

She grabbed her glass from him and took a long swallow, then said, "Let me have it. Don't hold back."

"I've seen Aaron."

"Are you about to tell me it's over? For if you are, I'm likely to throttle you with my bare hands."

"No, it's not over—although he'd like it to be."

"I hope to God you told him to grow up and stop complaining."

"I did, but it's complicated."

"Complicated in what way? Your son has been engaged for an entire year. The wedding is in three weeks. It's a little late to whine about complications."

"Don't bark at me, Claudia. I completely agree with you."

They stood, glowering like combatants in the ring, neither able to land the crucial, decisive blow.

"I need you to deal with a situation that's arisen," George said. "Actually, Priscilla needs to, but I have to ask you if you feel she's up to the challenge."

"The challenge? I won't try to guess what you're implying."

"He's met someone," George bluntly stated.

"Who has? Aaron?"

"Yes."

"Meaning what? He would wed her instead of Priscilla?"

"Yes, which is totally out of the question."

"Of course it is," Claudia concurred. "But...?"

"The woman is at Fox Run. Her name is Evangeline Etherton."

"Evangeline? What sort of name is that? She sounds like a missionary's daughter."

"She's a schoolteacher."

"A schoolteacher?" The news made Claudia so angry that red dots formed in her vision, and she wondered if she wasn't about to suffer an apoplexy.

"And not just any schoolteacher," George said. "She worked at Miss Peabody's school with Amelia Hubbard. They're...friends."

George placed special emphasis on the word *friends,* figuring that reference to Miss Hubbard would galvanize Claudia as nothing else possibly could.

Despite Claudia's efforts to prevent the marriage, Miss Hubbard was about to join the Drake family as Lucas's wife—if she hadn't already. But one of her friends might join too? Aaron might shame Priscilla with Amelia Hubbard's bosom companion?

It was all too much to absorb.

"What are you asking me, George? Whatever it is, I'll do it."

"Aaron is at Fox Run with Miss Etherton."

"Marvelous," Claudia sarcastically seethed. "Is he planning to return for the wedding?"

"I'm nervous, so I thought we should ensure Miss Etherton leaves Fox Run so she is no longer there to distract him. Once she's gone, he'll come to his senses."

"How—pray tell—would we make her leave?"

"From what I've learned about Miss Etherton, she had a very sheltered upbringing. She's a very moral, very honorable young woman."

"I'm certain she's a veritable paragon of integrity."

"She wouldn't tolerate deceit or dishonesty, and Aaron hasn't bothered to inform her that he's engaged."

Claudia gasped. "She doesn't know?"

"Apparently not."

"How could he suppose to keep such a secret? A servant could simply mention it in passing, and it would blow up in his face."

"He's not thinking clearly."

"Obviously not."

"So I decided I should be thinking for him."

"And your thinking is…?"

"Initially, I was opposed to Priscilla visiting Fox Run, but she hasn't been there in ages, and it's about to be her home. She should tour the manor and jot down a list of the redecorating projects she'd like to attempt."

Claudia nodded. "I should probably travel with her. We could stay a few days."

"Yes, several days are definitely in order."

"After we arrive, we're to chase Miss Etherton away? Is that the plan?"

"I'm expecting—when Priscilla introduces herself—Miss Etherton will go on her own. You and Priscilla won't have to do anything at all."

"What about Aaron? Won't he be angry?"

"Briefly, but he can't deny Priscilla's identity or her desire to inspect the property. Miss Etherton seems to have a strange hold over him, but if she departs, her influence will evaporate, and he'll be right as rain."

"Consider it done, George."

"Before you so firmly reply, Claudia, I must caution you. This will take an enormous amount of finesse. I would only advise your participation if you can coach Priscilla as to how the visit should be managed."

Claudia scoffed. "Don't worry, George. She's my daughter. Once I explain what's at stake, there will be no need to *coach* her."

"When can you leave?" he asked.

"First thing in the morning."

"Wonderful."

He downed his drink, then walked to the door and yanked it open. "Send me a note as soon as there's news."

"I will."

He slipped out, and she downed her own drink, then set down the glass with a hard thud.

Aaron, having an affair! Aaron, imagining Claudia and his father would let him cry off! The stupid idiot had a marital noose around his neck, and she'd be more than happy to strangle him with it.

She hurried back to the party to find Priscilla so they could head home and pack their bags.

CHAPTER THIRTEEN

No, no, I want to stay with you...
Evangeline thrashed in her sleep, trying to push herself out of her dream.

"Don't make me go with them!" she moaned, the haunting remark jabbing at an old wound she'd never understood.

She grabbed for someone's hand—she couldn't see who it was—but bigger, stronger hands yanked her away. She wailed with fear and lurched awake, her heart pounding, tears on her cheeks. It took her a moment to calm, to remember where she was: her bedchamber at Fox Run.

She was in her bed, safely snuggled under the covers. The room was dark, but out in the sitting room the remnants of a fire still burned. She rolled onto her side so she could be comforted by that bit of light, so she wouldn't feel so alone.

To her surprise, Aaron was in a chair a few feet away, drinking a glass of liquor and quietly watching her.

She gasped with delight. When he'd left for London, he hadn't said how long he'd be away, and she'd been on pins and needles every second, staring down the lane, hoping to find him riding in.

"Hello, you." She smiled. Everything would be all right now. Finally.

"Hello."

"When did you get back?"

"Awhile ago."

"You sneaked in, you bounder."

"I was just about to wake you. It sounded as if you were having a nightmare. Was it your same dream again?"

"Yes."

"Were there any new details?"

"No, it's always exactly the same. I'm very young, and someone is taking me away, but I don't want to go."

"I wish I had an idea of what it indicates."

"Believe me, so do I."

"If we could unravel it, we might learn about your past."

"When I was tiny, I yearned to figure it out, but as I grew older, I started to think that maybe I wasn't meant to know my history. Maybe it would be horrid and I'd be crushed."

"Or maybe it would be grand, and you'd discover you had an entire family out there that's dying to meet you."

"If I have a huge, mythical family, how was I lost in the first place?"

"That's an intriguing question, isn't it?"

He stood and came over to the bed. As he eased a hip onto the mattress, he seemed troubled.

"Are you all right?" she asked.

"I'm fine." He paused, pondered, then shook his head. "Actually, I'm not fine. Why do people always say they are? We're all so bloody polite."

His crude language disturbed her. It signified he'd probably had more to drink than she'd suspected.

"You must have been traveling for hours. Were you riding alone in the dark?"

"Yes."

"I'm guessing you were *drinking* and riding. Was that wise? I'd have been panicked if I'd known."

"I was eager to return."

"To see me?"

"Yes, to see you, you scamp. What would you suppose?"

"Well, I was hoping it wasn't to sit around reading your account ledgers, but you can be such a stern fellow. How can a girl be sure?"

"I missed you," he murmured.

"I missed you too."

He pulled her into his arms, lifting her off the mattress to bestow a stirring, exhilarating kiss that went on and on. He seemed particularly driven as he'd never previously been with her. He caressed her everywhere, as if needing to feel she was solid and real, that she wasn't an illusion.

"I'm glad you're still here," he said as he drew away. "I'm glad you didn't leave."

"I told you I wouldn't."

"I was afraid you'd be gone."

"Silly man. I wouldn't go anywhere without you."

"Good. Let's keep it that way."

What did he mean? Was he saying he wanted to be with her forever?

"How was London?" she asked.

"Oh, about as awful as I could have predicted."

"Were you able to settle your family issues?"

"No, but with my family, nothing is ever easy." He studied her, then—almost as if he was testing her—he inquired, "Do you know any of my relatives other than the Bosworths?"

"I know your brother. I met him once."

"You never mentioned it."

"It never came up. Besides, it was just a quick introduction. He briefly stopped by the school where I was teaching."

"So you know his fiancée, Amelia Hubbard."

"She's a great friend of mine, but are you certain they're still betrothed? Last I heard, they'd decided not to proceed."

"And last I heard, they'd decided they should."

"Should I celebrate or not?"

"Time will tell if it's for the best. I love my brother, and I'm an optimist, so I'll keep my fingers crossed."

Aaron chuckled, but it wasn't very merry. He looked distressed and a tad lost.

She rested a palm on his cheek. "It was difficult for you to go home, wasn't it?"

"It always is. My father is a hard man."

"Your issues involved him?"

"Yes, and other...things, but guess what, Evangeline?"

"What?"

"I don't want to talk about London or my father. I've *talked* lately until I'm blue in the face."

She tugged on the covers and patted the mattress. "Then lie down with me. Let's just hold each other. You'll be better very soon."

She shouldn't have asked, and he gazed at her for an eternity, clearly debating whether he should agree, but finally, he slipped under the blankets and stretched out. He slid an arm under her shoulders and pulled her to him, so she was draped over his chest, her ear directly over his heart. She could hear its steady beating.

Immediately, she realized it was the most thrilling moment of her life. He was big and warm and solid, and with him touching her all the way down, she felt safe and secure and cherished as she'd never been.

He stared at the ceiling, obviously torn by weighty thoughts. She yearned to inquire, *What about us? What will happen?*

He'd claimed they would eventually be together. Had he spoken to Lord Sidwell? Had they quarreled over her?

If so, she had to do whatever she could to make Aaron see it wasn't the end of the world. Once they were married—even if the earl was initially furious—Evangeline would wear him down so he accepted her.

She had excellent instincts with people, could charm them

with her pretty manners. She'd charm the earl too. Of that fact, she had no doubt.

"You're not angry with me, are you?" she asked.

"With you? Never. Why would I be?"

"My presence here is creating so many problems."

"No, you're wrong. You're the only good thing I have at all."

He kissed her again, the embrace quickly growing heated as he shifted her onto her back, as he also shifted so he was on top of her.

"Have you visited my cousin?"

His query vexed her. It seemed an odd time to discuss her betrothal or the vicar.

"You asked me not to. I sent a message to the vicarage that I had a cold, so he's stayed away."

"You haven't severed the engagement?"

"No, but now that you're home, I'll do it right away. I'll go to him tomorrow."

"I couldn't bear it if you married him."

"I couldn't either. We're completely incompatible. I shouldn't have agreed without meeting him, but when I was first informed of the betrothal, I was pressured to make a decision."

"You deserve someone much better than him."

"That's what I've been thinking too."

She paused, on tenterhooks, waiting, expecting him to propose, but he was silent.

Blasted man!

He simply began kissing her again, sweeping her into the spiral of desire.

There was a frantic level to it that had never arisen previously. They grappled and pawed at each other as if they were struggling through barriers, fighting their way to a gripping conclusion. She couldn't hold him tightly enough, couldn't bring him near enough. He appeared to feel the same, as if it was impossible to satisfy their need to connect.

When he'd sneaked into her room, she'd been asleep and attired in her nightgown. Gradually, he was removing it, tugging up the hem, untying the bow on the bodice, so he could yank the garment over her head. He tossed it on the floor.

She should have protested, but she didn't, and before she realized what the result would be, she was naked. The entire episode was escalating out of her control. She didn't know how to stop it, and she didn't exactly *want* to stop it.

She understood that men and women performed salacious acts when they were in a bed. In his elevated world, there was a different standard as to what was allowed and what wasn't. She was anxious to prove she could belong in that world.

He'd taught her some of the behaviors he enjoyed, and there were others that hadn't been explained or described. Apparently, that's what he was intending—to go farther than they had prior. He was honorable and wouldn't push her into immoral conduct. It would be her choice, and if they proceeded to decadence, she was certain it would draw them closer.

He abandoned her lips and nibbled a trail down her neck, her chest, to her breasts. He kissed them, biting and massaging, sucking on the nipples. The sensations he evoked were sinfully delicious and, rapidly, she was goaded beyond her limit.

As he reached down and touched her between her legs, she suffered an exhilarating tremor of ecstasy. He'd previously spurred her to a similar reaction when down on the sofa in the music room, but this one was much more potent. She cried out with amazement, with a blinding sort of terror, as she seemed to soar through the sky and float back down.

He was grinning, preening, his masculine pride on full display as he murmured, "You are such a gem."

"I am? What type of gem? A diamond? A ruby?"

He thought about it, then said, "A beautiful blue sapphire that is the precise color of your eyes."

"If you keep spewing compliments like that, I'll get a big head."

"Heaven forbid."

They smiled, a poignant silence growing. She was dying to ask him if they would marry now, but she'd raised the issue once before and had bungled it. *He* was the man. *He* had to propose, and she was positive that was his plan. If it wasn't, why was he in her bed when she wasn't wearing any clothes?

"I need you to do something for me," he said.

"What is it?"

"There's more to this than what we've shared."

"What more?"

"Well"—his cheeks flushed—"you just experienced a wave of passion, and the same kind of thing can happen to me."

"It can?" She was such a naïve ninny that the prospect hadn't occurred to her. "Can I make it transpire? Tell me what to do."

"It's easier if I show you."

"All right." But he didn't move. He continued to stare, and she asked, "What's wrong?"

"Nothing's wrong. I...want to engage in marital behavior. It's what a husband and wife would do. I'd join my body to yours. Here."

He cupped his palm at the vee of her thighs, at the entrance to her woman's sheath.

She frowned. "I don't know what that means."

"That's why it's easier to show you."

"We're not husband and wife though, so how could we?"

"It's just physical conduct. You don't have to be wed to accomplish it."

"But," she countered, "you're *supposed* to be wed."

He shrugged. "It's what the preachers claim."

"You disagree?"

"It's simply pleasure. There's no sin or damnation attached to it."

She gazed at him, and she was so perplexed!

While she didn't grasp the technicalities, she recognized that he was expecting her to surrender her virginity. It was a bride's role on her wedding night. It wasn't ever what a female would contemplate during a quick tumble with a libertine, and she viewed him as being such a stellar person.

If he was truly requesting she perform the ultimate carnal act, what was she to think?

She couldn't imagine refusing him, and if they proceeded, they'd *have* to marry. Wouldn't they? The law demanded it. The Church required it. Societal rules wouldn't allow for any other ending.

"If I say *yes*," she hesitantly started, "there's no going back."

"No."

"I wouldn't be a maiden anymore."

"No," he said again, "but Evangeline, you're such a wildly sexual creature. You'll be better off for having done this with me, and I'm desperate to know you this way."

His use of the word *desperate* made her realize she should consent. Hadn't she felt that everything between them was a tad desperate from the moment he'd lain down?

"We'd have to marry afterward." She watched his eyes, searching for prevarication. "We'd have to be together forever."

"Of course we will be."

"Swear it."

"I swear."

She kept watching him, but he didn't give the slightest indication of dishonesty. He looked resolute, determined, and—dare she say it?—madly in love with her. She was being pelted by his affection, showered with it, deluged by it.

"Let me," he whispered.

"I don't know..." she whispered in reply. "I'm so confused."

"Don't be confused. I love you!" he suddenly, fervidly announced.

"I love you too," she responded, more delighted than she'd ever been. How could she deny him? Why vacillate a single second?

"Tell me it's for the best," she urged.

"Yes, my darling, Evangeline. It is absolutely for the best."

She studied him again, still torn and conflicted, but he looked so happy! She couldn't bear to disappoint him.

Finally, she said, "I believe you, Aaron. Show me how it can be between us."

Aaron sat back on his knees and drew off his shirt.

His heart was hammering in his chest, thundering so violently it might simply burst through his ribs.

He loved her! He'd said it out loud! What had come over him?

She loved him too, and with their mutual declarations on the table, he couldn't decide if it improved matters or not. What benefit was there in professing deep fondness? It didn't change anything. It didn't fix any of their problems.

Still, he felt grand. He felt like he was king of the world, like a god that walked on water. If he lived to be a hundred, he didn't suppose he'd ever enjoy a moment quite so much.

He lie down, his chest crushed to her own, and as they connected for the first time—bare skin to bare skin—they both hissed with pleasure. The air sizzled, the temperature of the room rising by a good twenty degrees.

He was behaving very badly, and he'd had too much to drink, so he wasn't thinking clearly. He should have been proving how much he respected and cherished her, but instead he was deceiving her, pressuring her to give him what he craved, and she was so besotted that she'd agreed.

She couldn't truly understand what she'd offered until it was over, and by then, it would be too late. But once she was his, the future would be set for both of them.

He couldn't marry her, but he could keep her with him forever, the trick being to persuade her. He had to convince her to stay by his side—unwed but together—and to accept his vision as to how that could be accomplished.

He had two weeks, and with her breaking off her engagement, she had no ties to bind her, no family to protest an affair. There was no reason to decline, and their fornication would seal her fate. She would belong to him, and he wouldn't listen to any further nonsense.

Events were barreling toward them, so he didn't have time to dawdle or seduce. They would spend every second of the next fourteen days in her bedchamber. They would love and tease and play, and when he had to depart for London, she would have no option but to remain with him.

If he was lucky, she might even wind up pregnant with his child, and there was no more weighty fetter with which he could shackle her. He'd always told himself he was honorable and decent, but unless he took drastic measures to stop her, she might slip through his grasp.

His scheme was dastardly. It was cruel and despicable and shameful, but he would proceed anyway. In the end, she'd recognize that it was for the best.

He started kissing her again, quickly and easily driving her up the spiral of desire. She was so eager, so attuned to his every touch. With a few laves of his tongue across her nipple, a few flicks of his thumb down below, she soared to the heavens again.

As her orgasm exploded, as it peaked and waned, she was laughing, merry, sputtering with amazement and delight.

Don't do it! Don't hurt her like this! Yet he was too intent on ensnaring her so she could never leave.

"What are you thinking about?" she inquired, noting his confusion, his doubt.

"I want you to be happy."

"You oaf. I'm the happiest woman in the whole world."

"I'd hate to have you regret this later on."

"Regret it?" She scowled. "I never could."

"I'm doing this for us—so we'll always be together."

"Yes, together forever," she agreed, but her definition and his definition of being *together* were two completely different things.

The life he planned for them—the cozy house, the rambunctious children running in the halls, the quiet nights reading by the fire, the slow glide into their elder years—would be exactly what they could have had through marriage.

The only item missing would be the official license, and with so much contentment at stake, a license was a foolish impediment.

He gripped her thighs, wedging his torso in between. He loosened his trousers, yanked them down, then he inserted the tip of his cock in her sheath. She inhaled a sharp breath, her eyes widening with alarm.

"What are you doing?"

"I'm going to attach our bodies, remember?"

"Yes, but I told you I don't know what that means."

"We're built differently—in our private parts."

"I see..." she mumbled, but clearly she didn't.

"It will be over in a minute. Try to relax."

"If I can, I will. It just feels...strange."

"It always is the first time."

He kissed her, toying with her nipples, distracting her as he flexed with his hips. But as she'd mentioned, the episode was too peculiar, and she was too unschooled as to the mechanics.

He'd never been so aroused and couldn't delay to let her acclimate, to let her accept what was coming. He raised her hips to his loins and thrust inside. There was a tear, the rush of her virgin's blood. He held himself very still.

"Is that it?" she asked. "Are we finished?"

"No, there's a bit more."

"Will it take long?"

"No."

She was gazing at him, her uncertainty evident, but her love and affection were shining through.

"Does it hurt?" he inquired.

"A little."

"It will fade."

"It already is."

Gradually, her bodily tension lessened, and he started to flex.

"Better?" he asked.

"Yes."

"Move with me."

"Like this?"

"Yes, just like that."

He'd wanted her for too long and was far past the edge of sanity. He couldn't temper the pace, couldn't delay the conclusion. But then he had all night to do it again. He had the next two weeks, and the next year, and the rest of their lives.

He gave a handful of fierce thrusts, and his seed swelled to his loins and burst into her womb in a passionate wave that went on and on until he began to doubt he'd ever get to the end.

Finally, the last drop was spent, and he collapsed onto her. He tried to muster some remorse for his pushing ahead, but he didn't feel an ounce of guilt. He'd pressed the issue, had abused her trusting nature, but she would be his forevermore.

He slid away, and she rolled with him so they were nose to nose. They were grinning, ecstatic, thrilled with what they'd perpetrated.

"What did you think?" he asked.

"I'm not a...a..."

"No, you're not."

A tiny twinge of conscience pricked him. She was such an innocent, she couldn't even verbalize the word *virgin*, but he tamped down any regret, refusing to focus on the negative.

Everything was perfect now! Perfect!

"It gets better," he said.

"I'm sure it does."

"It won't hurt ever again either."

"It didn't hurt much this time."

"From here on out, it will always be marvelous."

"Good."

"It will last longer too. You've had me so titillated I couldn't restrain myself."

"*I* had you titillated?"

"Yes, you vixen, but now we'll be able to slow down and become familiar with one another."

"Husbands and wives, they do this often?"

"Some often, some not, but yes, it's the marital behavior that's kept such a secret from you females. With you being the weaker sex, people are afraid you'd swoon if you knew what was required."

"It's more physical than I thought it would be."

"Yes, that's why I couldn't explain it."

She chuckled. "I wouldn't have believed you. It would have sounded too farfetched."

They both sighed, and he turned her and spooned himself to her back. His cock stirred, eager to start in again, and he smiled.

She noticed right away. "You're smiling. Why?"

"I'm happy."

"So am I."

"I'm so enticed by you, my body is already anxious to try it again."

"Is that common?"

"Not usually. It's a sign of how much I adore you."

At the compliment, she nestled closer and gave a very unladylike yawn.

"I'm so tired all of a sudden," she said.

"Carnal conduct can be exhausting."

"I can hardly keep my eyes open."

"Doze off. I don't mind."

"You can't doze with me though. If the maids caught you in here in the morning, I'd die of embarrassment."

"I'll snuggle with you until you fall asleep. Then I'll go."

They were quiet, the room cooling, her respiration slowing.

"This fixed everything, right?" she asked.

"Yes."

"We'll always be together?"

"Always, Evangeline. We will always be together. I swear it to you."

"I'm *so* glad," she murmured, and she plunged into a deep slumber. He lay with her, imprinting every detail into his memory so he'd never forget.

It was their wedding night of sorts, the night she'd given

herself to him, the night that would set the tone for the remainder of their life, and he had to remember it all, her scent, her warmth, her size.

When he began drifting off too, he forced himself to slip away. He stood next to the bed, straightening his trousers, tugging on his shirt. He glanced down at his feet and shook his head with chagrin.

He'd been so intent on deflowering her that he hadn't paused to remove his boots. He'd been in that big of a hurry, was that smitten, and he was liking the idea of *forever* more and more. Their relationship would only improve from this point on.

He spun and tiptoed out—while he had the fortitude to make himself go.

CHAPTER FOURTEEN

Evangeline was seated at the writing desk in the front parlor. It was situated by a window and provided a view of the park and the lane that led out to the main road.

The butler had mentioned that a housemaid was headed to the village and would be taking the mail with her, so Evangeline had hurried to draft yet another letter to Rose. A few days earlier, Evangeline had written to inform Rose that Evangeline would be leaving Fox Run and would travel to the Summerfield estate where Rose was living with her new husband, James Talbot.

At least, Evangeline thought Mr. Talbot was Rose's husband. Rose hadn't answered Evangeline's increasingly frantic messages, so any debacle could have occurred.

Except now, Evangeline was telling Rose she wasn't departing after all. Her cheeks flushing, she recalled the previous evening, how she and Aaron had sealed their future by getting a jump on their wedding night.

She supposed she shouldn't have agreed—every female knew to have a ring on her finger first—but she'd been so overwhelmed. Afterward, he'd been so pleased! He'd said he loved her! He'd announced it with no hesitation or restraint. And she'd told him the same, that she loved him with all her heart.

It was interesting how those simple words could change everything. The morning was so beautiful, the sky so blue, the grass so green. Her smile was so wide her face hurt, but her emotions were jumbled, and she wanted to laugh and weep at the same time.

Though he had portrayed their behavior merely as physical conduct, it had altered her in ways she hadn't expected. She felt raw and exposed, ragged with sentiment she didn't understand.

Her letter finished, she placed it on the table by the door in the foyer. Then she went back to the parlor and sat on the small sofa. She stared outside, wondering what to do with herself.

While eating breakfast, she'd heard the servants whispering that Aaron was off handling some business. Bryce was with him, and they wouldn't be back for hours. Initially, the news had irked her, but she'd shaken off her aggravation. Like a silly ninny, she'd jumped out of bed and raced downstairs, hoping Aaron would be pacing, waiting with bated breath for her to appear.

But he had a busy life and an estate to run, and his world wouldn't suddenly revolve around her. Yet how could he focus on business?

She couldn't concentrate at all. She was so fidgety, so restless. Fleetingly, she considered walking into the village too. She could stop by the vicarage and talk to Vicar Bosworth. He'd sent a note, asking after her health, and his courtesy made her ashamed. She had to break it off, but she was too agitated to think rationally.

In her current condition, if she tried to explain her decision, she'd babble like an idiot. So...she'd go first thing in the morning.

As she waffled and debated, a carriage turned up the drive, and she winced. Who could it be? With Aaron out of the house, she would have to clarify her presence, but how would she describe herself?

She and Aaron hadn't discussed a single detail about their marriage, and until he declared the situation to his father and friends, she couldn't claim a close acquaintance. She would have to say she was the vicar's fiancée, which—in view of her new circumstance—she shouldn't keep repeating.

She continued to watch the vehicle and saw that it was very fancy, being pulled by four matching white horses. The animals had ribbons braided in their manes and tails, and the coach had a crest on the door that indicated an elevated lineage.

There was an awful lot of luggage attached, as if—whoever it was—they planned an extended stay, and Evangeline's spirits flagged. She didn't want company! She and Aaron had vital matters to sort out, and she needed to be alone with him while they figured out how the future would unfold.

For a frightening instant, she worried that Aaron's father had arrived. What if he'd come to chase Evangeline away? She'd been too much of a coward to press Aaron about his visit to London, so she didn't know if he'd told his father about her. If they'd fought, how had they left things?

What if it was Lord Sidwell and he was angry and abrasive? Aaron wouldn't return for ages, and the notion of facing his father was terrifying.

The carriage passed by the window and rolled out of sight. Evangeline dawdled, wondering if she shouldn't go to her room, but hating to feel she should hide. She'd been living in the manor for several weeks, and though it was wrong, she was starting to think of it as her own. Especially after what she and Aaron had done.

Eventually, she would be mistress of Fox Run, so it seemed she should be allowed to greet guests, to welcome them inside. But for the moment, she was simply a guest herself and had to remain in the shadows until Aaron pushed her into the light.

Soon, the front door opened, and servants tramped in and out. The butler's voice wafted toward her, and Evangeline frowned as a female answered him.

Who could it be?

She stood and, shortly, the butler approached and stepped into the parlor.

"If you'll wait here, ladies," he said, "I'll have refreshments served."

"Thank you," two women said in unison as they skirted by him.

They were obviously mother and daughter, the younger one very beautiful with white-blond hair, striking blue eyes, and a voluptuous figure. The mother was an exact replica, perhaps twenty years older. They looked rich and sophisticated.

The butler noticed her hovering. "Miss Etherton, I didn't realize you were still in here."

"I was finishing my letter. It's on the table in the foyer."

She walked to the trio as the butler puffed himself up and announced, "We have important guests."

Evangeline smiled. "I see that."

He gestured dramatically. "May I present Lord Run's fiancée, Miss Priscilla Cummings? And her mother, Mrs. Cummings?"

Evangeline gasped. She didn't mean to; it just slipped out.

"What did you say?"

But he didn't respond. Instead, he introduced Evangeline. "This is Miss Etherton. She's engaged to the vicar, and she's staying at Fox Run until her wedding." He glanced at the women. "I believe you know the vicar. It's Mr. Bosworth? He and Lord Run are cousins."

"Yes, we know him," Mrs. Cummings said.

Their stares condescending, their disdain blatant, mother and daughter studied Evangeline. In her gray dress, with her messy chignon that had strands falling everywhere, she might have been a beleaguered governess.

Clearly, they didn't like to find her in the house. With a subtle nod to each other, they spun away as if Evangeline was invisible.

"Is Aaron at home?" Priscilla Cummings asked the butler.

"No, he's out. We don't expect him for hours."

"Lovely," she purred. Her tone was so soft and soothing she'd probably had elocution lessons.

Miss Cummings spoke to her mother. "While he's away, we'll be able to take all sorts of measurements."

"Yes," her mother replied, "and we can sneak into his bedchamber and poke around. You've always hated those maroon drapes."

"And that wallpaper!" Miss Cummings simpered. "It will all have to go. I don't care how he complains."

She and her mother chuckled as if her complaints about the wallpaper were a running joke with Aaron.

Miss Cummings told Evangeline, "The wedding is very close, so I've been busy. Aaron would like me to redecorate, but I've been swamped and haven't had a chance to think about it."

Evangeline had no idea how she remained on her feet. She really and truly thought she was about to faint. Could they see how she was shaking?

"The wedding is close?" Evangeline forced out.

"In three weeks."

If Miss Cummings had pulled out a pistol and shot Evangeline right between the eyes, Evangeline couldn't have been anymore shocked.

"Three weeks?" she breathed, but no one paid her any attention.

Miss Cummings was talking to the butler. "Would you ask Cook if she has any of those little blueberry cakes she bakes? I love those. If she doesn't have any this morning, could we have some for tea this afternoon?"

"I'll inquire for you." The butler was all smiles, all fawning obsequiousness. "Please make yourselves comfortable, and I'll notify you when your rooms are ready."

He swept out, and Evangeline was alone with the two women. They went over to a sofa and confidently plopped down—as if they owned the place, as if it had been theirs forever.

"How long have you known Aa..." Evangeline caught herself before she inappropriately used his given name. "How long have you known Lord Run?"

"Since I was a baby," Miss Cummings said. "Our estate borders Sidwell. We grew up together."

Evangeline was so dizzy she could barely stand. "When were you betrothed?"

Her mother answered. "His father and I had discussed it ever since Priscilla was born. We always planned on it, but it's only been official the past year."

Miss Cummings held out a hand, displaying an emerald ring with a stone that was as big as a bird's egg. Fat diamonds circled it. "This is the engagement ring of the Sidwell heir. It was his mother's. Isn't it gorgeous? I realize it's horrid to flaunt it, but I just love to show it off."

Evangeline was swaying, about to collapse, and she grabbed the back of a chair to keep from toppling over.

"Sit, Miss Etherton." Mrs. Cummings waved to the sofa across. "Tell us about you and Cousin Iggy. You must be so excited to have your own wedding coming."

Miss Cummings said, "We had heard Iggy was betrothed. Lord Sidwell—my father-in-law—was very helpful in arranging it. Have you met Lord Sidwell? He's such a dear, always thinking of everyone but himself."

She smiled a feline smile, and there was a hint of cruelty behind it. If she'd been a venomous snake, Evangeline would already have been bitten, would already have been dead on the floor.

Had Miss Cummings and her mother learned about Aaron and Evangeline? Were they aware of how Evangeline had misbehaved with him? They couldn't be. Could they? No one knew! Evangeline had been so discreet. Yet what was she to assume? The Cummings women oozed malice.

"I'm not feeling very well," Evangeline mumbled.

"That's too bad." Mrs. Cummings evinced no inkling of concern.

"I was up late. I'm probably just tired."

"Then a nap is certainly in order." Miss Cummings gestured to the door. "Don't let us keep you."

"Yes, if you'll excuse me?"

She started out, when Miss Cummings called, "Oh, and Miss Etherton?"

Evangeline glanced back. "Yes?"

"Aaron and I would like to have an intimate supper. The dining room will be off limits to you this evening."

Her mother spitefully added, "We'll have a tray sent up to you, so the bride and groom won't be interrupted."

Evangeline staggered out. The world seemed to have tipped off its axis, and she couldn't find her balance. She made it to the hall, but had to press a palm to the wall so she didn't fall down.

He was engaged to be married? He'd been engaged for a whole year? His wedding was in three weeks?

She'd spent the prior month, letting him charm her, letting him seduce and woo her. She'd known better, but she'd never met a man like him before, so she'd forgotten all the lessons Miss Peabody had taught her.

She'd tossed it all away, and for what?

With a wail of despair, she lurched toward the stairs,

wondering what to do.

"To heck with business," Aaron announced. "I'd much rather play."

Aaron grinned at Bryce, and Bryce was taken aback.

"Are you ill?" Bryce asked.

"Why?"

"I don't believe I've ever heard you say you would ignore your chores."

"I'm turning over a new leaf."

"It's about damn time, too. You should enjoy a frenzy of pleasurable activities for I'm sure that being shackled to Priscilla will be a bit of a trial."

Aaron chuckled. "You could be right about that."

They had ridden out early, with Aaron expecting to visit a neighboring farm to look at some horses that were for sale. But he'd quickly realized he was too unsettled to be away from the estate, away from Evangeline.

Upon arising, he'd been so overwhelmed by what had happened between them that he'd been confused as to how he should behave, so he'd reverted to form. He'd tried to go about his day as if it was any other. Yet they'd only traveled a few miles down the road.

He didn't care about how he was *supposed* to act, how he would usually act. There was such a short period remaining where he could truly be with Evangeline as frequently as he liked. He was like a man facing the gallows, counting down to the end.

They were back at Fox Run, having left their horses with a stable boy, and they were headed for the front door. Aaron was so excited to see Evangeline, he felt as if he was floating, as if his feet didn't touch the ground.

"Could I ask you something?" Bryce suddenly said, and at his solemn tone, Aaron stopped walking.

"What is it?"

"Have you…ah…told Evangeline about your wedding?"

Aaron frowned, frantic questions racing through his mind. Did Bryce suspect Aaron's infatuation? Had Aaron given himself away? He thought he'd been discreet, but then he and Bryce had been friends a long time.

"Why would you ask me that?" Aaron was stalling, struggling to figure out what notion he wished to convey.

Appearing troubled, Bryce frowned too. "Look, I'll just come out and say it. You can tell me to sod off if you want."

"I will if it's deserved. What is it you need to know?"

"Are you in love with her?"

"In love?" Aaron pronounced the word *love* as if he'd never heard it before.

"I understand it's none of my affair, but I saw you two riding the other day. Your affection for her was blatant and shocking."

Aaron tepidly stated, "I'm charmed by her."

"Aren't we all? What is your plan? And please don't insult my intelligence by claiming you're barely acquainted."

Aaron should have denied any fondness, but he doubted he could hide his sentiment from Bryce.

"I have no idea what I'm going to do."

"Why have you kept your engagement a secret from her? Are you pretending you might marry *her* instead? I'm afraid that's the impression you're creating."

"Why would you imagine that?"

"The poor girl is not from our world, Aaron. She hasn't the sophistication to involve herself with you."

"Probably not."

"Have you encouraged her to cry off from her betrothal?" Aaron's cheeks flushed with chagrin, and Bryce bristled, "Oh, you horse's ass! What will happen to her if she doesn't wed the vicar? Will you let her stay at Fox Run? Until when? Until you stroll in with your wife on your arm?"

Aaron hemmed and hawed. He was aware of how badly he'd treated Evangeline, so he couldn't paint himself in a more flattering light.

Still, he tried to insist, "It's not what you think."

"It's not? Have you seduced her? Are you fornicating with her?"

"I'd like to marry her!" Aaron said, avoiding any confession as to carnal dalliance. "When I went to London last week, it was to inform my father I would separate from Priscilla so I could wed Evangeline."

"I hope to God Lord Sidwell yanked you back to your senses."

"He did, so I'm working to convince Evangeline to be my mistress. I raised the possibility when we'd first met, but she was opposed. We're much closer now, and I'm certain I can change her mind."

Aaron was almost desperate in his assertions, as if he was persuading himself rather than Bryce, and Bryce was regarding him so skeptically.

"I like her, Aaron. I like her very much."

"Well, I *love* her."

"You have to tell her about Priscilla." It looked as if Aaron might argue the point, so Bryce stated more firmly, "You have to!

Why, she might learn of it in passing from one of the servants. What if she discovered it that way?" More grimly, more sternly, Bryce added, "She has to hear it from you."

"Then she won't keep on with me," Aaron bleakly replied, "and I couldn't bear it if she left. Can't you understand? I'm finally happy!"

"So bloody what?" Bryce fumed. "You're happy. Bully for you, but I don't want her hurt, and if you won't tell her, I will."

"Please don't."

"Aaron..." Bryce shook his head with disgust. "You're putting me in a horrid position. When this all blows up—"

"It won't."

"It will! I'd hate to realize I could have protected her, but I didn't."

"She doesn't need your protection, Bryce."

"Doesn't she?" Bryce seethed.

"Just give me two weeks," Aaron begged. "If I can get her to agree to be my mistress, everything will be fine. I'll move her to London and set her up in a house in a nice neighborhood."

"A little love nest, Aaron? You'd actually arrange it the same week as your wedding? What is wrong with you?"

"I'm simply bowled over by her. I can't imagine my life without her in it."

"If she won't agree, and you have to rush off to London to marry Priscilla, what then? What will become of her?"

"Let's not contemplate my failing. Let's proceed with the expectation that I'll wear her down."

"I doubt you will."

"And I'm *sure* I will." They paused, on the verge of a major quarrel, and Aaron begged again, "Please, Bryce? Two weeks?"

"All right, but *only* two weeks. I won't wait a second more."

"Thank you. You're a good friend."

"I'm a foolish friend."

"That too."

Aaron's retort dragged a smile from Bryce. They hurried on to the manor, and Aaron practically bounded up the stairs, being that thrilled to be back with Evangeline.

As they approached the door, the butler opened it and, as Aaron was shucking off his coat, the man said, "We have guests, Lord Run."

"Guests?" He wasn't really paying attention. "Who is it?"

"Your fiancée has arrived—with her mother."

Aaron froze. He couldn't have heard correctly. "Priscilla and Claudia are here?"

"Yes."

Behind him, Bryce muttered, "Dammit."

"They're in the front parlor," the butler said, "having refreshments while the maids prepare their rooms." He noted Aaron's consternation and hesitantly added, "They'll be with us for a few days? I didn't suppose you'd mind."

Before Aaron could muster a response, Evangeline staggered into the hall. She was stumbling along, looking ill, as if she might faint.

"Evangeline!" he murmured, forgetting himself with the familiar form of address. He hastened over to her and took her arm.

"What's wrong?" he asked, though he absolutely knew.

"I just met your fiancée," she said, "and I'd like to be alone."

She jerked away and continued on, and Aaron felt as if he'd been poleaxed. The butler was confused, staring, and Bryce was glowering, his fury obvious.

"I told you so," Bryce spat, as Claudia appeared in the doorway to the parlor.

"Aaron, is that you?" she inquired. "We weren't expecting you so soon. Could I speak with you?"

That feeling of facing the gallows was back. That feeling that his life was over, that time had run out, covered him like a dark cloud.

He gazed at Bryce, visually seeking advice, seeking support, but Bryce merely shrugged. "Go on. See what she has to say. What else can you do?"

Aaron trudged down the hall.

Gertrude Bosworth sat in her bedroom suite, reading and rereading the letter Mrs. Turner had brought from Fox Run.

The message Miss Etherton had penned was so galling that—if she'd been present—Gertrude would have grabbed a poker from the fireplace and beat her bloody.

Miss Etherton deemed herself too grand to join the Bosworth family. She was in love and excited to tell her friend, Miss Ralston, about her new swain.

Love, bah! Gertrude fumed.

Who put any stock in love? It was fleeting and ridiculous, the stuff of fairytales and romantic novels. It always faded away, and once it waned, the parties were left with no foundation.

No man's name had been mentioned—clearly, his name *couldn't* be mentioned—and Gertrude was trying to guess who the lucky fellow might be. It was probably that scoundrel Bryce Blair. The only other choice would be Aaron.

Was Miss Etherton that brazen? Was she that bold?

If Miss Etherton was sniffing after Aaron, what was Aaron's opinion? Did Miss Etherton presume Aaron would marry her? Hadn't it occurred to her that Aaron might have other obligations?

Gertrude snickered cruelly. Aaron's fiancée could enlighten Miss Etherton as to what some of those obligations entailed.

During Mrs. Turner's brief visit, she'd told Gertrude that the staff at Fox Run was in a dither, that Priscilla Cummings and her mother had arrived without warning. Oh, wouldn't Gertrude like to be a mouse in the corner, watching as they were introduced to Miss Etherton!

The little slattern! The disloyal, fickle slut!

Gertrude detested it when Ignatius was hurt, when he was slighted or made to feel inferior. Fortunately, she'd had the foresight to invite her cousin's daughter to live with them. The girl was quiet and obedient, and she seemed in awe of Ignatius. She was religiously devout and hung on his every word. So there was a benefit in knowing—after they were shed of Miss Etherton—there was another bride, a more appropriate bride, lined up to take her place.

And—praise be!—Gertrude hadn't had to do anything to be shed of Miss Etherton. By her own conduct, she'd condemned herself.

Gertrude wished she didn't ever have to inform Ignatius, but then there was relief in having discovered Miss Etherton's true character before the wedding. What if they'd found out after the marriage had been finalized? Gad, what then?

Gertrude went to the stairs and started down. Ignatius was in the library, writing his Sunday sermon. When pursuing such an important task, he hated to be interrupted, but this news couldn't wait.

She knocked and called, "Ignatius?"

"What is it, Mother? I'm busy."

She opened the door and peeked in. "We must confer. I'm afraid it's dire."

"Come in, come in." His exasperation evident, he motioned for her to enter.

She approached the desk and laid the letter in front of him.

"I'm sorry to be the bearer of these bad tidings, but maybe it's not so bad. After you're over the shock of it, you may decide it's very, very good."

He scowled. "What are you talking about?"

"It's a note from Miss Etherton to one of her friends."

"Where did you get it?"

"It doesn't matter. Just be glad I did."

His temper short, he demanded, "Why? What does she say?"

"Read it, Ignatius. Read it and learn everything about Miss Etherton you will ever need to know."

CHAPTER FIFTEEN

"Leave us, Priscilla."

"Must I, Mother?"

"Yes, I'd like to meet with Aaron alone."

"May I stay and listen?"

"I'd rather you didn't."

"Fine." Priscilla breathed out an exasperated sigh. "I'll be in my room. Once the two of you are through, please come upstairs and tell me what he's decided."

"I will," Claudia said.

Then Priscilla turned to Aaron.

"I know you've been upset with me, Aaron."

He made a waffling gesture with his hand. "Let's not go into it now."

"I've been difficult and immature, but I'm trying to improve so I can be the bride you'd like me to be."

How was he to answer such a statement? "We'll discuss it later."

"I'm praying that you'll agree to continue with our wedding. If you cry off, I'll be crushed. It would humiliate me before the entire world"—tears flooded her eyes—"and while you may not care about that, I couldn't bear it."

He kept his face blank, shielding any reaction. How in the hell had she learned about his affair? Were their spies among the servants?

She looked majestic and grand, but very young too, and he felt like the cad he was, like vermin that should be squashed under a boot heel. He'd broken her heart—he hadn't realized she *had* a heart—had infuriated her mother, and all he could think about was how he needed to rush upstairs so he could explain himself to Evangeline.

"We'll talk later," he said again.

She scowled and sauntered out, regal as any queen, and he and Claudia stood like statues, listening as her strides faded down the hall.

Claudia pointed to a sofa. "Sit, would you?"

He was on the verge of refusing, of stomping out, but he didn't. "I suppose I might as well."

First, he detoured to the sideboard and poured himself a whiskey. He gulped it down, then went to the sofa. What was he to say? How was a man to behave in such a situation? He had no idea.

Claudia seated herself in the chair across, and for a long while she simply studied him, as if he were a curious bug she'd spotted on the floor. Eventually, she began.

"We've had our differences in the past, Aaron."

"We have."

"I hope we can put them aside for a few minutes."

"I'm sure we can."

"Tell me about Miss Etherton."

He frowned, feigning confusion. "What about her?"

"I had a lengthy conversation with your father."

The bastard! Aaron would have denied any affinity, but if Lord Sidwell had tattled, there was no reason to pretend.

"I see."

"George thought you and Priscilla should confer about it."

"He did, did he?" Aaron replied with more venom than he'd meant to display.

"But I decided *I* should speak with you instead. There aren't many women who are prepared to have a discussion like this, and I know Priscilla certainly isn't."

"What would you have me say, Claudia?"

"I want you to promise me you'll marry Priscilla—in three weeks as we've planned all year. I want to hear that it's still your intent."

Aaron's head was spinning. He was disoriented, as if he was walking around in a nightmare and couldn't find the route to escape.

Was he planning to wed Priscilla? That issue had been resolved after he'd visited his father. Hadn't it?

The previous evening, when he'd had too much to drink, it had seemed perfectly logical to deflower Evangeline so he could blackmail her into being his mistress. But in the light of day and being confronted by his future mother-in-law, it seemed tawdry and vile.

He had to talk to Evangeline and beg her forgiveness. Everything was ruined. She was likely packing her bags and would be gone before he and Claudia were finished.

"Yes, I guess I'm marrying Priscilla," he halfheartedly said.

"You *guess*? Or you know?"

"I know."

"Then please march upstairs right now and end your affair with Miss Etherton."

"I'm not Priscilla, Claudia. Don't tell me how to behave."

"I'm not telling you. I'm asking you. Miss Etherton appears to be a fine young woman."

"She is."

"When we introduced ourselves, she didn't realize you were betrothed, and the news was a great shock to her. She was devastated."

"No doubt she was."

"Send her away. At once. Swear to me that you will."

He wouldn't have to *send* Evangeline away. He was positive she would leave on her own. She'd need no coaxing.

But still, he snapped, "Stop bossing me, Claudia. You can't."

"Look, I'm not a child, Aaron, and it's clear the two of you have grown very close. I don't care what you do with her, but she can't stay here. It's horridly offensive to Priscilla, and I can't imagine how Miss Etherton is feeling. If you like, stash her away somewhere for a few weeks. Get her out of sight, then you can take up with her—discreetly—later on."

"That's big of you to give me your permission."

"Your relationship with her is interfering in all our lives. You can't keep on."

"Maybe if Priscilla hadn't shown up at Fox Run uninvited, we wouldn't be having this problem."

Claudia flashed such an enraged glare that, had he been standing, it would have knocked him over.

"You dare say that to my face?" Claudia seethed. "Priscilla shouldn't have come to Fox Run? My God, Aaron, this manor is about to be her home and your mistress is living here!"

He was so far in the wrong, he couldn't defend his conduct. He muttered, "I apologize."

"I want you to arrange for Miss Etherton's removal from the premises. Then I want you to return with us to London tomorrow. In the coming days, I expect you to exhibit the amiable, charming traits I've always witnessed from you, just as I expect you to courteously participate in all the events leading up to the wedding."

"Or...?"

"I will not let Priscilla marry you. We will break the engagement and file suit for breach of contract and alienation of affection. I'll drag you and Miss Etherton through the courts. I will smear your reputation—and hers—so thoroughly that you will both be pariahs. There will be nowhere you can go with her and have any kind of sane existence." She paused, seeming dangerous and deadly. "And I will demand your father repay the sums I have advanced toward the dowry. No judge in the land would deny my request to recoup it."

She raised a brow, informing him she was cognizant of Lord Sidwell's finances, that he'd already spent the money.

"I understand," he grumbled, feeling sick and furious.

"We'll depart for London at ten o'clock. I hope you'll come to your senses and ride with us." Her tirade ended, she stood. "At the moment, it's a bit past noon. If you don't mind, I'll ask the housekeeper to have supper served at eight. I would appreciate it if you could join us for the meal to give me your answer. I would hate to have you make us wait until morning."

"I'll be there." He had no idea if he was being truthful or not.

She swept out, and Aaron was all alone.

Priscilla was marching down the hall when, up ahead, a door opened and a very beautiful auburn-haired woman emerged. She turned to Priscilla, and she was smiling, about to say hello, when she noted Priscilla's condemning glower.

"Aren't you Florella Bernard?" Priscilla inquired.

"Yes, I am."

"I thought so. I've seen you on the stage in London."

"Oh. I'm always delighted to meet a fan."

"I'm not a fan. I am Priscilla Cummings, Lord Run's fiancée. I'm visiting Fox Run. My mother is with me too."

"How nice." Miss Bernard struggled to keep her smile in place.

"Though Lord Run occasionally consorts with actresses and other low persons, I don't believe I should have to."

"No, no, certainly not."

"My mother wouldn't deem you to be appropriate company."

"Of course not."

"You're leaving this afternoon, aren't you? Isn't that what I heard? You were called back to London unexpectedly?"

Priscilla scowled at Miss Bernard, watching as a dozen replies flitted through her mind. Possibly she was thinking she'd like to speak to Aaron first. Possibly she'd like to announce that she was a guest and Priscilla had no right to boss her.

But she didn't dare. Priscilla was so far above her in station that it was a wonder they could see each other across the distance separating them.

Ultimately, Miss Bernard nodded. "Yes, Miss Cummings, I was just on my way downstairs to find my maid so we can pack."

"It shouldn't take more than an hour or two, should it?"

"I can be gone by then."

"Marvelous."

Priscilla kept on down the hall, and she was so angry, she was trembling. For weeks, her mother had been haranguing at Priscilla about how she had to act around Aaron. Priscilla was trying her best, but honestly, there was a limit as to what she should have to endure.

An actress! Staying in Priscilla's home! The outrage of it was almost greater than the fact that Aaron's mistress was present too.

Priscilla didn't care what her mother said. Once Priscilla and Aaron were married, they would have to establish some rules as to what was allowed and what wasn't.

She arrived at Miss Etherton's door, knocked, then strolled in without waiting for a response. The sitting room was empty, but in the bedchamber, Miss Etherton was leaned against the edge of the bed.

She was in a state of shock, had seen Priscilla enter, but didn't move. She simply stared, her blue eyes wide and tormented.

Priscilla approached until she was directly in front of Miss Etherton. She'd planned to be rude and cruel, but Miss Etherton's desolation was so obvious, Priscilla couldn't bear to chastise her. It would have been like kicking a puppy.

"You know who I am, Miss Etherton."

"Yes, I know."

"And *I* know who you are. Lord Sidwell told me all about you. It's why I've traveled to Fox Run. Each minute that you're in residence is an insult to me."

Miss Etherton's cheeks flushed a bright shade of scarlet. "I'm terribly sorry."

"I must say a few things to you, Miss Etherton."

"No, Miss Cummings, I believe *I* should say them to you."

"Let me start," Priscilla insisted, "and I must be very blunt."

Miss Etherton chuckled miserably. "I doubt there's any other way to have a conversation like this. Yes, please be blunt."

"You didn't know about my wedding."

"No, I didn't."

"If you had been apprised, I'm positive you wouldn't have been here in my home."

"You're correct."

"It was awful of Aaron to have put you in such a predicament."

"Well..." Miss Etherton couldn't finish her sentence.

"You seem like a nice person. In other circumstances, we might have been cordial."

"Yes, we might have been." Miss Etherton didn't sound as if she meant it.

"You understand, don't you, that you must leave Fox Run immediately?"

"Yes, I understand. Absolutely." Miss Etherton straightened. "I was about to begin packing."

"Good. I'm glad there won't be a fuss over it."

"No, there's no need to fuss. I was a tad...surprised by your arrival. I was catching my breath, but I'm better now. I'll get my bag and be gone in a thrice."

She and Miss Etherton were the same height, but that was the only similarity. Miss Etherton was older than Priscilla, was more slender than Priscilla. While Priscilla never left the house unless she was immaculately coifed and tailored, Miss Etherton wasn't overly concerned as to her appearance. Her hair was in a haphazard chignon, and she was attired in a dowdy gray dress such as a nanny or governess might wear.

Yet despite her lack of wardrobe or polish, she was very pretty, very appealing, and she exuded a confidence Priscilla would probably never be able to match. Priscilla could definitely comprehend why a man might be attracted to Miss Etherton. If she'd been decked out in a ball gown and jewels, she'd have been stunning.

Priscilla had brought her reticule, and she opened it and pulled out a sack full of coins.

Miss Etherton frowned. "What's this?"

"It's for you. Please take it."

"Why?"

"Have you anywhere to go, Miss Etherton?"

"Yes, I think I do."

"Is it a location Aaron might recognize? Might he come there in search of you?"

Miss Etherton pondered, then her shoulders drooped. "Yes, he would figure it out eventually."

"Then I'm asking you—no, I'm begging you—to use this money to go somewhere else."

"You assume he would look for me?"

"I'm convinced of it, Miss Etherton. He's very fond of you, and I can see you were very fond of him."

"Perhaps," Miss Etherton muttered.

"I'm about to be a bride, Miss Etherton. My wedding day is an event I've dreamed about and planned for since I was a little girl."

"Of course you have," Miss Etherton gently said.

"I'm afraid Aaron won't show up for the ceremony. He's so infatuated by you! He's dawdling here, but it's keeping him from his responsibilities in London. If he left me standing at the altar, I'd just die!"

"He would never do that," Miss Etherton loyally declared.

"I believed that about him once, but since he met you, I'm not so sure."

"I'm very sorry," Miss Etherton murmured.

"I want to start my married life on a good note, Miss Etherton, and I'm aware of how charming Aaron can be. If he knows where you are, he'll seek you out and persuade you to dally with him again. Sooner or later, I'd learn of it, and it would kill me."

"It will never happen," Miss Etherton insisted.

"I'd like to be certain of that." She forced the money into Miss Etherton's hand. "Take it, would you? Don't travel to the location you were envisioning. Go where he would never find you. Consider this a nest egg that will help you get settled."

Priscilla stared, her expression concerned and sympathetic, and Miss Etherton gaped at the sack of coins. Finally, she sighed.

"Yes, it's probably for the best."

"And you oughtn't to tarry."

"No. There's no reason to delay my departure."

"I heard Miss Bernard is leaving for London."

"Is she?"

"Yes—within the hour. Maybe you could ride with her."

"Yes, maybe I could."

Priscilla studied Miss Etherton, wondering what would become of her. Ruined by a scoundrel. Deceived by his lies. Abandoned by him when push came to shove. It was like a scene out of a tragic novel.

She reached out and squeezed Miss Etherton's wrist in a supportive way.

"Let me have him, Miss Etherton. Give him up forever so he can be mine. Don't allow him to shame me further."

"Yes, yes, he's all yours. He always has been."

"Swear it to me."

"I swear."

Priscilla nodded and smiled. "Thank you."

She hovered, expecting Miss Etherton to add a pithy or profound comment, but she didn't, and her silence made Priscilla feel as if *she* should comment, but she couldn't imagine what it might be. They seemed to have hashed it out to the bitter end.

"I appreciate your listening to me," Priscilla said. "Goodbye."

She spun and left, and she could sense Miss Etherton's weary eyes digging into her back. Head high, shoulders straight, Priscilla continued on. She stepped into the hall and quietly closed the door. She would have liked to slam it—she was in that kind of dark mood—but she minded her manners.

She walked on, and as she turned the corner and there was no chance Miss Etherton might peek out and see her, she grinned from ear to ear.

CHAPTER SIXTEEN

Evangeline was in her bedchamber, packing her meager pile of belongings, when the door opened again. Annoyance rippled through her. No doubt it was Miss Cummings having returned to twist the knife, and Evangeline had listened to every word she ever intended to hear from the horrid girl.

She had to give credit to Miss Cummings though. Prior to her barging in, Evangeline had been too stunned to react or figure out a plan. Miss Cummings had forced Evangeline to realize she had to get moving and flee Fox Run before Lord Run tried to talk to her—and he would try. She had to find somewhere safe where she could rest and regroup and decide what to do next.

Having shaken off her stupor, she'd hurried to Florella's room and found Miss Cummings had been telling the truth. Florella was leaving immediately, and Evangeline was going with her.

Evangeline hadn't confessed her sins to Florella who—at the moment—appeared to be Evangeline's only friend in the world. But from Florella's expression, she seemed to be aware of Evangeline's affair with Lord Run. How would she have learned of it? Did the whole kingdom know?

Evangeline had one goal and that was to depart the premises before Lord Run crept upstairs.

The poor, poor man, she caustically mused. In love with one woman but about to marry another.

He'd be anxious to persuade Evangeline that she was completely wrong about him, but if he tried to *explain,* if he tried to justify his conduct, Evangeline couldn't predict how she might lash out.

She'd already lingered much too long, and with each passing minute, she was risking a confrontation she couldn't bear to have. She wouldn't listen or commiserate or attempt to *understand.* Gad, just from considering the conversation they might have, a wave of nausea swirled in her stomach.

Footsteps sounded as someone marched across her floor, and she scowled, recognizing they were much too heavy for it to be

Miss Cummings. Evangeline sighed with disgust and whipped around as Lord Run entered the room. They stared and stared, the silence so fraught with fury and regret that she felt dizzy.

"Don't say anything to me," Evangeline told him.

His gaze shifted to her portmanteau on the bed.

"You're leaving?" he inquired.

"Of course I'm leaving."

He shook his head. "No. I can't let you."

"You can't *let* me?" His idiotic comment was so galling, she wanted to hit him. "You don't own me. In fact, you have no connection to me at all. You have no authority over me, and you've squandered any glimmer of friendship. You're insane if you assume you can prevent me."

Like the incredible boor he could apparently be, he tromped over, grabbed the portmanteau, and carried it to the wardrobe. He dumped her clothes into it in a messy pile and tossed the bag on top of them.

His blue eyes flamed with temper. "You will not go until I tell you you can."

"Oh, for pity's sake." Mockingly, she added, "Yes, my lord and master. By all means, permit me to stay. Please! I'll hide in my bedchamber, and you can pop in for a visit whenever your fiancée isn't looking."

He stomped over and wagged an angry finger in her face. "I didn't ask her to come here."

"So what? She's here and I'm here, and one of us has to depart. Shall we inform Miss Cummings you've decided it should be her?"

The question stopped him in his tracks for it was painfully obvious he'd tell Miss Cummings no such thing. He and Miss Cummings had known each other since they were children. Their parents had discussed a marriage when Miss Cummings was in the cradle. They'd been engaged for an entire year.

How bizarre, how humiliating that he would wedge Evangeline into the middle of such a long-established plan. And at the very end too!

The man was mad as a hatter.

His expression softened, his shoulders drooped. "I'm sorry."

"Are you?"

"Yes. I'm sorry to the marrow of my bones."

"Were you ever going to mention her to me?"

"I wanted to."

"I'm sure you did," she sarcastically fumed.

"If you knew, I didn't think you'd keep on with me—"

"You're bloody right about that."

"And I can't imagine my world without you in it."

"Have you any idea how mortified I am or how stupid I feel?"

"I'm sorry." It seemed to be the only remark he could utter.

"What now?" she asked. "Your fiancée is here, and you refuse to let me leave. Are you expecting we'll cohabitate? Will we spend a week or two becoming chums? For I must point out, having met Miss Cummings *and* her mother, I doubt cordiality is possible."

"You're making too much of this," he claimed.

Evangeline gasped with affront. "*I* am making too much of it?"

"Yes. I apologize for how you found out, but it doesn't have to change things between us."

"Not change things?" She gaped at him as if he'd spoken in a foreign language.

"We can continue on," he insisted.

"How?"

"I love you, Evangeline."

"Be silent, Lord Run."

"Don't call me Lord Run," he imperiously commanded. "My name is Aaron."

"*Lord Run,* you're embarrassing yourself—and me."

Fleetingly, he looked as if he'd argue over her mode of address but, evidently, he was eager to move on to more pertinent issues. "You told me you loved me too. Such a potent amount of affection can't have vanished over night."

"When we declared heightened sentiment, I think *one* of us was sincere, but I think one of us may have been lying. One of us may have merely been hoping for a quick tumble."

"You're wrong," he furiously said. "I love you with all my heart, and I've asked you—from the moment we met—to let me take care of you. Haven't I asked you? Haven't I begged you?"

"If I remember correctly, you *asked* me to be your mistress."

"Yes, and I'm asking again. Let me take you to London. I'll buy us a house, and we'll start a family. We don't need a marriage license to prove we belong together."

She studied him, wondering if he hadn't been possessed by demons.

They would live openly in sin? They didn't need a marriage license? Who talked that way? Who acted that way? Such fraternization wasn't legal! They could be arrested for illicit consorting. Their children would bear the stain of bastardry. Evangeline would be a fallen woman, the type no decent female could invite inside for a cup of tea.

That was the future he envisioned for them? That was the life he was offering?

"I firmly believe, Lord Run, that you have gone insane. Are you feeling all right? Perhaps we should summon a footman and have you put to bed until you've recovered your wits."

"We could be happy!" He grabbed her shoulders and shook her.

"If that's what you suppose, then you don't know me at all."

"But if you love me, Evangeline—"

"I loved a mirage. I loved a man who doesn't exist."

"You know me better than anyone ever has. You understand me better."

"I don't understand you at all, and clearly, *you* don't understand me. I would never agree to be your mistress. I want to wed and have a husband and family. I want to be respectable—and respected."

"You wish to wed?" he snidely said. "Who? Iggy Bosworth? Is that your idea of an appropriate husband?"

"At least he asked me. At least he was prepared to behave honorably—as opposed to some men of my acquaintance."

Her insult hit its target, and he flushed with chagrin. "How does it make sense to live with someone horrid because you have a piece of paper—a marriage license—that says it's all right? With me, you could be rich and happy and pampered, but you'd give it all up for a piece of paper? You'd pick Iggy over me because of a piece of paper?"

"I'm not marrying Vicar Bosworth. I can't now, can I? Not when I'm ruined."

"You're not ruined."

"What would you call it then?"

"You're cherished and adored as you will never be by another person."

"Fine, then. I'm cherished and adored. Go downstairs and tell your fiancée that it's over. Tell her you had to choose between her and me, and you choose *me*."

A muscle ticked in his cheek. "I can't."

"Why can't you?"

"It's complicated."

"How is it complicated?" she asked. "It actually seems quite simple to me. You want us to be together, yet you deride me because I demand a paltry license for it to be official. So give me the license I'm yearning to have."

He huffed out a heavy sigh. "Evangeline, don't be so difficult."

"I'm not. Just marry me instead of her. In my book, that's not difficult."

They glared, fuming, at an impasse. She couldn't abide the tension and wished he'd leave so she could get to Florella's room before Florella grew tired of waiting and left without her.

Ultimately, she said, "Explain something to me."

"If I can."

"You insist you love me. Are you in love with her too?"

"No," he scoffed. "I don't love her."

"Then why would you wed her?"

"It's a business arrangement."

"I feel sorry for both of you."

"Don't be sorry. Priscilla and I entered into it with our eyes open. Neither of us would expect elevated sentiment. It's not how marriages happen in our world."

At the way he said *world,* Evangeline was very sad. It underscored the differences between him and her. It made her realize what a fool she'd been to dream and plan.

"Wouldn't you like to be happy, Lord Run?"

"Of course I would. It's why I keep asking you to be my mistress."

"You have a strange view of life. How could you wed one woman, but bind yourself to another? How exactly would that work?"

"She doesn't have anything to do with you and me," he practically shouted.

"If that's what you assume, then we've arrived back at the spot where I must repeat that I am gravely concerned as to your mental state."

They stared again, and he tried to take her hand, but she yanked away, and he appeared very hurt. He was insane! No doubt about it.

"Calm down," he snapped.

"I'm very calm."

"This disaster unfolded so fast, and we all have to catch our breath."

"I've caught my breath."

"Well, I haven't, and you must listen to me. You can't run off half-cocked. I need a chance to figure out somewhere for you to go that's safe and stable."

"Where would that be?"

"I thought I'd write to my brother, Lucas. I believe he's married your friend, Miss Hubbard. I'll ask if you can stay with them. You'd like that, wouldn't you?"

She recalled Miss Cummings's assertion that Lord Run would search for Evangeline, that he'd coerce her into restarting their affair. She recalled her promise to remove to a location where Lord Run could never find her.

So she lied and said, "Yes, I'd like to be with Amelia."

"Good. We have to be in close contact in case there are...consequences."

She didn't grasp the implication, and she frowned. "What consequences?"

"In case you're...ah...increasing."

She gasped with alarm. "I could be with child now? Is that what you're telling me?"

He shrugged. "It's not likely, but it's possible."

The prospect hadn't occurred to her, and she was aghast. "Can it happen from just one time?"

"It can. Not often, but it can."

Shame rocking her, she felt as if she might faint, and she staggered over to the bed and eased her hips onto the mattress.

"I proceeded with you," she murmured, "because I presumed we'd wed afterward, because you swore we'd be together."

"And we will be—if you'd stop being so contrary."

"But you didn't mean marriage, did you? You meant I could be your mistress."

"I was hoping."

"What were you hoping? Were you hoping a babe would catch so I'd have to remain with you?"

He shrugged again. "I won't deny it, Evangeline. I'm that desperate to keep you by my side."

"I'm such an idiot," she muttered. "I'm a blithering, idiotic dunce!"

She gazed at him, curious if she'd ever really known him. She'd seen only the part of his personality that was sunny and light, was kind and considerate. She hadn't realized he possessed this hard, callous edge, hadn't realized how driven he could be to get what he wanted.

Yet hadn't Rose warned her? Rose was his cousin, and she'd been disavowed by the Drake men her entire life—merely because her mother had wed without permission thirty years earlier. The Drakes had attached that old transgression to Rose, and she hadn't been able to shed it.

Hadn't Rose mentioned the ruthless nature of her male kin? Hadn't she commented on how merciless they could be? Why hadn't Evangeline listened?

She thought—if she turned out to be increasing—she would buy a gun. She would buy a very big, very lethal gun, and she would hunt him down and shoot him right between the eyes.

"I'll contact my brother immediately," he said, "but I need you to promise me you'll remain at Fox Run until I hear back."

"What about Miss Cummings and her mother?"

"They're leaving in the morning, so you don't have to fret about them."

"Are you going to London with them?"

"Yes, I'm going to London."

She hadn't expected anything else from him, but still, the admission was brutal. She nearly collapsed to the rug in a bereft heap.

"I'm glad you're accompanying them," she lied again. "I'm sure it's for the best."

"It's not for the best, but I've always done my duty. I don't know how to act any differently, but the only way I'll follow through is if you stay put. You can't run off the second I walk out the door."

"I won't run off," she said.

"Swear it to me," he demanded. "Swear you'll stay until we hear from Lucas."

"It's not as if I have any choice." She used the answer to keep from giving her vow. "What if your brother doesn't want me in his home?"

"We'll devise another solution. Just don't traipse off alone."

"I won't."

He studied her, looking bereft too, as if he might fall to his knees and beg for forgiveness, which she couldn't bear to imagine.

She'd lived a sheltered life and had been instantly fascinated by him. She had no defense against him, had never been able to resist him or behave as she ought. If he was forlorn and remorseful, she could picture herself missing him, relenting, letting him describe the future he envisioned and hoping it would transpire.

"Would you go?" she asked. "Your fiancée is downstairs, Lord Run. You need to be with her now. You shouldn't be up here with me."

"Will you come down to supper?" he absurdly inquired.

"No!"

"Then, I'll see you in the morning before I depart. We'll talk."

"All right."

"I'm sorry, Evangeline." He reached out to stroke her cheek, but she lurched away so he couldn't.

"I'm sorry too."

"I wish…"

"Don't tell me what you wish. Just go."

She spun away and went to the window, showing him her back.

He dawdled and fidgeted and, finally, he left.

She was frozen in place, in a state of shock, wondering how her heart kept beating. She was so weary, so sad.

Eventually, a knock sounded, and Florella called, "Evangeline?"

Evangeline had been so distraught, she'd forgotten about Florella.

"Yes, I'm here," she replied as Florella stepped inside.

"Are you ready?"

"In a minute."

Evangeline hurried to the wardrobe and scooped up the clothes Lord Run had dumped out. She stuffed them into her portmanteau without bothering to fold any of it. Then she grabbed the sack of coins Miss Cummings had given her and stuffed it under the clothes.

She probably should have felt awful about accepting the money but, actually, she was relieved to have it. It would take her far away from Aaron Drake, and it would take her very fast.

"I need your assistance," she said.

"With what?" Florella asked.

"Lord Run told me not to leave"—Florella frowned at the news—"and I agreed I wouldn't, but I really have to get away from him."

"I think that's wise."

"Would you carry my portmanteau?"

"Certainly."

"I'll walk through the park—as if I'm simply taking a stroll. I'll meet you on the road."

"Yes, that's fine."

"Is Bryce coming with us?" Evangeline inquired.

"No. The idiot refused to let Miss Cummings chase him away. He's looking for Aaron right now to tell him how rude Miss Cummings was to me, but I'm not waiting around so that little harridan can accost me again."

"My feeling exactly," Evangeline concurred.

"So...let's go."

"Yes, let's do, but on the way, I have to stop in the village."

"What for?"

"I have to inform Vicar Bosworth that I'm breaking my engagement."

"Oh."

"Yes, oh," Evangeline said.

"Well then"—Florella forced a smile—"we'd best get a move on."

"I'll be out on the road, past the gate."

Florella picked up Evangeline's bag and left with it. Evangeline put on her cloak and bonnet, then tiptoed down the servants' stairs and went outside. No one saw her. She might have been invisible. She might have been a ghost flitting by, unnoticed and unremarked.

CHAPTER SEVENTEEN

"Hello, Miss Etherton."

"Hello, Vicar Bosworth."

"How *kind* of you to stop by."

Evangeline hovered in the doorway to his library. He was seated at his desk, glaring at her as if daring her to enter.

She shuddered, briefly reflecting that—had her path gone in a different direction—this would have been her fate. The notion was terrifying, and if there was one aspect to the debacle that provided any solace, it was the fact that she would never be Mrs. Ignatius Bosworth.

"May I come in?" she tentatively asked, feeling afraid of him, as if she was a stranger begging for a handout.

He gestured to the chair across, and she hurried over and slid onto it.

"How is your cold?" he inquired.

"My...cold?" She was so disoriented by events that she didn't know to what he referred.

"Yes, your *cold*. It's all I've heard all week. You were too ill to socialize."

"Ah...I'm much better."

"Thank goodness," he sarcastically said.

She'd understood that the conversation would be difficult but, apparently, it would be even more horrid than she'd assumed. He continued to glare, not furnishing an opening for small talk that would have eased them toward more thorny topics.

There was no hope for it. She'd have to simply blurt it out, but she didn't imagine he'd mind very much. His mother would certainly celebrate.

"I have to tell you something," she murmured.

"Speak up," he snapped. "I can't hear you."

"I have to tell you something," she repeated more loudly.

"Let's have it, Miss Etherton." When she couldn't spit it out, he mockingly chided, "Come now, where's your spirit? Is the flamboyant Miss Etherton at a loss for words?"

"No, it's a sad day for me, so it's hard to start. I can't figure out how."

"Why is that? Could it be that you realize how you'll shame yourself?"

A sinking sensation crept over her, as if there was a cliff approaching and she couldn't avoid it. She was about to fall into a very deep hole.

"What do you mean?"

"You've been staying at Fox Run, Miss Etherton. The manor is filled with servants, and as anyone can apprise you, servants know all. Can you actually presume there are any genuine secrets in such a place?"

Gad, had he learned of her affair too? From how he was glowering, he definitely seemed to be aware of it. Or was it another infraction entirely?

She straightened, mustered her courage, and announced, "I can't marry you, Vicar Bosworth."

To her surprise, he exhibited no reaction whatsoever. Not shock. Not outrage. Not even a mild curiosity.

A sly smile creased his lips. "Is that right?"

"Yes. I'm very grateful to you and your mother for inviting me here and extending your hospitality."

"Oh, Mother is nothing if not gracious."

"Yes, she was wonderful," Evangeline fibbed. She had her goddess statue in her pocket, and she slipped her hand to it and rubbed her fingers across the smooth ivory.

"What is it that has led you to this decision?" He appeared snide and spiteful. "I suppose I'm entitled to know."

"We don't suit at all."

"We don't suit?"

"No. Surely you agree. You don't really like me, and you don't approve of my character or habits."

She thought he might at least feign a bit of courtesy, but he said, "You're correct. There is very little about you that would make you an appropriate wife for a man of my calling and station."

"I'm sorry you feel that way."

"Are you? For I must say that you don't look sorry."

"I am." She shrugged, not inclined to argue the point.

"When did you come to this conclusion?"

The moment I met you! "I've been pondering it for a while."

"Have you?" His gaze was condemning and a tad cruel.

"Actually, I wasn't sick this past week. I lied to you about my health. I simply needed a break so I could consider my options."

"Your options," he nastily mused. "And the number one choice just happened to be a severing of our betrothal?"

"Not the number *one* choice. Not at all."

"Tell me, Miss Etherton, what were some of the other *choices* you were contemplating?"

"I apologize, Vicar, but I'm very upset this afternoon, and I guess I'm not being clear."

"Trust me, you're being extremely clear." Suddenly, he pushed back his chair, leaping to his feet so abruptly that it tipped over and clanged to the floor. He slapped his palms on the wood of the desk, leaned nearer, and hissed, "Harlot!"

At his use of the harsh term, she was startled, and she sputtered, "What?"

"Harlot!" he seethed. "You dare show your face in my home? You dare come here after you have lain—like a common whore—with my cousin? You dare speak to me—*me!* a man of the cloth—as if I am an ordinary person of no stature? You dare foul the air under my roof?"

With each remark, he was rounding the desk, lumbering toward her. His fury was frightening to witness, and as she peered up at him, he looked mad.

He stopped in front of her and bent down so they were eye to eye. "Did you enjoy yourself, Miss Etherton? When you were fornicating with my cousin, when you were deceiving and betraying me, was it worth it? Did the two of you laugh and talk about me? Were you humored to assume I would never find out?"

She was too astonished to realize she should deny the affair, and she insisted, "No, no, it wasn't like that."

"Wasn't it? You have squandered your good name and your chastity, and for what? A few minutes of pleasure? Why would you? What is left to you now? Is there anything?"

"No, there's nothing."

"Precisely, Miss Etherton, which is why I'm trying to figure out your motivation. Were you in love? Is that what you assert? That *love* excuses your behavior?"

"I thought I was in love," she shamed herself by admitting.

"And my cousin must have pretended he'd marry you and install you as Countess of Sidwell someday."

"No, he never said that."

"Were you so overcome by lust you couldn't resist?"

"No!"

"I'm betting your paltry attempts were amusing to his fiancée. How is Miss Cummings, by the way? I'm told she's visiting."

He smirked, his condescending leer making her squirm, making her afraid. She wanted to leave, but wasn't sure how.

"I'm sorry, Vicar Bosworth," she said again. She wouldn't

justify her conduct, for there was no justification, and as he'd pointed out, she'd squandered everything. And for what?

"You're sorry," he spat in reply.

"I am. I truly, truly am."

"To think I let Lord Sidwell convince me to bring you here. To think I agreed to have someone of your low character. To think you've been allowed to drink tea with my mother!"

Before she grasped what he intended, he raised his arm and slapped her. She'd never been hit in her life, and the blow astounded her. She was paralyzed by fear, and while she needed to run out, she was too stunned to move.

"Harlot!" he accused, and he slapped her again.

The second clout was more vicious. It landed squarely on her cheek, and the force of it was so powerful it knocked her off the chair and onto the rug.

She'd had her hand in her pocket, clutching her statute, and as she reached out to catch herself, the statue skittered across the floor.

"What is this?" the vicar fumed as he marched over and snatched it up. He studied it, then scoffed. "Pagan idolatry? Is that what this is? You worship idols? You fornicate and worship idols?"

His voice thundered through the house, rattling the rafters, and she pushed herself to her feet and held out her hand like a supplicant.

"It belonged to my mother," she claimed. "Please let me have it."

"Get out, Miss Etherton. Get out! Your very presence offends me."

"It was my mother's!"

He stuck it into the pocket of his vest, and he stood there, glowering, disdain rolling off him in waves.

"Please?" she begged a final time, distraught over the prospect of losing it.

"Get out!" he bellowed. "I'm sick to death of you."

The door opened behind her, and she glanced around to see his mother.

"You've been asked to leave," Mrs. Bosworth said. "Go—before we call the servants and have them throw you out."

Evangeline hovered, desperate to heal the wounds she'd inflicted, or at least calm their hatred, but from their reproachful stares, it was obvious there was naught she could do.

Her cheek was hot, pounding from where he'd hit her. She laid a palm on it and dashed for the door. Mrs. Bosworth partially blocked her way so Evangeline had to brush against her as she passed.

"Whore!" Mrs. Bosworth hissed.

Evangeline raced out.

"Where are you going?"

At the question cast down the stairs from up above, Aaron peered up at Claudia who glared at him over the banister railing. He was in the foyer, stuffing his arms in the sleeves of his coat and ready to hurry out and mount his horse that was saddled and awaiting him in the driveway.

"I have an appointment in the village, Claudia," he told her.

"We're departing in half an hour."

"You'll have to go without me."

She sniffed with affront and stomped down, her heels clacking with precision as he watched her come. He steeled himself, bracing so he didn't shout at her, so he didn't tell her to sod off.

Generally, he was courteous and civil, particularly with someone of Claudia's station. But for once he was so on edge that he truly felt—should she provide the smallest excuse—he might toss her out bodily.

She approached until they were toe-to-toe and demanded, "Is Miss Etherton gone?"

"Yes, she's gone."

"Then why can't you travel with us?"

"Because I don't wish to. I'm not your slave, and I've been entirely too accommodating."

She searched his eyes for prevarication or deceit and, of course, there was plenty. It was impossible to hide it all.

"If she's no longer in residence," Claudia said, "there's no reason for you to tarry."

"No, there's not, but I plan to anyway."

"You told me last night at supper that you would be returning with us to the city."

"Yes, I did."

"You swore it to me!"

"Well, I changed my mind."

He spun away and headed to the door, and she barked, "Aaron!"

He whipped around. "What?"

"Don't you dare walk out of here."

He took a deep breath, struggling for composure, for sanity, then he marched back to her. He was much taller than she was, and he towered over her.

"Madam," he seethed, "this is my home and my foyer. Don't you ever raise your voice in it to me ever again."

"You will not leave!" She was so angry she was trembling. "You will ride to London with us as promised!"

"You barged in without invitation." He stuck a finger in her face and rattled off her transgressions. "You have interfered in my personal affairs, insulted my guests, and enraged me to the point of madness. Now, I am not riding to London with you this morning, and I suggest—for your own good—that you not boss me about it. Have I made myself clear, Mrs. Cummings?"

For a moment, he thought she might slap him. But she stepped away and said, "Yes, Lord Run, you've made yourself very clear."

"The boys in the stable will have your carriage ready. I assume you and your daughter can get in it without my assistance?"

"Yes, we can."

"Marvelous."

"Will you...will you join us in London?"

"I should be there tomorrow."

He whirled away, and though she called to him again, he continued on. Behind him, Priscilla was on the stairs saying, "Mother, what is it? What's happening?"

"Go to your room, Priscilla."

"Is Aaron leaving? Why?"

Aaron raced down to the driveway, the butler closing the door so he couldn't hear anymore. Not that he needed to. He'd heard enough from those two to last ten lifetimes.

He was in a frenzy, bursting with grief and ire. How could so much catastrophe be crammed into twenty-four short hours? Just the previous day, he'd been wildly in love, gloriously happy about his future with Evangeline.

Then, with Claudia's carriage rolling in, it had all unraveled. Aaron's dreams had been dashed, his fantastical plans exposed for the naïve nonsense they were.

After his hideous conversation with Evangeline, he'd spent the rest of the torturous afternoon fretting and stewing, anxious to figure out how it had all been destroyed.

As Claudia had requested, he'd shown up in the dining room at supper to inform her he would follow through with the wedding. Wouldn't he? Was there any other possible ending?

He'd tossed and turned all night, wondering what to do, but the only conclusion that appeared was for him to sever his engagement and marry a woman he'd known for four weeks.

He couldn't imagine doing something so reckless, but he couldn't imagine *not* doing it either. He'd survived the grueling interval by remembering he'd get to talk to Evangeline in the morning.

But when he'd gone to her bedchamber, he'd been stunned to find she'd left. She'd promised she wouldn't. She'd sworn to him! Yet she'd left anyway.

He'd been questioning the staff, trying to ascertain when she was last observed in the manor. No one had seen her exit the property, and a housemaid—the dour Mrs. Turner—mentioned that Miss Etherton had been spotted at the vicarage the prior afternoon. So he was stopping there first.

He couldn't picture her seeking assistance from Cousin Iggy—and Iggy was hardly the type to offer it—so why would she have been there? Had she cried off? Was she telling him goodbye?

Florella had fled Fox Run too, apparently having been ordered to vacate by Priscilla, and he suspected Evangeline might be with Florella, but he wasn't sure.

Would she cast her lot with Florella? And where would Florella take her? To London? To live there? Or would Evangeline continue on? To where?

Aaron was so vain and self-centered that he hadn't bothered to learn much about her and was aware of just two friends: Amelia Hubbard and Rose Ralston, who was Aaron's cousin and James Talbot's bride.

Would Evangeline go to one of them? James's estate was on the Scottish border. Was that Evangeline's plan? Would she travel so far by herself? Where would she have gotten the money for the journey? If instead she hoped to go to Amelia Hubbard, how would she have discovered Miss Hubbard's location? Aaron didn't think anyone knew Miss Hubbard's whereabouts.

When Aaron finished his visit to Iggy, he would pen a dozen frantic letters—to James Talbot, to Lucas—and would send them out by messengers riding his fastest horses. He wanted them watching for her.

In a matter of minutes, he arrived in the village, and he reined in at the vicarage and tied his horse. Then he dashed to the front door and pounded on it. There was no answer, so he blustered in just as a startled housemaid was walking into the vestibule.

"Where is my cousin?" he demanded, and she motioned toward the rear of the house, which likely indicated Iggy was in his library.

Aaron pushed by her and marched down the hall, delighted by his cousin's astonished expression as Aaron strutted into the library unannounced. Iggy was seated at his desk, and he sat back in his chair, his lips pursed in an unbecoming pout.

"Cousin Aaron," Iggy tightly said, "this is a surprise. What brings you by?"

"I'll come right to the point."

"Please do."

"I'm looking for Miss Etherton. Is she here?"

"No. Why would she be?"

"I was told she stopped by yesterday."

Iggy nodded curtly. "She did."

"She didn't spend the night?"

"That wouldn't have been appropriate."

"Why was she here?"

"I don't see how that is any of your affair."

"I'm making it my affair. What did she want?"

Gertrude entered and inquired, "Is he bothering you, Ignatius?"

"No, Mother."

Aaron glared at her. "This is a private conversation, Gertrude."

"Nonsense. If it concerns Ignatius, it concerns me."

Aaron was undeterred. "If you'll excuse us?"

"I won't," Gertrude huffed. "You can't barge in and presume to—"

Before she could complete her sentence, Aaron was across the room. He seized her arm and escorted her out, then slammed the door in her face. He went back to the desk, his fury escalating with each passing second.

"I'm out of patience, Iggy, so I suggest you answer me. Why was Miss Etherton here?"

Iggy shook his head with disgust. "You have an enormous amount of gall to be asking about her."

"Yes, I have an enormous amount of gall. Now where is she?"

Iggy stood, probably thinking he looked very grand when, actually, he looked like an angry, skinny scarecrow.

"For shame, Cousin Aaron! For shame!"

"What are you babbling about?"

"Your fiancée is at Fox Run, yet you're chasing about the neighborhood in search of your paramour. Does Miss Cummings know where you are? Shall I send her a note and invite her to join us?"

Aaron was amazed that Iggy had the temerity to scold Aaron, but he ignored his cousin's fit of pique and kept on. "My personal life is none of your business."

"Not my business?" Iggy sputtered. "You cheat on your fiancée. You betray me, your blood kin. You're so unable to control your rampant lust that you ruin *my* engagement. You woo my fiancée until she ridiculously believes you might marry her. You make her your whore, and you—"

"What did you call her?"

"She's a whore! How else should I describe a woman who has squandered her virginity on a worthless libertine such as yourself?"

Aaron was around the desk in a flash. He hit Iggy so hard that the pathetic idiot flew back and crashed into his bookshelf. Books tumbled down and pummeled him on the head and shoulders.

Aaron bent over and grabbed Iggy by his shirt, pulling him up so they were nose to nose. "Don't you speak a derogatory word about her ever again. In fact, don't ever *speak* about her again."

The door banged open, and Gertrude rushed in. As she saw Iggy on the floor, she shrieked, "Oh my Lord! Aaron, are you mad? Ignatius, my darling boy!"

She hurried over and tried to muscle Aaron out of the way, but he wouldn't budge, wouldn't release Iggy's shirt. She hovered on the edge of their quarrel, nervously ringing her hands.

"Did Miss Etherton say where she was going?" Aaron asked Iggy.

"I don't care where that whore went."

"You're a slow learner, aren't you, Iggy?"

Gertrude wailed with dismay as Aaron hit him again and he slumped down. Aaron straightened, and as he did, he was stunned to find Evangeline's goddess statue on one of the bookshelves. The discovery was terribly unsettling.

She would never have parted with it. Why would Iggy have it? Had he harmed Evangeline? When she'd cried off, had he grown enraged and murdered her? Was she locked in the basement and being tortured for spurning him? What? What?

Wild, violent scenarios careened through his mind, but he shook them away. Mrs. Turner had seen Evangeline leave the vicarage unmolested.

He stuck the statue in Iggy's face and demanded, "Where did you get this?"

"I took it from your harl—" Iggy stopped just in time so he didn't utter the term *harlot*. "I took it from Miss Etherton. Despite what you seem to assume, I am the vicar in this parish. I will not condone illicit fornication, and I will not tolerate idolatry."

Aaron slipped the statue into his pocket.

"I'm searching for her, Iggy, and you'd better hope she's all right."

"Why should I worry about that?"

"She would never have willingly given you this statue."

"Of course not, but I will not abide pagan rituals, and I won't pretend about it. Not even for you, Cousin."

Iggy spat the word *cousin,* apprising Aaron of how tediously he'd overstayed his welcome.

"If you've hurt her," Aaron warned, "if you bruised so much as a single hair on her head, I'll come back and kill you."

"Aaron!" Gertrude wheezed. "What is wrong with you? I've had enough. Get out of here, and the minute you depart, I'm writing to your father to tell him how you've acted toward us."

"Yes, please tell him everything, and in the interim, know this."

"What?" Gertrude mulishly asked.

"The two of you need to start packing."

"Packing!" Iggy snapped. "Why?"

"The people of this parish—myself included—are sick of both of you. The moment my affairs calm, I intend to have you removed as vicar."

"You can't fire me," Iggy claimed.

"We'll see what I can do," Aaron said.

He whipped away and stormed out.

CHAPTER EIGHTEEN

"What now?"

"What...now? You think I have an answer?"

Aaron spun away from Bryce and hurled his brandy glass to the floor. It shattered into a dozen pieces, shards flying everywhere.

"Feel better?" Bryce snidely asked.

"No, and why are you still here? Why didn't you sneak away with Florella?"

"I was smart enough to cower in my room so Miss Cummings had no chance to threaten me."

"She must have scared the devil out of Florella to convince her to skitter off like that."

"Florella wasn't scared," Bryce scoffed. "She was simply worried that—if she'd stayed on—she might have taken after Miss Cummings with a fireplace poker. She has that sort of temper, so she figured she should leave rather than remain and make matters worse."

"I don't see how they could have been *worse*," Aaron glumly said.

"Tell me you're not marrying that little harridan."

Aaron threw up his hands. "What can I do? The ceremony is in two weeks, and my father has frittered away the dowry money. We can't repay it."

"He spent *your* money?"

"He claimed it belonged to the estate, not to me."

"That was brash of him."

"If I cried off and there had to be a reimbursement to Claudia, I'm sure Lord Sidwell would insist that—even though he spent the money—I am the groom so *I* should square the accounts."

"Oh, of course, he would. He has you roped in."

"Yes."

"What about Evangeline?"

"What about her?" Aaron petulantly responded.

"I should probably urge you to honor your commitments and

all that nonsense."

"But...?"

"But if you marry Priscilla, you'll be miserable forever."

"That's what my brother told me."

"Usually I'd declare Lucas to be an unreliable idiot, but in this case, he might be on to something."

They were in the main parlor at Fox Run, the day having waned, the house quiet with everyone gone. Aaron had passed the afternoon in a frenzy of activity, organizing searches, writing letters to James Talbot and Lucas. He'd stirred up the neighborhood by sending out footmen to inquire after Evangeline. No one had seen her, and word that she was missing had spread like wildfire.

Iggy was generally loathed, so people were tittering over what he might have done to Evangeline to chase her away. They were angry about the situation too. She'd charmed them, and they'd wanted her to be Iggy's bride so she'd be part of the community. With the congregation already deeming Iggy a fool, the debacle didn't bode well for his reputation as their spiritual leader.

Aaron glared at Bryce. "Are you positive Florella didn't mention she was taking Evangeline to London with her?"

"No, Aaron. As I've explained a thousand times, she went alone."

"If Florella *did* take her, would she let Evangeline stay with her once they arrived?"

"I suppose. She liked Evangeline very much. I don't know how Evangeline would feel about it though. Florella's morals might have been too relaxed for Evangeline."

"Yes, they were."

"It's why I can't imagine them totting off together."

"Neither can I," Aaron muttered, "but still, we'd better head to London first thing in the morning."

"Yes, we'd better."

"I'm just sick about this. As far as I'm aware, Evangeline didn't have a penny in her purse, and if she's in trouble, it's all my fault."

Bryce smirked. "May I please say, *I told you so?*"

"No, you may not."

Bryce ignored Aaron and continued with his chastisement. "I specifically warned you about the mess you'd stirred."

"I don't need to hear about it now."

"In fact, right before we realized Miss Cummings and her mother were on the premises, I swore you'd never be able to keep your liaison a secret."

"Shut up, Bryce!"

"Who tattled to them about her? Are your servants paid spies? Are they sending reports to Mrs. Cummings?"

"It was my father."

Bryce scoffed. "Nice family you have, Aaron. It makes me glad I'm an orphan."

"When I informed him I wanted to cry off from Priscilla and wed Evangeline instead, he about had an apoplexy."

"So did I when you initially suggested it, but I've changed my mind."

"What? You think I should marry Evangeline?"

"I have no opinion about that, and I'm not about to advise you on the subject. What I *can* tell you is that you shouldn't marry Priscilla."

"That seems to be the common view—well, according to everyone but my father and her mother. I'm so sick of both of them. They order me about as if I'm still a lad in short pants. I'd like to elope with Evangeline just to spite them."

"You'll have to find her first," Bryce chided, "and you'll have to convince her that you're not a lying, deceitful swine. You're not that persuasive."

"She was crazy about me once. She could be again."

"In your dreams maybe."

Their conversation dwindled, and Bryce forced himself over to the sideboard and poured Aaron another glass of brandy—which he definitely didn't need—then plopped down in his chair again.

Aaron was staring into the fire, lost in contemplation, and he reached into his pocket and pulled out Evangeline's goddess statue. He ran his thumb over the intricate carving.

Where are you, Evangeline? Will you ever forgive me?

"Let me see that," Bryce suddenly said.

"What?"

Bryce leaned forward. "What have you there? Let me see it."

"It's nothing." Aaron was as reluctant to relinquish it as Evangeline had been.

"Where did you get it?" Bryce yanked it out of Aaron's hand, and he gaped at, appearing stricken.

"It's Evangeline's. She always carried it. She'd set it on the harpsichord when she played. She liked looking at it."

"Oh, my God..." Bryce murmured.

"When she stopped by the vicarage, I'm not certain if she dropped it or what, but Iggy found it somehow and took it from her."

"It can't be true, but it must be!"

"What, Bryce? You're scaring me."

"How did she come to have it?"

"She thought it might have been her mother's, but she wasn't sure. It was given to her when she was very small."

"And she kept it all these years," Bryce breathed.

"What are you talking about?" Aaron asked.

"It was her mother's." Bryce pointed to the bottom of the statue where two very faint initials, *AB,* were visible. "See? AB. Anne Blair. Her mother."

"You know this because...?"

"She was my mother too."

"But then...that would make Evangeline your sister."

"Yes, but her name isn't Evangeline. It's Anne Blair, just like our mother."

Bryce was so shocked that Aaron wouldn't have been surprised if he'd slid to the rug in a total and very unmanly swoon.

"I have a thousand questions," Aaron said. "Where should I begin?"

"I never told you much about my past."

"No, you were always very cryptic with the information you were willing to share."

"I know *some* of it, but I could never bear to discuss it—and it was extremely traumatic. Someone warned me *not* to tell. Someone scared me so I wouldn't."

"You don't recall who it was?"

"No, and I suspect my mother was convicted of a crime."

"A crime!"

"Yes, and she might have been transported to the colonies. I was so young; I didn't understand what was happening."

"Why do you think she was transported?"

"We were at the docks with her."

"You and Evangeline?"

"Yes, and we have two brothers as well."

"My goodness."

"My mother's last words to me were to watch out for them but, of course, I was a child myself and I couldn't. She was taken onto a ship. She was crying; we were screaming. It was very hectic, very disturbing."

"I can't believe this," Aaron told him.

"After my mother was on board, we were separated."

"By who?"

"A man named Mr. Etherton. He might have been my father's clerk. Or maybe his lawyer or friend. I was never certain. There were some other people there too, but I don't remember who they were."

"Etherton..." Aaron mused. "He gave Evangeline his name. Why couldn't she have kept her own? You did."

"I have no idea. As I mentioned, it was so hectic, and I was so young. I hardly had a chance to say goodbye to them. Anne—Evangeline—was holding my hand, and she was jerked away from me."

Aaron gasped. "She dreams about that all the time. It haunts her."

"Really? Gad, it was so horrid. I ponder it constantly. Whenever I pass a blond woman on the street, I wonder if it might be her." He chuckled miserably and shook his head. "This explains why I liked her so much. Right from the start, I liked her. I even asked her once if we might have met before, but she was sure we hadn't."

"I'm stunned," Aaron said.

"So am I." Bryce leapt to his feet, and he glanced around the room as if he didn't know where he was. "I have to go to London."

"Now? It's so late. Let's go at dawn. We'd travel faster in the daylight."

"Aaron, I've been searching for her for over twenty years. I have to learn if she's with Florella. And Aaron?"

"Yes?"

"It appears you've ruined my sister."

Aaron's cheeks flushed with chagrin. "Oh, yes, it appears I have."

"Amends will have to be made."

"Such as?"

"I'll devise an appropriate compensation. Marriage, for instance?"

"I'm engaged to someone else, Bryce. That's been my problem from the beginning."

"Engagements can be broken."

"Sometimes they can. Sometimes they can't. We'll see which of those times this turns out to be."

"We definitely will."

Bryce hurried out as Aaron stood.

"If you're going to London," Aaron said, "I'm going too."

But Bryce was already dashing up the stairs to pack his bag.

"I suppose you could head to Summerfield."

"It's probably for the best."

Evangeline gazed at Florella. Except for a bruise on her cheek where Vicar Bosworth had slapped her, she was in fair condition. Florella had graciously offered to let her stay for a bit, but Evangeline grasped that the invitation wasn't permanent, that she had to make plans for herself.

They were having tea at a shop in London and discussing

Evangeline's future.

She was still trying to catch her breath. Everything moved so fast in the city. There were crowds and horses and carriages and noise. She couldn't steel her nerves so she didn't jump at every sound.

Too much had happened too rapidly. She was exhausted and overwhelmed, and though she was appalled to admit it, she was incredibly heartbroken. She'd never been in love, so she hadn't known it could end in such a grueling way. It had concluded so abruptly too. She couldn't figure out how to forge on in a stable and sane manner, but she had to.

"Didn't you tell me," Florella was saying, "that this friend at Summerfield, this Rose Ralston, never answered any of your letters?"

"I don't understand it. She's not the sort who would fail to respond."

"Precisely, so I'm worried she's suffered a mishap. You might journey north only to find she isn't there. Then what would you do?"

"I imagine I'd come back to London and search for Amelia."

"Your other friend?"

"Yes."

"The other one who never replied, so we can't guess what's become of her either, and I'm intimately acquainted with Lucas Drake. There's an excellent chance she's not married to him, so she could be anywhere and in any situation."

"Lord Run said they had married."

"Aaron *said* a lot of things, didn't he?"

Evangeline snorted with disgust. "He certainly did."

"Here's what I was thinking." Looking shrewd and sly, Florella peered at Evangeline over the rim of her cup. "Why leave London? I mean, Miss Cummings gave you funds so you're set for a few months. Remain here."

"And do what?"

"Sing. Act. Use your talents instead of hiding them."

Evangeline's pulse raced. "Sing?"

"Why not? You're so good. I'm positive you could support yourself."

"But...sing! My! I hadn't considered it."

"What is your other option? Will you beg Miss Ralston to let you live with her and her husband? Until when? Until he mentions that you've overstayed your welcome? You'd be like the proverbial poor relative, except you're not even kin to them. It seems awfully precarious."

"It would be embarrassing to impose—especially with their

being newlyweds."

"Quite right, Evangeline. Or perhaps you could return to teaching and have some old fusspot bossing you constantly. Could you bear it? Haven't you groveled and obeyed long enough?"

"I can't decide, Florella."

"Or you could track down Miss Hubbard and move in with her and Lucas Drake. You could sit on pins and needles, waiting for the day Aaron arrives for a visit to show off his bride. You could hear all about their wedding."

"Oh, my Lord, that would be the worst."

"It definitely would be."

"The world is spinning so fast," Evangeline complained.

"There's nothing wrong with that," Florella said. "It beats plodding away in some country village where no one notices you and you die of boredom. Wouldn't you like to stand out for a change? Don't tell me you haven't thought of it."

"Of course I've thought of it, but to actually *do* it! The prospect is terrifying."

"Why would it be? What if you're remarkable and all of London falls in love with you?"

Evangeline chuckled. "My whole life, I was scolded for my talent and grandiose ambitions. I was deluged with horror stories about girls who brazenly ran off to London. They always ended up wrecked and ruined."

"Not me. My path went in the precise direction I dreamed. Besides"—Florella flashed a perceptive grin—"you're wrecked and ruined anyway, and it occurred before you ever made it to London."

"Too true."

Evangeline flushed with shame.

In a moment of weakness, she'd confessed her liaison to Florella, but Florella had already been apprised. By Bryce. Luckily, Florella hadn't been shocked. She was used to women leading scandalous lives and having affairs. She was in the middle of one herself with Bryce.

"I have an idea for you," Florella said.

"What is it?"

"I asked a friend to listen to you sing."

"You didn't!"

"I did. If he likes you, you'll have work right away. And if you build up a following—which I'm sure you'll manage—your situation will improve very quickly."

"Meaning what?"

"He owns a gentleman's club so, occasionally, it can be a bit wild"—Florella waved a hand as if describing a pretty flower or hat—"but the customers are rich and top-lofty, and if they like you, anything is possible."

"I don't know," Evangeline said again.

"Why not try it?" Florella pressed. "What have you got to lose?"

"My reputation? My morals? My dignity?"

"You lost those when you crawled into bed with Aaron."

"Oh."

They stared for a minute, and Evangeline realized she was too weary to make such an important decision. She yearned to go somewhere quiet, to rest and regroup, but where would that be? To Rose at Summerfield? What if Evangeline traveled to the estate and Rose wasn't there? Then what?

Evangeline would be alone in a strange place, her funds swiftly dwindling.

Wasn't it better to find a job in London? Florella was a friend, and she'd arranged an audition. Shouldn't Evangeline be grateful? Shouldn't she agree?

Still though, it seemed wrong. She was tired and worn down by events. She was about to refuse, when Florella gulped the last of her tea and said, "Let's go."

"Where?" Evangeline inquired.

"To sing for my acquaintance. He's dying to meet you. No time like the present, is there?"

Evangeline dithered and debated, but Florella was so excited.

"All right," Evangeline murmured. "What could it hurt?"

"My feeling exactly."

"He might not even like me."

"I don't believe we'll have to worry about that."

Florella took Evangeline's arm and led her outside to their carriage.

"What in God's name were you thinking?"

Aaron glared at his father and retorted, "I could ask you the same. You're the one who sent Claudia and Priscilla to Fox Run. What did you suppose would happen when they arrived?"

"I *supposed* that the appearance of your fiancée would yank you back to your senses."

"It didn't."

"So I hear," Lord Sidwell snapped.

Aaron was in London, at his father's house—though why he bothered was a mystery. Each successive visit was more contentious.

They were in the drawing room, having a whiskey before Lord Sidwell traipsed off to his nightly entertainments. For once, Lord Sidwell was not glad to see Aaron, and Aaron wasn't glad to see his father.

He was brooding over Evangeline, over the mistakes he'd made, the choices he faced. The entire journey to London, he'd talked to Bryce, probing his memories of Evangeline when she was a little girl.

With Bryce suddenly popping up as Evangeline's brother, there were even more problems created.

"You humiliated Priscilla," his father complained, "insulted Claudia, gave Ignatius a thrashing—"

"He deserved it."

"In front of his mother. She'll probably harangue about it forever."

"Don't listen to her."

"She claims you wish to have him removed from his post as vicar."

"I've had enough of him—and Gertrude. They've prevailed on us one too many times, and Iggy has none of the traits required to be a minister. He has to go."

"And then—after you've offended practically everyone we know—you stumble to London and immediately begin nagging at me about your doxy."

At the slight to Evangeline, Aaron bristled. "If you call her a doxy again, I'll beat you to a pulp. If you'd like to risk it, we could write to Iggy and ask how it feels."

Lord Sidwell was aghast. "You'll *beat* me? Your own father?"

"Her name is Evangeline. Or you can use Miss Etherton if you prefer."

"Let me tell you something, Aaron—"

"No, let me tell *you* something, Father."

Aaron had reached his limit. He'd spent his life, ignoring his father's faults, ignoring the punishments Lord Sidwell had inflicted on Lucas, making excuses and convincing himself that his father had to be respected and obeyed.

But did he?

Aaron was exhausted from trying to please his father, which was nigh on impossible. Lucas had always said so. Lucas had always seen their father as he really was. Only Aaron had been blind. Only Aaron had refused to accept the truth.

He shoved himself to his feet. "I shouldn't have stopped by."

"Don't be ridiculous. Of course you should have. This is your home."

"No. I shouldn't be here. I'll stay at my club."

"You absolutely will not."

"I will, and after you hear me out, you'll want me to leave."

"What now? Don't you dare upset me more than you have

already."

"The past few days, I've had a lot of time to reflect."

"So have I," Lord Sidwell replied, "and I'm wondering why I had children. Why should I care if there's an heir to this bloody estate? After I'm dead, how can it matter?"

"I agree, so I'm not marrying Priscilla."

"You...what? You are marrying her! You are!"

"No. At Fox Run, I was confronted yet again with her genuine nature, and I simply can't proceed." He shrugged. "I'd say I'm sorry, but I'm not."

"You will wed her!" Lord Sidwell thundered. "You will, or I swear, you will be disinherited. You and your brother both! I will cut you out of my life and my will."

"That's fine with me, Father, and Lucas won't mind either. Besides, wasn't he previously disinherited? And as for myself, Fox Run is profitable, so it's an idle threat."

"You will not mention your scapegrace brother to me!" Lord Sidwell raged. "You will not be impertinent!"

"You're correct; I shouldn't be, so I'll just be going."

Aaron spun away, and Lord Sidwell's shouting ceased. His voice became cajoling.

"Aaron, wait," Lord Sidwell said. "Let's not quarrel."

"We're not quarreling."

"We have to talk. You're not thinking clearly. I believe Miss Etherton has driven you mad."

"No, I've been always insane, and I was pushed there by your vanities and posturing. She had nothing to do with it."

Panic flared in Lord Sidwell's eyes. "Aaron, listen to me. If you don't marry Priscilla, how will we repay the dowry? The money's gone."

"Whose fault is that, Father?"

Lord Sidwell had the grace to look chagrinned. Still, he puffed himself up. "If you cry off, Claudia will sue. She'll drag you through the courts. Your name will be ruined."

"This will come as a shock to you, Father, but we're not held in much esteem by anybody."

"You will not denigrate our ancestors," Lord Sidwell fumed.

"I'm not denigrating them. I'm merely telling you what people say. We're not that highly regarded, so if Claudia wants to ruin my *name,* she won't have to try very hard."

"You'll be shunned. You'll be a pariah."

"I don't care."

"You'll destroy *my* life."

"Poor you," Aaron sarcastically mused. "Instead, you'd like to destroy *my* life by shackling me to Priscilla."

"I've explained to you about having a bride like her. You'll live separately. You'll never have to see her. It will all work out."

"Yes, I suppose it could happen that way, except for one teeny, tiny thing."

"What is that?" Lord Sidwell asked.

"I won't accept such a dreary existence."

Aaron started out, and Lord Sidwell frantically called, "Aaron! Let's discuss this."

"No, I have urgent business to attend." Aaron had to find Evangeline, had to catch up with Bryce to learn if there was news from Florella.

"What could be more urgent than your wedding to Priscilla?"

"How about my wedding to Evangeline?"

Aaron's question fell between them so dramatically that Aaron might have shot off a gun.

"You will honor your betrothal to Priscilla!" His father was bellowing again.

Aaron sighed. He was weary and fatigued and couldn't abide his father for one more second. Respect be damned. Courtesy be damned. He was beside himself with worry for Evangeline, and he'd had enough of Lord Sidwell and his tirades.

Aaron was eager for something else, something better.

"You know what, Father? The greatest idea just occurred to me."

"What is it?"

"You claim Priscilla will be a terrific bride."

"She will. There's no finer girl for this family."

"If that's your opinion, why don't *you* marry her? You're a bachelor, and you're an earl already. She wouldn't have to wait to become a countess. I bet she'd jump at the chance."

"Me? Marry Priscilla?"

"Why not? You wouldn't have to fret about the dowry. You'd be free of your financial obligation to Claudia, and I'll be free of Priscilla—and you. Goodbye."

He walked out, and though his father screamed and yelled, Aaron kept on.

CHAPTER NINETEEN

"Thank you for allowing me to perform for you."
"You're welcome."
Evangeline smiled at the man seated in front of her. His name was Mr. Rafferty. She was up on a small stage, having just finished her audition. She'd done her best, but she didn't know what he thought. He simply studied her with a very critical eye, as if assessing her for many purposes besides singing.

As Florella had pointed out, it was a gentleman's club, and Evangeline didn't suppose it was a place she ought to seek employment. Florella had lived in London a long time, and she was used to a relaxed world where moral rules didn't apply.

The club was quite large, and there were dozens of tables for card playing, imbibing, and socializing. In the back, there were other smaller rooms, where high-stakes wagering was allowed. On a busy night, she imagined it would be loud and raucous. There were shelves filled with liquor decanters, so customers would likely become very inebriated. Could she tolerate it?

No.

The artwork on the walls unnerved her the most. There were paintings of nude women such as one might see in a bordello. The canvases were brightly colored, and the females posed in them seemed to glare at Evangeline and ask, *Why are you here? You don't belong.*

She couldn't agree more. Miss Peabody had to be rolling in her grave.

Mr. Rafferty came over and offered his hand to Evangeline to help her climb down.

"Could you start this weekend?" he inquired.
"So soon?"
"Florella was correct about you. You're amazing. You have a grand future in London."
"You're very kind." Evangeline's mind was reeling. How did she politely refuse without offending him? "I should speak to Florella. I'm not sure as to the salary I should request or the

logistics of your shows."

"Yes, by all means, speak with Florella, but she's a mercenary. Don't think you can demand a fortune. She knows what I pay, and I won't raise the amount. Not even for someone of your caliber."

"Oh, certainly not," Evangeline hastily concurred. "I wouldn't expect any special treatment."

His lewd gaze meandered down her torso. "I'd have to purchase some clothes for you."

Evangeline laughed, but with chagrin. "I apologize. My wardrobe is a bit drab."

"Yes, and my customers will expect gowns that are a tad more revealing. It will be an extra expense. I'll advance you the funds, but we'll have to take the cost out of your earnings. Florella can explain how it works." He paused and studied her even more intently. "Florella said you were new to London."

"Yes, it's my first visit to the city."

"So...you don't have any kin or acquaintances. You're all alone? There's no one to worry if you come home late?"

"No, no one at all. I'm staying with Florella—until I settle in. Then I'll be on my own."

"Florella is a gem, isn't she?" His meticulous scrutiny had her squirming, and he chuckled. "We'll have many roles for you to fill."

"I hope so."

"We'll discuss them all after you've talked to Florella. We'll decide where you'll fit in the best."

"I'll stop by again tomorrow. How about the same time?" she said, when in reality, she never planned to return.

"Yes, that fine."

Evangeline stepped away. He was hovering a little too close, and his nearness bothered her. Actually, everything about the establishment bothered her. Even though it was the middle of the day, there were several male customers scattered at the tables. They were drinking heavily and had listened to her performance. They were watching her in a fashion she couldn't abide—just as Mr. Rafferty kept watching her.

He seemed to be evaluating her for illicit purposes, but as Evangeline considered the possibility, she shoved it away. Florella was a friend, and she wouldn't have arranged a disreputable position for Evangeline. Would she?

"Is Florella back yet?" she asked him.

"No, but I expect her shortly."

After introducing Evangeline, Florella had scooted out, claiming she hadn't wanted her presence to distract from

Evangeline's singing. The theater where she worked was down the street, and she'd walked there, promising to be back in an hour.

"I'll wait for her in the foyer," Evangeline said. "If that's all right?"

He nodded and gave a slight bow, his disturbing eyes never leaving her as a maid escorted Evangeline out. She was holding Evangeline's cloak and bonnet.

Evangeline was anxious over the entire situation and wouldn't tarry inside. She'd stand out on the sidewalk, which wasn't the wisest idea either, but then it was three o'clock in the afternoon. What could happen?

But when they arrived in the foyer, the maid opened the door a crack so Evangeline could peek out. It was pouring rain, the street awash with a deluge. Would Florella be delayed? How long would Evangeline be trapped?

Her consternation must have shown because the maid said, "If you'd rather not dawdle here in the entrance, we have a nice parlor you could use."

Evangeline dithered, peeked out again. "I guess I should."

The maid led her down a dark hall and ushered her into a cozy salon. There was wine and cheese on a tray, a fire burning in the grate, a sofa in front of it.

The maid gestured for her to sit, and Evangeline smiled.

"This is lovely," Evangeline told her.

"Make yourself comfortable. I'll come for you the moment Miss Bernard returns."

"You're very kind."

The maid laid Evangeline's cloak and bonnet on a chair in the corner, then she left. Evangeline went to the table to grab a bite of cheese when—to her astonishment—it sounded as if the maid locked the door.

Evangeline frowned, positive she was mistaken. Tentatively, she tiptoed over and spun the knob, being greatly shocked when her worst fear was realized. She rattled the knob, pulled on it to be sure, but it was definitely locked. How bizarre.

She knocked and said, "Hello?"

She pressed her ear to the wood and listened for motion or footsteps, but there were none.

"What the devil?" she grumbled. She knocked again and called more loudly, "Hello? Hello? Is anyone there? I've been locked in."

Yet there was no answer, and no one hurried over to let her out.

Florella leapt out of her carriage, dashed through the rain, and banged on the door at Lord Sidwell's town house.

She probably shouldn't have stopped, and if Lord Sidwell strolled by and saw her, there'd be hell to pay. But she'd heard Aaron was in London. Bryce had traveled with him, but she hadn't crossed paths with either man, and she had to speak to one of them immediately.

She didn't know what else to do.

She'd delivered Evangeline to her audition, then had popped up the street to the theater where she was currently performing. She'd informed them her holiday had ended early, and she could get back to work.

When she'd returned to the club, Evangeline was gone. Rafferty claimed she'd dazzled him and had been offered a position—which she'd accepted. Then she'd departed, telling him she'd watch for Florella out on the sidewalk.

But Evangeline hadn't been there, and it had been pouring, so Florella couldn't imagine she would have stood out in the rain. As to Rafferty's story, Florella couldn't decide what she believed. She'd questioned him, but he'd been so bloody evasive.

Florella had been acquainted with Rafferty for years and considered him a friend, but no person in her world was truly a friend. Occasionally, there were rumors about him and how he treated the women he employed, but then there were rumors about everyone.

With Evangeline being at the club only a short time, Florella hadn't supposed she'd needed to warn Evangeline to be careful around Rafferty, but should she have? When Florella had scolded Rafferty for losing Evangeline, she'd been promptly escorted to the door.

Florella was growing desperate, and she banged the knocker again. The butler opened wide and waved her in. She practically fell inside, grateful to be out of the torrent. Rain dripped from her cloak and pooled at her feet.

"I am Miss Florella Bernard," she advised.

"I know you, Miss Bernard. I've seen you on the stage."

"Lovely." She flashed a wide smile. "I apologize for barging in, but it's vitally important that I talk to Lord Run. Is he available?"

"I'm sorry, Miss Bernard, but he's out."

"When do you expect him to return?"

"I really couldn't say."

"Drat it," she mumbled. "My mission is extremely urgent. Might I...leave him a note?"

"Certainly."

The man ushered her into a nearby parlor and led her to a writing desk. She sat and penned an explanation of her visit to

Rafferty, of Evangeline's disappearance. She begged Aaron to investigate for himself—starting with Rafferty—and to take Bryce with him. No doubt the two men would have more luck intimidating Rafferty than Florella had had.

She sealed the note, then handed it to the butler.

"Give it to him at once," she said.

"I will, Miss Bernard. The moment he's back."

"Thank you for your assistance."

"It's my pleasure."

He beamed at her as if she was a grand celebrity, and he escorted her out, actually opening an umbrella and following her to her carriage.

He helped her in, getting himself soaked in the process, and as her driver clicked the reins and the horse pulled away, he stood in place, transfixed, watching her go. She leaned out the window and blew him a kiss, and he grinned and was merrily waving as she rounded the corner and lost sight of him.

Her next move would be to stop by all the clubs and taverns where Bryce and Aaron might spend a cold, stormy afternoon. She'd leave messages everywhere. Hopefully, they'd receive one of them.

"Was that Florella Bernard?"

"Ah...yes."

Priscilla entered the foyer. She'd heard Aaron was back—her mother paid a Sidwell housemaid to tattle—so Priscilla had come to speak with him, but he'd been out. She'd asked to wait, and the butler hadn't known if it was all right, but he hadn't felt he could deny her request.

She'd been dawdling in a drawing room when she'd glanced out and had observed the notorious actress slinking in.

"She seems an odd visitor," Priscilla said. "Is she a friend of Lord Sidwell?"

"No...ah...Lord Run. She was looking for Lord Run."

"Too bad she missed him," Priscilla casually mused. "I'm sure she was disappointed."

"She was."

The butler was a bit dazed, perhaps from the rain on his clothes, or perhaps from his encounter with Miss Bernard. A lower sort of person—a servant for instance—might deem her to be splendid.

But as to Priscilla, it was the second time in a matter of days that she'd been standing under the same roof as the actress. It was such an outrage that she wanted to reach over, shake him, and complain, *How could you let her in the door when I am in residence?*

"If you'll excuse me, Miss Cummings?" he said.

"Oh, yes, of course. You must find a towel and dry yourself. I'd hate to have you catch a cold."

"Do you need anything?" he asked.

"No, no, I'm fine. You go on."

He tottered off as she peeked over at the table in the corner and saw a letter laying there. Since Priscilla had arrived, Miss Bernard was the only one to pass through. Had she written it to Aaron?

What gall! What nerve!

Priscilla scooped it up and took it into the parlor where a warm fire burned. She sat on the sofa and broke the seal. She probably should have felt guilty, but she didn't. If Aaron ever learned about the letter and that it hadn't been given to him, she'd be more than happy to implicate the butler.

Servants were scandalously unreliable, and he was getting older. It wouldn't be surprising if he'd forgotten to hand over an important piece of correspondence.

The words were penned in a tidy, feminine script, and as she read them, her temper soared to such an astonishing height she was amazed she didn't swoon.

Miss Etherton was in London? She'd vanished? Miss Bernard wanted Aaron to search for the blasted woman?

Priscilla absolutely would not permit him to shame her by chasing around the city, hunting for his missing concubine. Aaron would generate tons of gossip, and Priscilla would be a laughingstock.

"Sorry, Miss Etherton," she muttered, "but if you're having difficulty, no one will ride to your rescue—especially not my fiancé." She rose and went over to the fire. "Goodbye," she nastily said, "and wherever you are, good luck."

She tossed the letter into the flames, just as a male voice asked, "What are you doing?"

She jumped and whirled to see Aaron. She suffered a moment of terrifying panic, then she regrouped and forced a wide smile.

"Aaron, I didn't realize you were back."

"I repeat, Priscilla, what are you doing?"

He glowered at her, and she shrugged. "Waiting for you. I thought we could spend the afternoon together."

As he stomped over to her, she was aggravated to discover that the letter had hit the grate, that only a small portion of it had landed in the flames. Aaron stooped down and retrieved it, blowing on the spot where it had begun to burn.

"What were you saying about Miss Etherton?" he demanded,

the damning evidence dangling from his fingers.

"Ah...nothing?"

"I was directly behind you, Priscilla. You mentioned her very clearly."

"You're mad if you think so."

"Am I?"

"Yes. Why must you always be so horrid? Why must you always chastise and belittle me?"

But he was already ignoring her to read what Miss Bernard had written.

"Dammit," he cursed. "How did you get your filthy paws on this?"

Her first impulse was to deny and deny and deny, but saner instincts prevailed. "It was on the table in the foyer."

"So you assumed you could open it and read it?"

"I'm about to be your wife. You shouldn't have any secrets from me."

His eyes narrowed, his gaze growing angry. "And after perusing it, you felt I shouldn't be allowed to see it?"

"Why should I have to sit idly by while an actress visits you? When Miss Bernard arrived, I nearly fainted. She blustered in as if it was perfectly acceptable."

"As she's a friend of mine, yes, it's perfectly acceptable."

"Well, it's not acceptable to me! I had to endure her company for several minutes. If Mother knew, she'd just die!"

She paused, expecting an apology or empathy as to her plight, but her dramatic announcement had no effect whatsoever.

"Go home, Priscilla."

"What? No. It's raining, and we haven't talked."

"Trust me, we've talked plenty. Now go!"

"I won't."

He stormed over and clasped her arm, and he was pulling her down the hall as she dragged her feet and tried to refuse to depart. All the while, he was calling for the butler, for the servants, to fetch her cloak and bonnet, for her carriage to be brought to the door.

To her disgust, Bryce Blair was in the foyer, and when he saw her, he smirked and chided, "Look who's back—like a bad penny."

"I won't be insulted by the likes of you," she huffed.

"Too late," he blithely replied. "You already have been."

Mr. Blair said to Aaron, "Who let her in?"

"Believe me, she wasn't invited."

"I insisted we shouldn't have stopped by," Mr. Blair said. "May I please say, *I told you so?* Just once, can I say it?"

"Be silent, Bryce," Aaron snapped.

The butler rushed up, several servants dashing behind him, everyone in a dither over Aaron's irate shouting.

"Is there a problem, Lord Run?" the butler inquired.

"Miss Cummings is leaving," Aaron advised him, "and she is not to be permitted inside again."

There was a gasp of surprise, and the butler stammered, "I...understand, Lord Run. I didn't realize she was...ah..."

"It's all right." Aaron's gaze drifted over the assembled group. "You didn't know before, but you know now. If she ever manages to slither in again, I'll have your hides. Am I making myself clear?"

There was frantic nodding all around.

She leaned in and whispered, "Aaron, you're embarrassing me in front of the servants. If they watch you berating me, how will I ever earn their respect?"

"You don't need to earn their respect."

"What do you mean?"

"Tell your mother I'll be by tomorrow at noon to speak with her."

"About what?"

"I'll tell both of you then." He glared at the butler. "I want her out of here in the next thirty seconds. If her carriage isn't ready, she can wait out in the rain."

This elicited more gasps from the staff and had the butler stammering again.

"Yes, Lord Run...ah...yes, I'll see to it."

Aaron turned to Mr. Blair. "Evangeline is in trouble. Let's go."

He and Mr. Blair raced out.

CHAPTER TWENTY

"I have great plans for you, Evangeline."

"Would you call me Miss Etherton?"

"There's no need to be so formal, is there?"

Evangeline glared at Mr. Rafferty, wondering if he wasn't mad.

She'd been locked in the small parlor for hours. She'd paced and knocked and begged for help, but no one had passed by.

Rafferty had finally arrived, but a servant had swiftly barred the door behind him. He was grinning, trying to appear charming and unthreatening, which was impossible.

He was built like a pugilist, with broad shoulders and big hands, and his nose was crooked—as if it had been broken in a fight. He had a scar too, a dangerous looking one over his eye.

She was thirsty and starving, and the tray of wine and cheese was still on the table—mostly untouched. In the beginning, she'd poured herself a glass of wine, but after taking a few sips, she'd grown very dizzy, gradually becoming so disoriented that she suspected he'd drugged it.

She'd increased her pacing, had let her temper flare, had pinched and slapped and talked to herself, all in an effort to keep herself focused, to ward off any narcotic effect.

Had he hoped to render her unconscious? And then what? What was his scheme? Would he use her for illicit purposes? Sell her into slavery? In the desperate period she'd been secreted away, a thousand anxious scenarios had arisen. He had to be disappointed to find her hale and alert. What would he try next?

"I want to explain our procedures," he said.

"You don't have to explain. I'm grateful that you offered me a position, but I can't accept it."

He chuckled. "You're sassy, aren't you?"

She continued on as if he hadn't spoken. "I'm sure Florella is looking for me." Evangeline stepped to the door, acting as if she could simply stroll out. "She's probably frantic."

"Don't worry about Florella. I sent her packing, and she won't be back."

"Why would you do that?" Evangeline employed her most stern, schoolteacher's tone. "How am I to get home?"

"You *are* home."

"No. I'm not staying, Mr. Rafferty. I've been very clear."

"I've been very clear too. So...this is how it works."

"Mr. Rafferty! You're not listening to me."

"And you're not listening to me. We'll have a contract for five years."

"Five years!"

"Yes, and at the end of it, we'll review your status and earnings. I'll decide if I should renew."

"I don't mean to insult you, sir, but I truly believe you may be insane."

"Not insane. Not about you. You'll make me a fortune. I can feel it in my bones."

"I won't make you a bent penny. Now I must be going. I have to locate Florella."

"She thinks you walked out of here and suffered a mishap."

"Why would she think that?"

"Because I told her you left, and we hadn't seen you again. If she's searching at all—and I hate to tell you this, but she has a very short attention span—she's searching out on the street."

Evangeline pounded on the door. Quick as a flash, he yanked her away. His expression turned stony, any pretense of courtesy abandoned.

"You can't leave, Evangeline. Not until I'm through with you."

"And you can't keep me here. I'm engaged to be married. People will be alarmed over my disappearance."

He pointed to her hand—that had no ring on it. "You're engaged? Who is the lucky fellow?"

"Aaron Drake, Lord Run," she lied, figuring mention of an illustrious person would frighten him. "His father is Earl of Sidwell."

"I know George Drake. He owes me a fortune, and as to Lord Run, I could have sworn he was betrothed to Priscilla Cummings."

"He was," she blustered, "but he changed his mind and asked me instead."

"Really? I would guess you haven't a farthing to your name, while Miss Cummings is rich as Croesus, and Lord Sidwell is in debt up to his eyeballs. Why would Lord Run toss her over for the likes of you?"

Why indeed?

She'd never been a good liar, and her cheeks heated, a red

flush coloring them. Still, she persisted. "He'll be very angry if I'm harmed. *Very* angry."

Rafferty's lewd gaze swept over her. "If you were anything to him at all, he lifted your skirt a few times, which means you were naught but a bit of fluff, and his kind is all the same. He'll move on to his next doxy without a second thought."

She was quite sure his description was accurate. In fact, Lord Run was probably glad she'd fled. She'd brought trouble and drama into his life, when he detested both. He was probably celebrating, toasting himself for being shed of her so easily.

Who would miss her? Who would realize she'd vanished? No one knew when or how she'd left Fox Run. No one but Florella knew she was in London, and she was barely acquainted with Florella. Florella had no duty to search or worry.

If Evangeline met with a bad end, who would ever be apprised?

It was such a sad, sobering prospect. She'd always been alone, with Miss Peabody the closest thing she'd had to a mother, and Rose and Amelia her only friends. They'd never learn what had happened, and London would be the last place they would assume her to be.

Mr. Rafferty could perpetrate any foul conclusion, so she had to muster her wits and prepare to escape. He couldn't watch her every minute. He couldn't remember to lock every door and every window. The instant she had the chance, she would run away.

"I should like to write to Lord Run," she pompously announced—as if she had his London address and could contact him there.

"No, and let's get back to our arrangement."

"We shall never have an arrangement, Mr. Rafferty."

He ignored her and continued. "Have you done any acting?"

She'd performed in theatricals at school, but she'd never admit it.

"Acting? No. I'm a schoolteacher."

"I presume you're a virgin, or has Lord Run relieved you of your only valuable asset?"

It was such a rude remark that she actually tried to slap him. But he grabbed her wrist, stopping any blow.

"You're feisty." He seemed tantalized by the notion. "I like that. My customers will too."

"Let go of me."

She fought to jerk away, but he tightened his grip and drew her to him so their bodies were pressed together. She struggled to put space between them, but he was wiry and tough, humored by her paltry attempts.

"I'm eager to determine"—he was leering, smirking—"if I should have you first, or if I should keep you chaste and drive up the price."

"The price of what?"

"We'll sell your virginity to the highest bidder, Evangeline. Then, depending on your acting skills, we'll sell it over and over."

She wanted to laugh. Any innocence she'd ever possessed had been destroyed by Lord Run. There was no virginity to sell, but she didn't suppose she should mention it.

"I don't care what schemes you concoct for me," she seethed. "I will never willingly participate in any of them."

"You won't? Not even when you realize that—in five short years—you can walk away rich beyond your imagination. You can take your earnings and move to Paris or Rome. You can live like a prosperous, sophisticated lady."

"Because you speak of such a future so confidently, I assume you often cross paths with women who would salivate over such a fate. Unfortunately for you, *I* am not one of them."

She managed to free her wrist, and she pounded on the door again, calling for help.

He clamped a palm over her mouth and pulled her away. She wrestled and scratched as he dragged her toward the sofa, but she refused to end up there. She understood what would happen if she did.

She'd surrendered her virtue to Lord Run, and he was the only man who would ever enjoy the privilege. She certainly wouldn't offer similar license to a rapacious brigand like Rafferty.

They were at the sofa's edge, and he was trying to force her down. She clawed her fingernails down his cheek, and he roared with outrage, the injury imbuing him with extra strength. He picked her up and tossed her onto the sofa, and he fell on her as she wailed and bit at him—but to no avail.

She was crying, begging for assistance, her pulse booming in her ears. There was banging and shouting too, that seemed to emanate from out in the hall, and the noises matched the rhythm of her thundering heart.

Suddenly, there was a loud hammering and a crash and...

Mr. Rafferty was yanked away so swiftly and so violently he might never have been there. Evangeline was dazed, and she slid to the floor. She wanted to stand, but couldn't find her balance.

The melee was so confusing and occurring so fast. She couldn't figure out what had transpired or who had arrived. Eventually, she was raised to her feet, and as she pushed her hair out of her eyes, she was staring up at Lord Run.

You came for me! You came for me!

The joyful sentence rang through her mind, and she yearned to hurl herself into his arms, to gush over how glad she was to see him, to ask how he'd discovered where she was, but she was too stunned.

"Evangeline, are you all right? Tell me he didn't hurt you."

Before she could utter a word, Bryce Blair was there, and he shoved Lord Run aside.

"Evangeline?" he said more gently, and he retrieved her goddess statue from his pocket.

She frowned, not understanding why he had it, how he'd gotten it. Then...he said the strangest thing.

"Anne—you kept it all these years."

"What?" she forced out.

"I've been looking for you everywhere, Anne, and I finally found you. You're home now. You're safe."

"Anne...?" she murmured.

She peered up at him, and a wave of anguished memories flooded in. It had been such a frightening day, and she'd been so tiny she could barely walk. She'd gazed up into one face. She remembered one face.

Her older brother—had Bryce been his name?—telling her to never lose the statue, telling her he'd find her someday and know who she was because she had it.

"Bryce?" she tentatively asked, sounding very young and not like herself at all.

"Yes, Anne. It's me. Bryce."

Her eyes rolled back in her head, and she fainted dead away.

"Hello, Aaron. Thank you for being prompt."

Aaron nodded at Claudia, the woman who might have been his mother-in-law. He supposed he should have been suffering a flicker of emotion—regret, remorse—but all he could think was that he'd dodged a bullet.

Priscilla was seated in a chair in the corner, but she didn't greet him or display any sign that she'd seen him.

"Have you talked to Priscilla?" he inquired.

"Briefly," Claudia replied. "She mentioned you had another quarrel."

"A quarrel? Is that how she described it?"

"Yes, and as I've previously explained, you mustn't let a spat interfere with your wedding plans. All couples fight. It's practically expected, and you've both been under a lot of pressure."

"I'm not under any pressure. In fact, I've never felt better." He spun to Priscilla. "Tell your mother what you did."

"I did nothing," Priscilla retorted, "and I have no idea why you constantly snipe at me."

"That's what you claim?" Aaron scolded. "You did nothing?"

Priscilla turned to Claudia. "Mother, how many times is he allowed to berate me? Surely there's a limit."

Claudia studied Priscilla, Aaron, Priscilla again. Apparently, Aaron's angry countenance unnerved her for she said, "Priscilla, go to your room. I'd like to meet with Aaron alone."

"No," Aaron protested. "I want her to stay. She has to hear this."

Claudia sighed. "All right. What is it?"

"Yesterday, she visited while I was out. It was raining, and she asked the butler if she could wait for me. She was permitted to dawdle in a front parlor."

"And...?"

"I came in shortly after and discovered she'd stolen an important piece of correspondence that had been addressed to me. She was burning it in the fire."

"You retrieved it," Priscilla snottily said. "You're acting as if it was destroyed, but it was fine. I don't know why you're raising such a fuss."

Claudia scowled at Priscilla. "You tried to burn his correspondence?"

Priscilla was mulishly aggrieved, debating her response, and finally admitted, "It was a note from that actress who'd been his guest at Fox Run. That Miss Bernard? She was begging him to reestablish his affair with Miss Etherton!"

Claudia frowned at Aaron. "Is this true? Have you taken up with Miss Etherton again? How long were you parted from her? Two days? Three? You couldn't have delayed until after the wedding? Is your passion for her so unwavering that you would shame Priscilla like this?"

Aaron rippled with disgust. "Is that all you have to say, Claudia? Your daughter interfered in my private business, and she sits here boasting about it."

Claudia countered with, "You haven't answered my question. Are you involved with Miss Etherton again?"

"I never stopped being involved with her, and if I hadn't stumbled on your daughter with that letter, Miss Etherton would have come to great harm."

Claudia bit down whatever horrid remark she was considering, but Priscilla was too stupid to keep her mouth shut.

"I wish you'd never seen that letter. I wish she *had* been harmed."

A deadly silence settled in, with Aaron staring at Claudia, and

Priscilla fidgeting, realizing she'd crossed the line.

"I'm crying off, Claudia," Aaron announced, "and I won't change my mind. You and my father can't dissuade me."

"I understand," Claudia said, as Priscilla leapt to her feet and shrieked, "He can't cry off, can he, Mother?"

Claudia spoke to Aaron. "I warned you about what would happen. I'll sue to recoup my money, and I'll drag your name—and Miss Etherton's—through the mud. After I'm finished, there won't be a family or venue that will allow you in the door." She sneered as if she'd bested him in every way that counted. "Is that the future you envision with her?"

"Do what you will, Claudia. I don't care. As to Miss Etherton, she and I will retire to Fox Run, and I don't anticipate our ever returning to the city. However you smear us, it will have no effect."

On uttering the statement, Aaron tamped down a shiver of dread, feeling extremely anxious over what Evangeline's opinion might be.

After the imbroglio the previous evening, he hadn't had a chance to confer with her. Bryce had carried her out of the despicable place, leaving Aaron behind to clean up the mess. Since then, matters had been so hectic he hadn't had an opportunity to call on Bryce to see how she was faring.

It had taken all night to wade through the disaster at the club. Mr. Rafferty was in jail, charged with pandering and numerous other crimes. The upstairs of the establishment was a brothel, and Aaron had stumbled on a dozen females like Evangeline who'd come to London, hoping to work as an actress or a singer, but who'd been kidnapped by Rafferty and forced into prostitution.

Aaron had occasionally heard such stories floating around the city, but he'd never actually met anyone who'd participated or been ruined in such a scheme. Every time he thought of Evangeline and what might have happened if he and Bryce hadn't arrived, he shuddered with alarm.

The blasted woman couldn't be left to her own devices. She *had* to wed him. He wouldn't consider any other ending.

"You can't stay at Fox Run forever," Claudia said. "How will you ever visit London? *You* might be able to survive the shame of it, but Miss Etherton never will."

"Your threats are pointless, Claudia, and as to the money we owe, I suggest you discuss the issue with my father."

"Oh, I definitely will."

"For I will be happy to defend myself in a court of law. I can easily prove that none of the funds were paid to me and none of them were spent by me. I don't owe you a single farthing."

"We paid it to your father with the intent that Priscilla would be a countess. If you're refusing to proceed, we've been significantly damaged, so you bear an enormous amount of the blame."

"Well, Claudia, as I told my father, and I'm delighted to tell you. *He* is a bachelor and an earl. He can avoid legal difficulty by marrying Priscilla himself. There's no reason he can't. She can be a countess immediately; she wouldn't have to wait."

It took a moment for the import of Aaron's idea to sink in, and when it did, Priscilla raged, "Marry that horrid old sot? You're joking! I absolutely won't."

"Goodbye," Aaron said to Claudia, and as he walked out, she was staring at Priscilla, a shrewd, calculating gleam in her eye.

If Aaron had been a betting man, he'd wager Priscilla would be wed to his father very soon.

He grinned and kept on.

"But she's all right, isn't she?"

"Yes, she's fine. A bit shaken, but fine."

Bryce glared at Florella. She was trying to bluster her way in, but he was firmly blocking the door.

He lived in a suite of rented rooms. Since he was a bachelor who never entertained, he didn't need a grand residence. *She* lived in a lovely house—that he provided—but she always complained about it. Perhaps it was time for her to move on to the rich fellow she liked to brag she would eventually find.

"I wasn't in league with Rafferty, Bryce. You must know that."

"I can't decide what to think, except you should head home. We'll talk later."

"Promise you'll apologize to Evangeline for me."

"Her name isn't Evangeline. It's Anne."

"What?"

"Never mind. Just go away."

She couldn't oblige him though. "I thought it would be a great place for her to sing. She'd have earned a lot of money and built her prestige very quickly."

"She's new to London, which means she's a lamb among the wolves. You left her there alone with Rafferty."

"Only for an hour! How could I guess he'd kidnap her?"

"Don't claim you haven't heard the rumors about him, for I'll never believe you."

"Well, of course there have been rumors, but how would I know they were true?"

There was no need to respond to such a ridiculous comment.

He simply glowered until her cheeks flushed with shame, making it even more difficult to discern guilt or innocence.

"Go home, Florella."

"I'm afraid about Aaron. Is he angry with me?"

"You can ask him yourself next time you see him, but as for me, your house will be put up for rent. You should probably start packing."

"So we're through? Because of Rafferty? I had naught to do with it!"

"You can try to convince me tomorrow. Today, I can't listen to you."

He closed the door in her face and spun the key in the lock. Then he went back up the stairs to his sitting room. Anne—Evangeline—was coming out of his bedchamber. She'd been taking a nap, exhaustion seeming to be her constant state.

"Who was at the door?" she inquired.

"Florella."

"She didn't stay?"

"She was busy," he lied. "She just popped by to check on you."

He didn't have the heart to share his suspicions and maybe he was wrong. Maybe it had merely been a mistake on Florella's part to leave her naïve friend with Rafferty. Or maybe, she'd been counting on a reward from Rafferty for delivering such a pretty creature.

Florella had worked frantically to get Bryce to locate Evangeline, so she might not have been Rafferty's partner. Or Rafferty might have double-crossed her and refused to pay up, so Florella had turned on him. With Florella, it was hard to guess.

"I have to write to Rose and Amelia," Evangeline said.

"I met Miss Hubbard. Did I mention that?"

"No, you didn't."

"I liked her very much. She had Lucas Drake wrapped around her little finger. By the end, he didn't know up from down."

"I can't picture her as a vixen. She was always plain, ordinary Amelia to me."

"Trust me, that woman had flirtation skills you couldn't imagine. Lucas didn't stand a chance."

"I need to tell her and Rose where I am—if I can get a letter to them. I kept writing to them when I was at Fox Run, but I never received a reply."

"Very mysterious," he mused. "You don't suppose the servants stole them, do you?"

"Stole them? Why would they?"

"There might have been a thief among them who assumed you were sending secrets or money."

"The prospect never occurred to me, but it would make sense. Rose and Amelia weren't the type to ignore a letter."

"Will they be surprised you're in London?"

"Extremely surprised. They were expecting by now that I was glumly wed to Vicar Bosworth."

"Perish the thought! If there is one silver lining to this debacle, it's that you were smart enough to skedaddle out of that engagement."

"Yes, I'd have been an awful vicar's wife."

"I wouldn't condemn any poor girl to being Iggy Bosworth's bride."

Bryce gave a mock shudder that made her laugh, and at the timbre in her voice, he was taken aback. From the moment they'd arrived home, she'd been stirring long-buried memories he'd forgotten.

He'd been five when his mother had left, and he had fleeting visions of her that he kept tucked away in his mind as if they were precious treasures locked in a box.

When he'd last seen her, she'd probably been the age Evangeline currently was—twenty-five—and as he studied Evangeline, it seemed as if his mother had waltzed into the room. They could have been twins.

"Tell me more about our parents," she said as she snuggled herself on his sofa.

"Mother was an actress and singer and, obviously, you inherited her talent."

"I'm happy to hear it."

"I've often wondered if she wasn't quite renowned."

"Why do you think she was?"

"It just seems to be true."

"Have you ever checked old newspapers or asked about her at the theaters."

"No."

"Why not?"

He shrugged. "I was afraid."

"Of what you'd learn?"

"No." He chuckled and shook his head. "This will sound silly."

"Just say it."

"That terrible day, I was warned not to boast about who I was. I carried that worry inside me—that no one should know. It's pathetic to still be rattled by it all these years later."

"It was a traumatic experience for you."

"Very traumatic."

"Why would my name have been changed but yours wasn't?"

"I have no idea."

She smiled his mother's smile. "But no brigand from your past ever came to haunt you?"

"No. I haven't encountered a single brigand."

"Who was our father? Do you remember him?"

"He was very dashing, very charming. I don't believe he lived with us though. He'd show up out of the blue and it was always exciting."

"Why was he away so much? Might he have been a soldier or a sailor?"

"He had two very fancy pistols on a belt. When he arrived, he would lock them in a cabinet in mother's bedchamber."

"Where was our home?"

"Here in London, but I don't recall the area."

"And our brothers? You've searched for them?"

"Not really. There were no clues to go on. Don't forget, I was five when it happened."

"I want to find them," she vehemently said.

"I definitely agree, but you shouldn't get your hopes up."

"I won't, but we have to try. For our mother maybe. I feel as if she's watching us. Don't you?"

He flushed, deeming it a ludicrous admission. "Yes, it appears she's been lurking about recently."

"If it takes my whole life, I have to locate them. I've always been alone, and I hate to imagine them being alone too."

"There's an attorney who used to come to my school to check on me. I don't think I was supposed to realize he was visiting, but another boy eavesdropped when he was in the dean's office. He was a portly old fellow named Thumberton."

"I know him! He was Miss Peabody's solicitor."

"We should contact him and schedule a meeting."

"He's very crafty," she said. "He might have been sworn to secrecy."

"We'll wear him down." Bryce glowered—as if he could be fierce and threatening. "We'll make him talk."

She laughed again, and he thought he might jest with her constantly merely so she'd keep laughing his mother's laugh.

Someone banged the knocker down on the street below. He employed a cook and two footmen, but they didn't live in, so he had no one to greet callers. He went down himself.

As he pulled the door open, he was irked to see Aaron, but then he'd been expecting Aaron all day. Bryce just hadn't determined how he would handle his friend.

They'd known each other a long time, but all of a sudden, Bryce had a family, that being his sister. His relationship with her trumped everything.

"I'm sorry it took so long to arrive," Aaron said. "The entire mess at Rafferty's club was a boondoggle."

"I received your message. He's in jail?"

"Yes, and the club is closed. I'm investigating to learn the identities of the investors, and when I do, they'll be persuaded not to start it up again. I intend to have Rafferty transported. He shouldn't be allowed to hang around London and commit further mischief."

"My feeling exactly."

Aaron moved as if to come inside, but Bryce blocked him as he had Florella.

Aaron frowned. "What's wrong?"

"I think you should go away."

"Go…away? No! I have to see Evangeline."

"I'd rather you didn't."

"Don't be ridiculous," Aaron huffed. "Let me in."

"No."

They engaged in a staring match that was odd for them, and typically Bryce would have backed down. He hated to quarrel as much as Aaron but—even before he'd discovered Evangeline was his sister—he'd thought Aaron had behaved very badly toward her. With their kinship revealed, he was even more incensed.

"You can't talk to her," Bryce said.

"Don't be an asshole."

"What were you planning to say? Were you planning to explain again how you'd like to buy her a house and set her up as your mistress?"

"No, you idiot. If you must know, I'm here to propose."

Bryce scowled. "Marriage?"

"Yes, marriage. What other kind of proposal is there?"

"Well, there are plenty of illicit ones—as you've so deftly indicated."

"Get out of the way," Aaron snapped.

"No."

Aaron blew out an exaggerated breath. "Bryce, what is your problem? I demand to speak with her."

"No."

"Ask her if she'll see me. Let *her* decide if we chat or not."

"No. *She* doesn't get to decide. She has a brother now, so she has me to look out for her interests."

"Really?" Aaron scoffed. "How will you?"

"By keeping her away from libertines and cads such as yourself. Go home to your fiancée, Aaron."

"I don't have a fiancée. I cried off."

"Bully for you." No emotion showed in Bryce's expression.

He was delighted that Aaron had come to his senses, but he didn't suppose for a second the betrothal was off permanently. There was too much money at stake, and Lord Sidwell was a master at coercing Aaron.

"I'm not marrying Priscilla," Aaron insisted. "I'm marrying Evangeline."

"So you've said. Are you claiming that—in twenty-four short hours—you dumped one fiancée and are ready to glom on to a different one?"

"Don't be smart. I love Evangeline. I have from the moment I met her."

"I don't believe you."

"You don't...*believe* me?"

"No."

Aaron leaned in and shouted, "Evangeline! Would you come down here please?"

They both waited, and Bryce was relieved that Evangeline didn't appear.

"There's your answer, Aaron. She doesn't wish to speak to you."

"Well, *I* wish to speak with her."

"You'll have to convince me that I should permit it."

"Permit it?" Aaron grabbed Bryce by his shirt and shook him. "Listen to me, you stupid prick, I intend to wed her, and you can't stop me."

"Is that right?" Bryce coolly replied.

"Yes. She'll be mine and no one else's."

"I'm fully aware of every low, conniving deceit you perpetrated against her."

"And I'm sorry for it!"

"Are you?" The question hung in the air between them, and Bryce pushed Aaron away and stepped back. "I might allow you to propose someday. I *might*. But you'll have to prove you're worthy of her."

"You ass!"

"Prove you're worthy, Aaron. Then you can sniff around her. If you dare."

Bryce slammed and locked the door, then he sprinted upstairs so he wouldn't have to hear Aaron sputtering and fuming out on the stoop.

CHAPTER TWENTY-ONE

"Home sweet home."

Evangeline gazed outside her carriage window at Miss Peabody's old school.

Though her mother had given her the name of Anne, she didn't remember being anyone but Evangeline and didn't think of herself as Anne.

From Bryce's stories, it was clear she had once lived with her mother and brothers in a house in London, but she didn't recollect any of it. She recalled only the school—and stern Miss Peabody who'd run it.

In light of all the horrid things that could have happened to her, she supposed she'd been lucky. She'd been safe, had been fed and clothed and educated. She'd had Rose and Amelia as her friends.

But she was curious as to who had arranged for her to be brought to the school, who had paid her tuition year after year. And someone had paid it, or Evangeline wouldn't have been allowed to remain. Miss Peabody had been a strict businesswoman. There had always been girls who were expelled because their parents were in arrears.

Evangeline's biggest question was why Miss Peabody had kept her as a teacher. Miss Peabody hadn't really liked Evangeline— Evangeline had never been able to act as Miss Peabody demanded—so they'd constantly butted heads. Their personalities had been too dissimilar, and with Evangeline having been engaged to Vicar Bosworth, she wondered if Miss Peabody's dislike hadn't actually risen to the level of hatred.

So it made no sense that Miss Peabody had offered employment to Evangeline, and Evangeline assumed Miss Peabody had been forced or bribed—probably by the mysterious Mr. Etherton—to retain Evangeline. Why?

She was desperate for answers and had been trying to schedule an appointment with Attorney Thumberton, but he was away from his office on a trip to Scotland and wouldn't return for several weeks. When he did, she and Bryce intended to sit down with him and have a long talk.

The carriage door was opened, the step lowered, and a footman helped her climb out. Once she was standing on the ground, she suffered an attack of vertigo that was so virulent she visibly swayed, and the footman grabbed her arm to steady her.

She'd been so dizzy lately, the feeling sweeping over her at the oddest moments. Occasionally, she was nauseous too—especially in the mornings—and her burgeoning malady was alarming. Her body seemed to have been altered, her internal anatomy different in ways she couldn't describe. What could be causing it?

Though she pretended to be hale and healthy, her symptoms were so severe that Bryce had noticed she was ailing. She couldn't hide her condition.

"Are you all right, Miss Etherton?" the footman asked.

"Yes, I'm fine. I'm just overwhelmed by the trip. I grew up here, and I'm glad to have this chance to visit."

A foolish rush of tears flooded her eyes. It was so comforting to be back.

Since she'd left, nothing good had transpired. Well, that wasn't precisely true. She'd met Bryce, so details of her past had been revealed. But those two events couldn't dispel the overarching impression of calamity.

Her teaching career had ended. Her engagement had been a disaster. She'd fallen in with bad company. She'd leapt into an affair with a scoundrel. She'd ruined herself and nearly been enslaved by a kidnapper. If Bryce and Lord Run hadn't found her, there was no telling where she'd be. Certainly not at Miss Peabody's school and eager to be hired as a teacher again by the new owner.

The interview had come as a huge surprise. Rose and Amelia had corresponded with her about it. They'd previously been told that the new owner wouldn't use the property as a school, that he planned another enterprise entirely. Now, apparently, he'd changed his mind. He was picking teachers and staff, getting ready to advertise for students.

Evangeline had been loafing in London, writing letters of introduction, searching for a post as a governess, which was about as boring a job as she could imagine.

Bryce insisted she could stay with him, but she wasn't a child and didn't need her brother watching over her like a nanny. And while she hadn't asked Bryce about his finances, she suspected he earned his living by gambling and sporadic work in the theater. He wasn't Lord Run, wasn't rich and prosperous, so he couldn't afford to have a lazy, indolent relative move in.

"Shall we wait for you, Miss Etherton?" the footman inquired.

"Would you please? This should take an hour or so. If it looks like it might be longer than that, I'll send someone out to apprise you."

He and the driver nodded, and she went inside, reflecting on how grand it was to be thinking about the future—instead of lamenting the past.

During her sojourn in London, she'd deliberately avoided hearing any news. Was Lord Run married to his precious Priscilla? Evangeline hoped he was and that he was miserably unhappy. It was a petty sentiment, but she couldn't set it aside.

He'd stopped by once, had made that one paltry attempt to see her, but Bryce had chased him off, and he hadn't bothered to return. His lack of interest disconcerted her. She thought his vanity would have spurred him to try again. Had their liaison been that meaningless to him? Had she been so inconsequential?

Yes. Obviously, it had been incredibly easy for him to let her go, and she had to accept that fact, galling though it was.

Well, she'd definitely learned her lesson. If she had any opinion about Lord Run, it was that he'd opened her eyes to the wickedness of the world. As any preacher could explain—Vicar Bosworth could probably write a book on the subject—the cost of sinning was very high, and she'd never be able to fully repay what she owed.

She had vowed to herself that she would spend the rest of her life doing good deeds and helping others. Maybe by the time she was a very elderly matron, she'd have squared her accounts.

In the main foyer, she smiled to see extensive remodeling was occurring. Walls had been painted. Wallpaper had been torn down and replaced. The colors were brighter, the ambiance livelier.

A maid hustled up. She was wearing a pristine black dress, a crisply-starched white apron. She appeared professional and well trained, which was encouraging. Evidently, competent people were being hired. Would Evangeline ultimately be one of them?

"Miss Etherton?" the girl asked.

"Yes, I'm here for an interview."

"We've been expecting you. If you'll come this way?"

Evangeline wanted to say, *You don't need to escort me. I know where the office is.*

Yet she simply tagged along, peeking into each room as they passed. Clearly, the new proprietor was very wealthy. There would be no lectures about scrimping and saving, no nagging to conserve and use less. Why, there would likely be plenty of coal for fires in the winter, and no one would have to wrap up in blankets and shawls to ward off the cold.

She was delivered to the headmistress's office and told to wait. As she sat in the chair by the desk, it seemed as if she'd never left, and any second Miss Peabody might stroll in.

The door opened behind her, and before she could turn around to see who'd entered, a familiar male voice said, "Hello, Miss Etherton."

Scowling, she froze. She recognized that voice. It sounded like...Aaron Drake. But Aaron Drake was on his honeymoon. Or perhaps by now, he was at Fox Run with his bride. The very last place he would be was at Miss Peabody's school.

Alarmed, she glanced over her shoulder and blanched with shock.

"Lord Run?"

"Yes, hello."

He was more handsome than she recalled. His hair was longer, as if he'd been too busy to visit his barber. It was pulled into a short ponytail, tied with a black ribbon, which gave him an air of a bandit or highwayman. He was casually attired, tan breeches, knee-high black boots, and a flowing white shirt that was partially unbuttoned at the front to reveal a bit of his chest.

A memory assailed her, of her palms running across that smooth flesh, and she pushed it away and leapt to her feet. She was suffering from an absurd yearning to throw herself into his arms but from an even more pressing need to race out of the room.

"What are you doing here?" she demanded.

"I'm preparing to interview you. Isn't that why you've come? To see if I'll hire you?"

"No, that can't be right."

"Why can't it be?" He gestured to her chair. "Sit, sit."

"I don't think I should."

He passed by very close, and she lurched back so her skirt wouldn't brush his legs. He'd always had a potent effect on her. She'd never been able to dawdle in his presence and behave like a normal, prudent person. She could smell him and feel his bodily heat. There was an aura around him, an essence of some sort that drew her like a magnet.

She was terribly afraid that—should he snap his fingers and suggest they start in again—she'd jump at the chance.

Was she mad? Had she no sense? No shame?

Her knees were quaking so hard, she truly thought she might collapse. She slid down onto her chair, reeling, perplexed, stunned beyond measure.

He seated himself at the desk, flashing a grin that was a tad smug. "It's marvelous to see you again, Miss Etherton."

"I can't say the same."

"Can't you?"

"No."

"Where is your sunny smile?"

"I left it in London."

"That's too bad. I was hoping you'd brought it with you."

Though the notion was ridiculous, it appeared he was flirting with her. Why would he? Was he about to proposition her? Would he play such a cruel jest? She wouldn't put anything past him. She'd assumed she was seeking an offer of genuine employment. Was she about to be offered another situation entirely?

"I asked you what you were doing here," she tentatively began. "I haven't received an answer."

"I bought the school."

"*You* bought it?"

"Not originally from Miss Peabody. Some other fellow did, but there was a death in the family and a bankruptcy. Nasty business. He suddenly had no money, so I swooped in and grabbed it. You wouldn't believe the low price I managed to negotiate."

"I didn't realize you were interested in education, Lord Run."

"I wasn't, but I spent the summer crossing paths with schoolteachers. You. Rose Ralston. Amelia Hubbard. It seemed like a sign."

"A sign of what?"

"That perhaps I should branch out."

"By purchasing a school?"

"Why not? It's a good investment. If I can find the right people to work for me, I'll be all set."

"Will you?" she coolly retorted, wishing she was anywhere else in the kingdom but trapped in a room with him.

"I'm betting you'll turn out to be exactly who I need."

Confusion rocking her, she frowned. "Aren't you a bit...*busy* for all this?"

"Why would I be busy?"

"With your wedding and your honeymoon and your bride." Her expression grew lethal. "By the way, how is married life treating you?"

She'd rather have cut off her tongue than mention any of it but, apparently, she was still smarting over how he'd tricked and deceived her.

"Haven't you heard?" he asked.

"Heard what?"

"I didn't marry Priscilla."

She gasped aloud. She couldn't hold it in. "You didn't?"

"No, and any minute now, I'm expecting to learn whether my father has agreed to wed her instead."

"Your father?" It was the strangest news ever. "Is he...was he...involved with her?"

"No, he just harangued so vociferously about what a terrific wife she would be that I finally told him—if he thought she was so grand—he should marry her himself."

"I see," she mumbled though she didn't *see* at all.

"Besides, her mother had paid a substantial part of the dowry, and my father squandered it and hasn't the funds to pay it back."

"Oh."

"It was the best resolution for them *and* for me."

"How could it be?"

"Claudia's goal was for Priscilla to be a countess someday. If Priscilla weds my father, she won't have to wait. She'll be a countess immediately, and *I* shall be free to do whatever I want."

"What is it you want to do?"

Again, she could have kicked herself rather than inquire, but she was so curious about how the whole debacle had unraveled. Due to his determination to marry Miss Cummings at all costs, he'd misled and betrayed Evangeline. He'd insisted the only role she could ever fill was an illicit one.

But now, he'd walked away from his betrothal? Now he was eager for his father to wed Miss Cummings? It made no sense.

He pulled some papers from a drawer, and he glanced through them, as if checking his notes. Then he studied her, looking smug again.

"Just so you know," he said, "I've discussed this with your brother. He's completely amenable."

"He's aware you're the owner and I'd be talking to you?"

"Yes, but then he and I have been friends since we were boys. We rarely have secrets from one another. Initially, he was opposed, but I wore him down. He's totally fine with it."

"Fine with what?"

"With this interview. What would you suppose?"

It occurred to her that Rose and Amelia had notified her about the job opening. They had both written and urged her to apply. Had they known he'd bought the school? Had they known—if she was hired—she'd be working for him? Why would they have humiliated her in such a way?

"What about Rose and Amelia?" she inquired. "Were they in on it too?"

"Absolutely. When I approached them, they were happy as larks."

"You spoke to them about me?"

"Yes, so you see, Miss Etherton, practically all of your close acquaintances have agreed this should happen."

"Well, Lord Run," she caustically replied, "they aren't as familiar with your character as I am. In this instance, they may not be the best judges."

"Yes, but your brother knows me inside and out. After I explained myself and my plan, *he* was ecstatic."

"Was he?" she muttered.

"Would you call me Aaron?" he suddenly requested.

"It wouldn't be appropriate."

"You used to think it was all right."

"That was before. This is now."

He grinned again and sat up straight, his elbows on the desktop. "Where were we?"

"We were about to begin our interview, but I must tell you that—whatever the salary—I don't want the job."

"Are you certain?"

"Quite certain."

"Let's read through a few of the requirements, shall we? Listen to them, and then you can decide if you feel you're qualified or not."

"If I'm...qualified?" she fumed. She'd had a stellar education at Miss Peabody's school, and she'd been a teacher for eight years. How dare he impugn her abilities!

"I'm offering a lifetime position," he said.

"Lifetime?"

"Yes, and I'm seeking a person who has very special, very unique talents."

"What are they?"

"I wrote them down so I wouldn't forget." He picked up a piece of paper and recited from a long list. "She has to be loyal and faithful. Kind. Merry. Generous, lively, and rambunctious. She must fill my halls with singing and music and laughter."

It was the most peculiar list ever. "So...you're hiring a music teacher?"

"Oh, much more than that. I insist on having someone who can charm the servants, charm the neighbors, and make friends wherever she goes."

"You want *charm*? In a teacher?"

He ignored her and continued. "I need someone who will overlook my faults, who will scold me when I need it, but praise me when I deserve it. I need someone who will stick by me and support me and make me the man I was always meant to be."

He was smiling, his gaze warm and affectionate, and she squirmed in her seat, not certain what to think.

"I don't understand this at all," she mumbled.

"And of course, she must be extremely beautiful, the most beautiful woman in the whole world."

She was even more confused. "Beautiful?"

"In other words, Miss Etherton, I need a candidate who is amazing and stunning and remarkable in every way. Do you know anyone like that?"

It took a moment for her to catch up. "Me? You're talking about me?"

"Yes."

He'd rendered her speechless. She gaped at him, and he stared back, then pushed to his feet and rounded the desk. She should have used it as her chance to run out as she should have from the minute he'd arrived, but she was paralyzed with indecision.

He kept coming until he was directly in front of her, and he braced his palms on the arms of her chair. She was trapped, and they were eye to eye, nose to nose.

"I love you, Evangeline."

"What?"

"I love you. I have from the very first."

She shook her head with dismay. "No, no, that's not true."

"It is. You know it is."

"You were lying! I was a trifle to you, a dalliance."

"No, Evangeline, I loved you, but I was a fool. I listened to my father and told myself I had to behave as he would behave, as my peers would behave, as my friends would behave, as every aristocrat in the kingdom would behave. But guess what I realized?"

"What?"

"I want to be happy, and *you* make me happy. Will you marry me?"

"What?" she said again.

She felt as if she'd stepped into a strangely altered universe where everything was backward. The earth seemed to have tipped off its axis, and she was positive—should she try to stand—she'd topple over.

"Will you marry me?" he repeated.

"I could have sworn you just proposed."

"I did. Say *yes*. Say you'll have me."

"*Have* you? Are you insane?"

"Yes, probably."

"You can't be serious. A few weeks ago, you were betrothed to someone else."

"A minor mistake, I assure you."

"Minor? You were engaged for an entire year."

"Yes, and I didn't recognize how miserable I was until I met you."

He fell to one knee and took her hand. "I was awful to you. I lied and deceived and hurt you, but I'm so sorry. Can you forgive me?"

"Well...yes, I suppose."

She was stumbling for words, for rational thought. She simply wanted to dash out of the room and get away from him. When he smiled at her like that, she couldn't think clearly.

"You told me once," he said, "that you loved me too. Don't you love me still? You'll never convince me all that sentiment has vanished."

"I don't know, I don't know," she wailed. She was so befuddled, so perplexed.

"After you left Fox Run, I kept telling myself I should be glad you were gone, that you'd made things easy for me. But since then, it's dawned on me that I can't live without you."

"You're being absurd, and I won't put up with this."

She shoved him away and jumped out of the chair, but she couldn't force herself to leave. She leaned on the wall, her back braced to hold herself steady.

"Why buy this school?" she asked. "Why bring me here?"

"I've been talking to Rose and Amelia. They explained how you were never allowed to sing, how you were never allowed to show off your talent."

"No, I wasn't. Miss Peabody never liked me to. She always admonished me for flaunting myself."

"I'm aware of how exceptional you are, and I can't imagine what those years must have been like."

"It was very difficult."

"You can guarantee it never happens to another girl. You can reopen the school and focus on music and writing and art and theatrics. You can encourage and mentor girls and furnish them with the chance to shine that you never had."

Her pulse was racing. It was such a dear, considerate idea. An academy for girls who liked to sing and perform and act in theatricals! A place where they wouldn't be chastised, where their abilities could be fostered and praised!

Her initial reaction was to graciously decline, but she simply couldn't.

"I would like that," she quietly said.

"Good. I was hoping you would. I'm giving you the school—as a gift."

"What? No. I could never agree to such an expensive present."

"No matter what ultimately transpires between us, it will be yours, but I'm asking—no, again I'm *hoping*—that you will accept it as your bride gift from me, as your loving, devoted husband."

She started to tremble so violently she could barely remain on her feet.

He came over to her and dropped to his knee again, took her hand in his again. He looked up at her, his beautiful blue eyes warm and pleading and seductive.

"Bryce told me an interesting detail about you."

"What was it?"

"Since you've been staying with him, you're constantly dizzy and nauseous."

She scowled, irked that her brother had tattled about her private business. "Yes, I have been unwell."

"I don't know much about female bodily conditions, but I know something you apparently don't."

"What?"

"You're exhibiting the classic signs of a woman who's increasing."

"Increasing?" At first, she didn't understand. Then she blanched with alarm. "Increasing with a child?"

"Yes, I believe that's where we've ended up on this odd journey."

"A child? A baby?"

She couldn't wrap her head around it, couldn't figure out how she was supposed to feel. A tiny glimmer of joy simmered inside her, and she couldn't tamp it down.

"So you see, Evangeline, it occurs to me that you're in dire need of a husband, and you need one right away." He grinned. "I'm going to ask my question again, and don't you dare say *no*."

She scoffed. "You're being ridiculous. I'm not even sure you *like* me."

"Now that, my darling, Evangeline, is where you're wrong. I love you, and if you'll be my wife, I will be happy until my dying day." He squeezed her hand. "Give me your answer. Will you marry me?"

"I don't know!" she wailed again.

"Blasted woman!" he scolded, but he was laughing. "How can I convince you?"

"It's happening so fast. I thought I was applying to be a teacher."

"You *are,* you silly goat. You will teach me to be a better man."

"Oh, Aaron..." It was so hard to resist him, so hard to refuse him.

"Fill my life with music, Evangeline. Rattle the rafters of my home. Sing and play and dance. Do it all for me, for if you won't, how will I go on without you?"

Behind him, the door opened, and she glanced over, stunned to see Bryce entering. To her astonishment, Rose and Amelia were with him too.

"Have you asked her?" Bryce said to Aaron.

"Yes, but she won't agree to have me." Aaron stood and shrugged. "Maybe you can talk some sense into her. I certainly can't."

Rose and Amelia came over, and they both gave Evangeline tight hugs that had tears flooding into her eyes and dripping down her cheeks. She had a thousand questions for them. When had they arrived? What scheme had they hatched with Aaron? What was their part in all of it?

But there would be time to pose them later.

"What's the problem, Evangeline?" Rose said.

"I'm afraid he doesn't mean it."

Aaron huffed with offense. "Not mean it? Me? Not mean it?" He peered over at Bryce. "We've been friends for twenty-five years, Bryce. Have you ever once known me to be insincere?"

"No, never." Bryce paused, then added, "Well, except at Fox Run when you were still engaged and you pretended to...ah...never mind."

Amelia asked Evangeline, "Do you love him?"

The room was silent, everyone on pins and needles for her response.

She gazed at Aaron, and he was smiling at her with such affection. She recalled those exhilarating days at Fox Run where she'd been so elated she'd often felt she might simply burst from trying to hold it all in. If she wed him, if she had him for her husband, she could have that sort of bliss forever.

Could she deny him? No.

"Yes, I love him so much I'm dying with it."

"Now we're getting somewhere," Aaron grumbled.

Rose laid a palm on Evangeline's tummy and said, "I've heard there might be some need to hurry."

"That's what he told me," Evangeline replied. "I hadn't realized it."

Bryce puffed himself up. "I've only just learned I have a sister, so I'm not very good at this yet, but if you think I'll allow you to trot around the countryside—with child and without husband—you're mad."

Evangeline chuckled as Aaron gently shoved Rose and Amelia away. He took her hands and said, "I'm asking you again, Evangeline—in front of your friends and family. You'd better give me the proper answer."

"Go ahead, Aaron," she murmured.

"Will you marry me and make me the happiest man alive?"

She delayed to study her surroundings. She wanted to imprint all of it in her memory so she would never forget a single detail.

Aaron grew impatient and shook her. "Evangeline! Will you?"

She laughed. "Yes, I will."

Bryce muttered, "About damn time."

Aaron ignored Bryce and inquired, "Will you have me right away? You won't make me wait, will you?"

"No, I won't make you wait."

"Because—in case I convinced you—I brought a Special License."

"You brought a Special License? You were awfully confident you could wear me down."

"I wasn't taking any chances. I couldn't let you ponder the situation or you might have changed your mind."

"I won't ever change my mind."

"Are you sure?"

"Very sure."

"We could hold the ceremony here at the school," he advised her. "Tomorrow. I already found a preacher."

She grinned at Rose and Amelia, at her brother. "What is your opinion? Does tomorrow sound like a good day for a wedding?"

"It sounds like a grand day," her brother said.

"Then *yes,* Aaron Drake, Lord Run. I would be delighted to marry you tomorrow."

"Wonderful, Evangeline. Absolutely wonderful."

EPILOGUE

"Does it seem as if everything has gone horribly wrong?"

Aaron glared at his brother, Lucas. "We're about to walk out to the altar so I can speak my vows. Why would you ask that?"

"We were bachelors. All of us." Lucas gestured to himself, to Aaron, then to his friend, James Talbot. "What happened?"

Aaron had assumed they'd hold the ceremony at the school but, ultimately, Evangeline had settled on the local church in the village. James and Lucas had ridden in to join their wives, Rose and Amelia. They were in a small room behind the altar. The two men would stand up with Aaron, and the two women would march down the aisle with Evangeline.

James scowled. "Yes, it's extremely peculiar that we're all suddenly married, isn't it? Maybe we were bewitched. Maybe that old harridan, Miss Peabody, cast a spell on us."

Lucas gave a mock shudder. "From the moment I met Amelia, I felt as if Fate had reached out and grabbed me by the throat. I couldn't escape."

"I felt the same," James agreed. He peered over at Aaron. "What about you?"

"If I was bewitched," Aaron said, "I can't complain because if I hadn't been, I'd currently be wed to Priscilla Cummings."

"Perish the thought," Lucas said. "Did I ever tell you I kissed Priscilla once?"

"No. Were you ever planning to?"

"No, and I have to admit, it was like kissing a block of ice. You were wise to scoot out of that mess."

"Yes, I've been celebrating ever since I broke it off."

"Any news from Father?" Lucas inquired. "Will he marry Priscilla himself?"

"I haven't a clue," Aaron replied. "I sent him an invitation to the wedding, but other than that, I've had no communication."

"Can you actually suppose he'd drag his sorry behind here? Should we expect him to stagger in at the last minute?"

"No, I don't expect him. My decision about Evangeline may

have pitched him into an apoplexy. He's likely too stunned to travel."

Lucas grinned. "It's nice to know it was you vexing him for a change instead of me."

"Glad to be of service."

James held up his hand, displaying his wedding ring. "Have you any idea how odd it is to have this gold band on my finger?"

Lucas raised his too. "It's like a permanent, weighty reminder that I'm good and thoroughly caught. I can't forget for a single instant."

"Speaking of rings," Aaron said to Lucas, "tell me you have mine."

Lucas patted his pockets, pretending to search for it. "Where did I put the damned thing?"

"Very funny," Aaron chided.

Lucas snatched it out and offered it to Aaron. "Are you sure you want to use it? If you're having second thoughts, we could just toss it out in the grass and climb out the window. You don't have to go through with it."

James added, "We could sneak to the tavern and drink ourselves silly rather than watch you have that leg-shackle pounded onto your ankle."

"It might be a more productive way to spend the afternoon," Lucas concurred.

They stared at Aaron as if he might realize he was making a huge mistake and should run like hell. As if he could ever regret picking Evangeline!

With how he'd betrayed and deceived her, he was lucky she'd have him. He'd be lucky everyday for the rest of his life.

There were some men—his father, for example—would think he was mad, but Lord Sidwell's opinion no longer mattered to Aaron.

Lord Sidwell was a cold, hard man, and very likely he'd never forgive Aaron for marrying Evangeline. Aaron hated that he'd caused such a rift in the family, and he hoped that, eventually, they would be able to move beyond it. He suspected—once Evangeline provided Lord Sidwell with a grandson or two—he might come around.

Aaron would pray it ended like that, but if it didn't?

Lucas had always been Aaron's favorite person in the world, and their relationship was quickly being repaired. His *family* was and always had been Lucas. Now it included James and his wife, Rose, who was Aaron's cousin. She'd been pushed away by Lord Sidwell too, and it was another loss for Aaron's father.

Lord Sidwell didn't want to know Rose, his niece, didn't want to meet the children she would have with James. It was infuriating and ridiculous, and if Lord Sidwell wasn't careful, he'd get the lonely old age he deserved.

Suddenly, Lucas wrapped an arm over Aaron's shoulder and gripped him in a headlock.

"Last chance to back out," Lucas said.

"I would never back out."

"Don't say we didn't warn you."

Lucas laughed and released Aaron, and it occurred to Aaron that he'd never observed Lucas so relaxed, so content. He gave all the credit to Amelia. Aaron had predicted from the start that Amelia would be good for his brother, and he was delighted to have been proved right.

For a fleeting moment, he suffered a maudlin wave of melancholy, wishing his mother could have been with them, wishing she was present to see how grand Lucas was looking, to see Aaron wed Evangeline.

By all accounts, Lucas was just like their mother: exasperating, remarkable, gifted, overly imprudent and reckless. She would have liked Evangeline, would have been ecstatic to learn who Aaron and Lucas had been fortunate enough to find.

The door opened, and the vicar peeked in. "Are you ready, Lord Run?"

"Yes, I'm ready," Aaron responded.

"Are you sure?" Lucas asked. "There's the window. We can be at the tavern in three or four minutes."

"I'm very sure." He glared at Lucas and James. "How about you two? Are you regretting your marriages? Is this your way of subtly hinting that you shouldn't have proceeded?"

James and Lucas gaped at each other, then vehemently shook their heads.

"I'm the happiest man alive," James declared.

"I'm happier than that," Lucas insisted.

"With Evangeline as my wife," Aaron said, "I shall be happier than both of you put together."

Lucas smiled a warm, supportive smile. "I'm betting you will be too, brother."

Lucas gestured for Aaron to lead them out, and as Aaron stepped toward the vicar, James teased, "What's that sound I hear? I believe it's the old ball-and-chain banging along behind him."

Aaron rolled his eyes at the vicar. "Please wed me to my bride as fast as you can so I can get away from these idiots."

"Idiots!" Lucas huffed. "I was smart enough to marry Amelia, wasn't I?"

"And I was smart enough to marry Rose," James pointed out.

"But I," Aaron said, "was smart enough to marry the most incredible woman of them all. Eat your hearts out, boys."

"If Miss Peabody was here, what do you suppose she would think?"

Evangeline peered over at Rose and Amelia.

Rose clucked her tongue like a mother hen. "She'd scold you for reaching too high in your choice of husband."

They all chuckled, knowing it was absolutely true.

Evangeline had always had big dreams, had envisioned a splendid future, but Miss Peabody had fought to quash Evangeline's optimism. Yet she hadn't been able to stamp it out completely. Evangeline had never stopped hoping for more.

Ha, Miss Peabody! she yearned to gloat. *It happened just as I planned, and I have everything I ever wanted.*

They were in the church's vestibule, the organ music playing quietly, and Evangeline could barely keep from dancing in merry circles.

"I doubt she'd have been overly thrilled with any of us," Evangeline told her two friends.

"Especially not with me," Rose said. "She betrothed me to James's grandfather. What sane person would have engineered such a dire fate? I nearly didn't escape it."

Amelia added, "I scarcely managed to wrangle mine into place. It was touch and go with Lucas. I couldn't figure out how it would end. I'm still surprised."

"If I recall correctly," Rose said, "you would rather have clobbered him with a stout log than have him as your husband."

"Look at me now." Amelia grinned and held up her wedding ring. "I snagged the worst rake in the world, and I'm so glad about it. Who would have ever guessed?"

"Life is so strange sometimes," Rose mused.

"And so amazing," Amelia said.

Up by the altar, a door opened, and the vicar emerged. Aaron followed him out, then Lucas and James. The organ began to blare, and people turned to glance back. For how swiftly they'd arranged the ceremony, there was a crowd in attendance. But then, Evangeline had boarded at the school, and the neighbors knew her.

Bryce asked, "Are you ready?"

Evangeline stared down the aisle at Aaron. "Yes, I'm ready."

Rose gave her a hug, then marched off. Amelia did the same. Then Evangeline was standing with her brother.

Evangeline gazed up at him. From the moment she'd agreed to

be Aaron's bride, she'd been weepy and emotional. Apparently, the heightened sentiment was catching. Bryce's eyes were a tad misty too.

"I wish our mother was here," she said.

"Oh gad, Evangeline, if you spew maudlin drivel like that, you'll have me bawling. I'll never be able to escort you."

"Sorry"—she was laughing—"but I wish she was."

"All right, I admit it. I wish she was here too." He offered his arm and she grabbed it. "Let's go. The groom is glowering at me. I think he's tired of waiting."

"Well, I want to proceed slowly and drag it out so I can remember every single detail."

"Women!" he huffed, and they started off, but he leaned down and murmured, "By the way, I believe Mother is probably with us. I believe she's watching."

"I believe she is too."

He straightened, struggling to appear very serious. "Now let me get you down to your husband—before you come to your senses and run out the back."

Aaron was smiling at her, his affection flowing out, luring her to him. She'd always been alone, an orphan who didn't know her history, who thought she was floating free and not connected to anyone or anything. But she'd been wrong.

She had friends. She had her brother—and two others besides. They were out there somewhere, practically begging to be found.

And she had handsome, dashing, wonderful Aaron Drake who would love her forever.

She peeked up at her brother and grinned. "You don't need to worry that I'll run away." She pointed to Aaron. "My future is there in front of me. Aren't I lucky?"

THE END

ABOUT THE AUTHOR

CHERYL HOLT is a *New York Times, USA Today,* and Amazon "Top 100" bestselling author of over thirty novels.

She's also a lawyer and mom, and at age forty, with two babies at home, she started a new career as a commercial fiction writer. She'd hoped to be a suspense novelist, but couldn't sell any of her manuscripts, so she ended up taking a detour into romance where she was stunned to discover that she has a knack for writing some of the world's greatest love stories.

Her books have been released to wide acclaim, and she has won or been nominated for many national awards. She has been hailed as "The Queen of Erotic Romance" as well as "The International Queen of Villains." She is particularly proud to have been named "Best Storyteller of the Year" by the trade magazine *Romantic Times* BOOK Reviews.

She lives and writes in Hollywood, California, and she loves to hear from fans. Visit her website at www.cherylholt.com.

6854650R00129

Printed in Great Britain
by Amazon.co.uk, Ltd.,
Marston Gate.